Obernewtyn

Don't get left behind!

STARSCAPE

Let the journey begin . . .

From the Two Rivers
  The Eye of the World: Part One
  by Robert Jordan

Ender's Game
  by Orson Scott Card

Mairelon the Magician
  by Patricia C. Wrede

Ender's Shadow
  by Orson Scott Card

Orvis
  by H. M. Hoover

The Dark Side of Nowhere
  by Neal Shusterman

The Magician's Ward
  by Patricia C. Wrede

Deep Secret
  by Diana Wynne Jones

Another Heaven, Another Earth
  by H. M. Hoover

Hidden Talents
  by David Lubar

To the Blight
  The Eye of the World: Part Two
  by Robert Jordan

The Cockatrice Boys
  by Joan Aiken

Dogland
  by Will Shetterly

The Whispering Mountain
  by Joan Aiken

The Garden Behind the Moon
  by Howard Pyle

Prince Ombra
  by Roderick MacLeish

A College of Magics
  by Caroline Stevermer

Pinocchio
  by Carlo Collodi

The Wonder Clock
  by Howard Pyle

The Shadow Guests
  by Joan Aiken

Obernewtyn

THE OBERNEWTYN CHRONICLES ✳ BOOK ONE

ISOBELLE CARMODY

A TOM DOHERTY ASSOCIATES BOOK
NEW YORK

This is a work of fiction. All the characters and events portrayed in this book are either products of the author's imagination or are used fictitiously.

OBERNEWTYN

A Starscape Book
Published by Tom Doherty Associates, LLC
175 Fifth Avenue
New York, NY 10010

www.starscapebooks.com

ISBN: 0-765-34267-7

First Starscape edition: February 2003

Printed in the United States of America

0 9 8 7 6 5 4 3 2 1

for Brenda

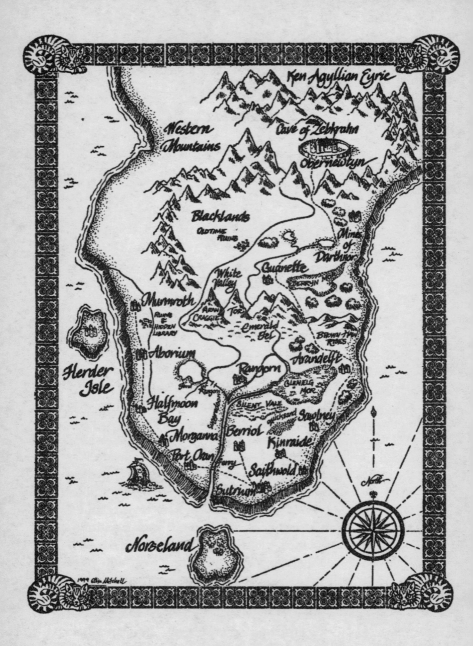

Introduction

In the days following the holocaust, which came to be known as the Great White, there was death and madness. In part, this was the effect of the lingering radiation rained on the world from the skies. Those fortunate enough to live on remote holdings and farms were spared the chemical destruction of the Great White, though they had seen the skies whiten and had understood that it meant death. These people preserved their untainted land and families ruthlessly, slaughtering the hundreds of refugees who poured from the poisoned cities.

This time of siege was called the Age of Chaos and lasted until no more came from the cities. Unaware that the cities were now only silent graveyards on endless black plains where nothing lived or grew, the most powerful farmers formed a Council to protect their community from further siege, and to mete out justice and aid.

As the years passed, more people did come to the land where the Council ruled, but they were few, and poor creatures half mad from their journey across the shattered lands, instinctively making their way for one of the few regions untainted by the black death that covered the earth. They learned quickly to swear allegiance to the

Council, only too grateful to join a settled society. And peace came to the land.

But time proved the remote community had not completely escaped the effects of the Great White. Mutations in both man and beast were high. Not fully understanding the reason for the mutations, the Council feared for the community and decreed any man or beast not born completely normal must be burned. To remove any qualms people might have about the killings, these burnings took on a ritual air, and were used by the Council to remind the people of their fortune in being spared in the holocaust, and of the time of Chaos.

They appointed a fledgling religious order to perform the burnings. The order, called the Herder Faction, believed that the holocaust was punishment from God, whom they called Lud. Gradually religious dogma and law fused and the honest way of the farmer was seen as the only right way. Machines, books, and all the artifacts of the old world that had perished, were abhorred and destroyed.

Some resisted the rigid lore but by now the Council had provided itself with a fanatical band of protectors, called soldierguards. Any who dared oppose the order were tried and burned as Seditioners, or given the lesser charge of being Unsafe and sent to work on the Councilfarms.

After some time, the Herder Faction advised the Council that not all mutancies were immediately apparent at birth. Such afflictions as those that attacked the mind could not be discerned until later.

This created some difficulty, for while the Council saw the opportunity to further manipulate the community, accusing anyone of whom they disapproved of hidden mutancy, it was more difficult to proceed with a ritual burning of someone who had been accepted as normal for most of his or her life. The Council eventually de-

creed all but the most horribly afflicted of this new kind
of mutant would not be burned, but would be sent instead to the Councilfarms to harvest a dangerously ra-
dioactive element called whitestick. A new name was
devised for anyone with an affliction not apparent at
birth—Misfit.

It was a dark and violent age, though the Land flour-
ished and even began cautiously to extend its boundaries
as the effects of the Great White began at last to wane.
New towns were established, all ruled by the iron hand
of the Council. So great was the death toll under Council
rule that hundreds of children were left orphaned each
year. The Council responded by setting up a network of
orphan homes to house those unclaimed by blood relatives.

The community regarded the inmates of orphan
homes with an abiding suspicion, since most were the
children of Misfits or Seditioners, and as such dangerous. . . .

Part I

The Lowlands

I

Before first light we set out for the Silent Vale.

It was a day's journey and we were led by a tall, gangling boy called Elii, who carried a small sword and two hunt knives at his belt. These were the only visible reminders that our journey involved danger.

Also traveling with us was a young Herder. He represented the true danger that lay ahead. Around our necks we wore the dull gray metal circlet that denoted our orphan status. This would protect us from robbers and gypsies, for as orphans we owned nothing. Normally the presence of a Herder would be enough to frighten off robbers who feared the wrath of the powerful Order.

But this was a very young Herder, little more than a boy with golden bum-fluff on his cheeks. His eyes held characteristic Herder zeal but there was a nervous tic in one of his eyelids. I guessed this was his first duty away from the cloisters and he seemed as nervous of us as of any supernatural dangers he might perceive. It was well known that Herders had the ability to see the ghosts of the Oldtimers flitting about as they had done in the terrible days when the sky was still white and radiant. This ability was Ludgiven so they could warn of the dangers that lay in following the evil ways of the Beforetimers.

I looked sideways, wondering if he could see anything yet. It was understood the visions came most often on tainted ground where the land had not long ago been untouchable. The Silent Vale was such a place, edging close on the Blacklands.

Ours was considered a perilous journey, but an important one. The expeditions to recover whitestick were vital to the orphan homes, enabling them to function independently. The Council had ruled that none but orphan homes might mine the rare substance, perhaps because orphans were the most expendable members of the community. Collection of the whitestick was fraught with danger, for the substance could only be found in areas verging on tainted. The whitestick was itself poisonous to the naked skin, and had to be passed through a special process designed to remove its poisons before it was of any use. Once cleansed it was marvelously versatile, serving in everything from sleeping potions to the potent medicines prepared by the Herders.

I had not been to the Silent Vale before. This was the Kinraide orphan home's area of collection and it yielded high-grade whitestick. But the Silent Vale was considered dangerously close to the Blacklands where the poisons of the Great White still ruled. It was even whispered there were traces of Oldtime dwellings nearby. I was thrilled, and terrified, to think I might see them.

We passed through a side gate in the walls of the Kinraide complex. The way from that door was a track leading steeply downward. Seldom traveled, it seemed a world apart from the neat, ordered gardens and paths within Kinraide. Bush creepers trailed unchecked from side to side, choking the path in places.

Elii chopped occasionally at the vines to clear the way. He was an odd boy. People tended to shun him because of his profession, and for his close connections with the orphan home, though he was no orphan. His own father had worked in the same capacity and his grandfather before that, until they had died of the rotting sickness that came from prolonged exposure to the whitestick. He lived in the grounds at Kinraide, but did not associate with us.

One of the girls in our party approached him. "Why not travel along the crevasse instead of going up this steep edge?" she panted.

For some way we had begun to climb a steep spur along one side of the rise. Northward the dale ran up into a glen of shadows.

"The path runs this way," Elii snapped, his eyes swiveling around to the rest of us, cold and contemptuous. "I don't want to hear any more whining questions from you lot. I'm the Lud of this expedition and I say there'll be no more talk."

The Herder flushed at his nearly blasphemous mention of Lud's name, but the restraint in his face showed he had been warned already about the rude but necessary youth. Few would choose to do his job, whatever the prize in the end. Elii turned on his heel and led us at a smart pace to the crest of the hill. From the top we could see a long way—the home behind us and beyond that the town center, and in front of us, far to the west, lay a belt of mountains, purpled with the distance. The boundary of untainted lands. Beyond those mountains, nothing lived. Hastily I averted my eyes, for no one understood all the dangers of the Blacklands. Even looking at them might do some harm.

The dawn came and went as we walked, a wan gray light seeping into the world. The path led us toward a pool of water in a small valley. It was utterly still and mirrored the dull overcast sky, its southern end dark in the shadow of the hills.

"I hope we are not going to swim that because it is in the way," said the same girl who had spoken before. I

stared at her defiant face, still stained with the red dye
used by Herders to mark the children of Seditioners. Elii
said nothing but the Herder gave her a look that would
have terrified me. A nervous young Herder is still a Herder, but the girl tossed her head.

We came to the pool at the shadowed end, only to find
the path cleaved to the very edge of the water.

"Touch this water not!" the Herder said suddenly in
a loud voice that made us all jump.

Elii looked over his shoulder with a sneering expression. A little farther on a cobbled border, crumbled in
places and overrun with sprouting weeds, ran alongside
the track. It was uncommon enough for me to wonder if
this was from the Beforetime. If so I was not much impressed, but the Herder made a warding-off sign at the
border.

"Avert your eyes," he cried, his voice squeaking at the
end. I wondered if he saw something. Perhaps there were
faint impressions of Oldtimers fleeing along this very
road, the Great White mushrooming behind them, filling
the sky with deadly white light.

An eastward bend in the path led us around the edge
of a natural stone wall and there we came suddenly upon
a thing that was unmistakably a product of the Oldtime.
A single unbroken gray stone grew straight up into the
sky like the trunk of a tree, marked at intervals with bi-
zarre symbols, an obelisk to the ancient past.

"This is where the other Herders spoke their prayers
to Lud," said Elii. "They saw no danger before this."

The young Herder flushed but kept his dignity as he
made us kneel as he asked Lud for protection. The prayer
lasted a very long time. Elii began to sigh loudly and
impatiently. Making a final sign of rejection at the unnatural gray pedestal, the young priest rose and self-
consciously brushed his habit.

The same girl spoke again. "Is that from the Beforetime then?" she asked. This time I did not look at her. She was dangerously careless and seemed not to think about what she was saying. And this Herder was nervous enough to report all of us because of the one stupid girl.

"It is a sign of the evil past," said the Herder finally, trembling with outrage. At last the girl seemed to sense she had gone too far and fell silent.

One of the others in our party, a girl I knew slightly, moved near and whispered in my ear, "That girl will be off to the Councilcourt if she keeps that up."

I nodded slightly but hoped she would not prolong her whispering. Her name, I remembered suddenly, was Rosamunde.

To my concern, she leaned close again. "Perhaps she doesn't care if they send her to the farms. I heard her whole family was burnt for Sedition, and she only escaped because of her age," she added. I shrugged and to my relief Rosamunde stepped back into line.

When we stopped for midmeal, Rosamunde sought me out again, sitting beside me and unwrapping her bread and curd cheese. I hoped there was nothing about her that would reflect on me. I had heard nothing of any detriment about her, but one never knew.

"That girl," Rosamunde said softly. "It must be unbearable to know that her whole family is dead except for her."

Unwillingly I looked to where the other girl sat alone, not eating, her body stiff with some inner tension. "I heard her father was mixed up with Henry Druid," Rosamunde continued.

I pretended not to be interested, but it was hard not to be curious about anyone linked with the mysterious rebel Herder priest.

Rosamunde leaned forward again, reaching for her cordial. "I know your brother," she said softly. I stiffened, wondering if he had sent her to spy on me. Unaware of my withdrawal, she went on. "He is fortunate to be so well thought of among the guardians. There is talk that the Herder wants to make him an assistant."

I was careful not to let the shock show. I had heard nothing of that and wondered if Jes knew. He would have seen no reason to tell me if he did.

Jes was the only person who knew the truth about me. What he knew was enough to burn me and I was frightened of him. My only comfort lay in the tendency of the Council to condemn all those in a family tainted by one Misfit birth; Jes might not be burned, but he would not like to be sentenced to the farms until he died. As long as it was safer for him to keep my secret, I was safe, but if it ever looked like I would be exposed, Jes would denounce me at once.

Suddenly I wondered if he had engineered my inclusion on the whitestick expedition. As a favored orphan, he had some influence. He was too pious to kill me himself, though that would have been his best solution, but if I died seeking whitestick, as many did, then he would be innocently free of me. Elii called us to move.

This time I positioned myself near him, where Rosamunde would not dare chatter. The Herder priest walked alongside, muttering his incantations. We had not gone far when a rushing noise came to our ears through the whispering greenery. We came shortly thereafter to a part of the path that curved steeply down. Here a subterranean waterway, swollen with the autumnal rains, had burst through the dark earth, using the path as its course until the next bend.

"Well now," Elii said sourly.

The Herder came up to stand uneasily beside him. "We will have to find another way," he said. "Lud will lead us."

Elii snorted rudely. "Your Lud had better help us on this path—there ain't no other way."

The priest's face grew red, then white. "You go too far," he gasped, but Elii was already preoccupied, drawing a length of rope from his pack and tying the end around a tree. Then he slung the other end down the flooded path.

The Herder watched these movements with horror.

Elii pulled at the rope, testing it, before swinging agilely down to the bottom. Back on dry ground, he called for us to do the same, one at a time.

"We'll be dashed to pieces," Rosamunde observed gloomily.

The Herder gave her a terrified look as one of the boys started to climb carefully down. Several others went, then Rosamunde and I. The rope was slippery now and hard to grip. As well, I found it difficult to lift my own weight. Two-thirds of the way down, my fingers became too numb to cling properly and I fell the last two feet, crashing heavily into a rock as I landed. The water soaked into my pants.

"Get her out. The water may be tainted," Elii growled, then yelled up for the priest to descend.

I was completely breathless and dazed from my fall and my head ached horribly where I had hit it on the rock.

"She's bleeding," Rosamunde told Elii.

"Won't hurt. Running blood cleans a wound," he muttered absently, watching the priest descend slowly and with much crying out for Lud's help. I seemed to be watching through a mist.

When the Herder reached the bottom, he knelt beside me quickly and began reciting a prayer for the dead.

"She's not dead," Rosamunde said gently.

Seeing that I was only stunned, the priest bandaged the cut on my temple with deft efficiency, and I reminded myself again that for all his youth, the Herder was fully trained in his calling.

"Come on," Elii said impatiently. "Though I doubt we'll make it in time now."

"Was the water tainted?" I asked, ignoring Rosamunde's audible gasp. There was no point in caution if I died from not speaking out.

The Herder shook his head and I wondered how he knew without doubting that he was right. Herder knowledge was wide-ranging and sometimes obscure, but generally reliable.

We walked quickly then, urged on by Elii. My head ached steadily, but I was relieved it was only a bump and not a serious infection. I had a sudden vision of my mother, applying a steaming herb poultice to my head. How quickly the pain had subsided on that occasion. Herbal lore was forbidden now, though it was said there were still those who secretly practiced the art of Healing. I walked into Elii, having failed to notice he had called a halt.

"Through the Weirwood lies the Silent Vale," he said. "If we are too late today, we will have to camp here and enter the Vale tomorrow."

"The Weirwood?" said someone nervously.

The Herder was not alone in his consternation at the thought of sleeping out. "It is dangerous to be out at night in these parts," he said, "where the spirits of the Beforetime rest uneasily."

Elii shrugged, saying there would be no help for it if the sun had gone. He had his orders. "Perhaps your Lud will cast his mantle of protection over us," he added with a faint glimmer of amusement. Elii cared little for convention, knowing his worth.

We entered the Weirwood and I shivered at the thought of spending a night there. It had an unnatural feel and I saw several in our group look around nervously. We had not walked far when we came to a clearing, and in the center of this was the ravine they called the Silent Vale. It was very narrow, a mere slit in the ground, with steps hewn into one end, descending into the gap. The light only reached a foot or so into the ravine, and the rest was in dense shadow.

I understood now Elii's haste, for only when the sun was directly overhead would it light the Vale, and it was almost overhead now.

Elii urged us again to hurry if we did not want to spend a night in the Weirwood. We entered the ravine gingerly and descended the slippery steps fearfully. By the time we reached the bottom, I was numb with the cold and we huddled together at the foot of the steps, afraid to move where we could not see. Moments passed and the sun reached its zenith, piercing the damp mists that filled the ravine and lighting up the Vale.

It was much wider at the base, and unexpectedly, there were trees growing, though they were stunted and diseased, with few leaves. A thick whitish moss covered the ground and some of the walls in a dense carpet, while the walls of the ravine exposed were scored and charred, possibly marked by the fire said to have rained from the skies during the first days of the holocaust. A faint charred stench still filled the air.

Elii handed out the gloves and bags for gathering the whitestick, instructing us needlessly to be quick and careful, never letting the substance touch our skins. Pulling on the slippery gloves, we spread out and set to work, searching for the telltale black nodules that concealed the deposits of whitestick.

The bags were only small, but took time to fill because the substance crumbled to dust if not handled carefully. Standing to ease my aching back once I had finished, I noticed that I had wandered out of sight of everyone else. I could hear nothing, though the others must be quite near. I had noticed at once the aptly named Vale was oddly silent, but now it struck me anew how unnatural that silence was, and how complete. Even the wind made no murmur. It was as if a special kind of death had come to the Silent Vale.

"Are you finished?" Rosamunde asked, apologizing when I jumped in fright. "This place is enough to give even a soldierguard a taste of the horrors. Do you notice how quiet it is, as though everything we say is absorbed?"

I nodded, thinking how all the places where whitestick was mined had the same aberrant feel.

Returning to where some of the others had gathered around the steps, we heard voices from somewhere near.

"What do they use this stuff for anyway?" one asked.

"Medicines and such, or so they say," said another voice with a bitter edge. It was the voice of the outspoken girl marked with Herder red. "But I have heard rumors the priests use it to make special poisons, and to torture their prisoners for information," she added softly.

Rosamunde looked at me in horror, but we said nothing. I was no informer and I did not think Rosamunde was. But that girl was bent on disaster, and she would take anyone with her stupid enough not to see the danger. Better to forget what we had overheard.

I left Rosamunde with the others, going to examine a deep fissure I had spotted in the ground. The Great White had savaged the earth and there were many such holes and chasms leading deep into the ground. I bent and looked in and a chill air seemed to strike at my face from those black depths.

Impulsively, I picked up a rock and dropped it in. My heart beat many times before I heard the faint sound of impact. It echoed in the Vale.

"What was that?" cried the Herder, who had been packing the bags of whitestick.

Elii strode purposefully over. "Idiot of a girl. This is a serious place, not the garden at Kinraide. Throw yourself in next time and make me happy." I looked at my feet with a fast-beating heart. That was twice now I had called attention to myself and that was dangerous. Suddenly there was a vague murmur from the ground beneath our feet.

"What was that?" the Herder cried again, edging closer to the steps.

"I don't know," Elii said with a frown. "Probably nothing but I don't like it. We are not far from the Blacklands. Come, the sun is going." The Herder, who came last, kept looking behind him fearfully as if he expected something to reach out and grab him.

An air of relief came over the group as we threw off the oppressive air of the Vale. Fortunately we had gathered enough whitestick and we made good time on our return, reaching Kinraide early in the evening.

To my private astonishment, Jes was among those who met us, and he wore the beaten potmetal armband of a Herders' assistant.

II

"Elspeth?"

It was Jes, and I willed him to go away. He knocked again, then stuck his head around the door. "How are you?" he asked with a hint of disapproval. Anger overcame caution.

"For Lud's sake, Jes, they're not going to condemn me because of a headache. If you think it looks suspicious, then why don't you report me," I retorted, staring pointedly at his armband.

He whitened and shut the door behind him. "Keep your voice down. There are people outside."

I bit my lip and forced myself to be calm. "What do you want?" I asked him coldly. I knew I was being stupid but I didn't care. Jes was the only one I could strike out at. And that, I thought, looking at his stiff face, was becoming increasingly dangerous.

"Maybe you don't care about being burned but I do. Much as you scorn it, caution has kept us safe until now. No thanks to you," he added, and I was bitterly reminded that our plight was my fault. "A headache is nothing, but you know how little things are blown out of all proportion. It is a short step from gossip to the Councilcourt in Sutrium."

"You have been made an assistant," I said flatly and now he reddened. A look of pride mingled with shame came over his face.

"How could you?" I asked him bleakly.

He clenched his jaw. "You will not ruin this for me," he said at last. "You are my sister. It is my sin that I do not denounce you."

"You would not dare denounce me," I said. "Your own life would be ruined if it was known you had a Misfit for a sister. Don't pretend you care for me."

A queer flicker passed over his face and I suddenly felt certain that this was the truth. When he had gone I lay back, my head aching dully, partly from tension.

For all my bravado, I was afraid of Jes. There had been a time when we were close. Not so much when we were young, for he had been a dutiful son and I too much of a wanderer to please anyone except my beloved mother, but after we had come into the orphan home system following the trial and execution of our parents, we had clung to each other. Jes had vowed then to have revenge on the Council and the Herder Faction for their evil work that day. He had wiped my eyes and sworn to protect me.

He had not known what that would entail. Neither of us had realized that I was more than the daughter of a Seditioner. Our remote childhood in Rangorn had kept us innocent of the knowledge that would come later. In those first years, we regarded our secretive behavior as a game. It was only as we grew older that we became increasingly aware of the dangers. Discovering the truth about myself made me more solitary than ever, while Jes developed a near obsession with caution. In those days his one desire had been to get a Normalcy Certificate and get out, then ask permission to have me with him. But somehow we had drifted apart, till the bonds that held us were fragile indeed. I knew Jes had become fas-

cinated with the Herder Faction and its ideas. But as an
orphan he would never be accepted into the cloister, so
I had thought little of it. I could not understand why he
was interested.

The fact that he had now been made an assistant drove
yet another wedge between us, for I still believed the
Herders and the Council to be the murderers of my parents.

Recently we had fought bitterly over his explanations
for why the Herders had burned our parents. I called
him a traitor and a dogmatic fool; in his turn he had
called me a Misfit. That he would even say the word
revealed how much he had changed.

Since then we had maintained an uneasy truce. He
said nothing of my secret and I had spoken no more than
was necessary to him. Lately I had seen him watching
me, with a look so bright and alien that I was chilled.
Those looks might have meant nothing, but instinct
warned me to beware.

People thought my headaches were the result of my
fall on the path to the Silent Vale that day. When I had
cried out in the night, the guardians came to hear of it.
I told them of the fall because I did not want them to
speculate, and had been given light duties and some bitter
powders by the Herder.

At first I told myself the headaches were simply a reaction to a change in the weather, for winds from the
Blacklands did cause fevers and rashes. But deep down I
knew they had nothing to do with either the fall or the
weather.

I shook my head and decided to go for a walk in the
garden. Perhaps Maruman would be back. I had missed
his gruff company.

I slipped out a side door into the fading sunset. Jes had
called me a Misfit, and according to Council lore, that
was what I was. But I did not feel like a monster. In a

queer mental leap I thought about my first visit with my
father to the great city of Sutrium. In my mind it seemed
we must have gone all that way just for the fabulous
Sutrium moon fair. Everyone who could walk, hobble,
or ride seemed to be on the road to the biggest town in
the land, bringing with them hay, wool, embroidery,
honey, perfume, and a hundred other things to trade.
They had come from Saithwold, Sawlney, Port Oran,
Morganna, and even Aborium and Murmroth.

I had not known then that Sutrium was also the home
of the main Councilcourt. That I had discovered on my
grim second visit. There had been no fair this time. It
was wintertime and the city was gray and cold. There
were no gay crowds filling the streets, only a few furtive
looks from people as we passed in the open carriage, our
faces stinging from the red dye. We had not known then
that Henry Druid had only recently disappeared, fleeing
the wrath of the Council, and that the entire community
was fearful of the consequences, since many had known
and openly agreed with the rebel. But what I did understand, even then, was the hatred and fear in the faces of
the people who looked at us. I felt then the terror of being
different that has never left me.

Shuddering, I thrust the grim memory away. Ludwill-
ing, I would never see such looks again.

The time of Changing was near and I sighed, thinking
it would be better for us both if Jes and I were sent this
time to separate homes. The Herder told us the custom
of moving orphans around regularly from home to home
had arisen to prevent the friendships forming that could
not be continued once leaving the homes, but it was
widely accepted that the Changing was engineered to
prevent alliances between the children of Seditioners,
which might lead to further trouble. But there was another effect evident only when the time for the Changing

approached. No one knew where they might go, and whom they might trust in the new home.

Even before the relocation, we learned to prepare mentally, withdrawing and preparing for the loneliness that must come until the new home was familiar, until it was possible to tell who could be trusted and who were the informers. Those who had before been friends, now became aloof and even slightly suspicious of one another.

I looked up. It was growing dark and soon I would have to go in. Fortunately, no one minded me wandering in the garden even on the coldest of days, but I never stayed out beyond nightfall—those dark hours belonged to the spirits of the Beforetime. I leaned against a statue of the founder of Kinraide. Here I was hidden from the windows by a big laurel tree and it was my favorite place.

The moon had risen early and the rapidly darkening sky made it glow. I frowned and an unnatural weakness coursed through me. I felt a sticky sweat break out on my forehead and thought I was going to faint. The pain in my head made me stagger to my knees.

I tried to force the vision not to come, but it was impossible. I stared up at the moon, which had become a penetrating yellow eye. I knew that eye sought me, and felt a scream rise within me.

Then abruptly there was only the pale moon, and I shivered violently and stood up. I would not let myself wonder about the vision or the others that had preceded it. Jes had told me long ago, when we could still talk of such things, that only Herders were permitted visions. "You must not imagine that you have them," he had said.

But I did not imagine them, either then or now, I thought, and walked shakily back across the garden. Those premonitions were warnings. I always had such visions. Yet, though I did not try to understand what they meant, a few days later the meaning forced itself on me.

III

Maruman confirmed it in the end.

It had been a cold year despite the sometimes muggy days that came whenever the wind blew in from the Blacklands. Most often even spring days were bitten with pale, frosted skies stretching away to the north and south, and over the seas to the icy poles of the legends.

Sometimes in the late afternoon I would sit and imagine the color fading out to where there is no color at all, as if the Great White again filled the skies, its lethal radiance leaching the natural blue. But unlike that age of terror when night was banished for days on end, I fancied that region would be permanently frozen into the white world of wintertime, the sea afloat with giant towers of ice such as those in the stories my mother had told.

"Stories!" Maruman snorted as he came up, having overheard the last of my thoughts. I smiled at him as he joined me beside the statue of the founder. I scratched his stomach, and he rolled about and stretched with familiar abandon.

He was not a pretty cat nor a pampered one. He had a battered head and a torn ear, and his wild eyes were of a fierce amber hue. He once told me he had fought a village dog over a bone and that the hound had cheated by biting him on the head.

"Never can trust them pap-fed funaga lovers," he observed disdainfully. Funaga was the thought symbol he used for men and women. "I'd no sooner trust a wild one any time; they'd bite me in half at one go."

Maruman possessed a dramatic and fanciful imagination. Perhaps that old war injury was to blame. It seemed to trouble him a good deal, though he never referred to it. Occasionally his thoughts would become muddled and disturbed. During those periods he could dream very vividly. Shortly after we had begun to communicate, he had undergone such a fit, only to tell me that one day the mountains would seek me. I had laughed because it was such a strange image.

Another time he confessed a Guanette bird had told him his destiny was twined with mine. This bird was a rather obscure symbol that appeared to have risen since the holocaust, representing an oraclelike wisdom or a preordained order of things, themselves archaic symbols from the Oldtime. The odd thing about the Guanette bird was the lack of origin for the legends surrounding it, and the whole meaning and reason behind the myths was a subject favored among scholars. In fact, there was such a bird, but it was said to be almost if not completely extinct. Maruman quite often attributed his insights or notions to the direct intervention of the mythical wise bird.

It was not always easy to understand Maruman. He was sensitive about birds, which struck me as unnatural, since he was their natural predator. However, I paid little attention to his predictions, though occasionally there was some substance to them.

For the rest of the time he was cynical, haughty, conceited; full of opinions- about everything. And how he loved to air them. Some of the things he said made me think twice about the Herder teachings.

Maruman was, he often told me, his own cat. Not so much wild, he would point out, as unencumbered. He once observed that life with a master was doubtless very nice, but for all that he preferred his own way. Having a master, he said, seemed to take the stuffing out of a beast. I reflected to myself that this was certainly true.

With a touch of cynicism, I thought that part of Maruman's devotion to me was because I fed him. But I looked at him fondly. There seemed little to love in this rude, unbalanced cat with an ear that looked half-devoured. Yet there was a kind of wild joy about him that I could only envy, for I was far from free.

If he had been human, I think he would have been a gypsy, and in fact he quite liked to visit the troupes that roved about. He told me they fed him scraps and sang rollicking songs and laughed more than other funaga. They were the descendants of those people in the community who had chosen not to cleave to the Council in those early years. Though tolerated now, they were neither liked nor trusted.

The bond between Maruman and myself had been an accident and without him I would never have discovered the full extent of my telepathic powers. He said it was destiny, but I doubted it.

Ironically, I had been seated right next to the statue of the founder when it happened. A scraggy-looking cat was stalking a bird. Normally I would have ignored them both, but that day I was struck by the carelessness of the bird. I thought it almost deserved its fate. As I concentrated on the pursuit, I had the sensation of something moving in my head. It was the queerest feeling and I gasped loudly.

Startled, the bird flew off with an irritated chirp. I had saved the wretched creature's life and it was annoyed.

Not even then did I wonder how I knew what the bird felt. The cat seemed to glare indignantly at me with its bright yellow eyes. I shrugged wryly and it looked away and began to clean itself.

I had the notion it was only pretending to ignore me. Then I laughed, thinking I must have sat too long in the sun. The cat looked at me again and for a moment I imagined a glint of amusement in its look. Maybe Jes was right and I was going mad.

"Stupid funaga," said a voice in my head. I knew it was the cat, but I didn't know how I knew. The cat glared at me balefully. "All funaga are stupid." Again I had heard what it was thinking.

"They are not!" I answered, without opening my mouth. Now it was the cat's turn to stare.

That first moment of mutual astonishment had given way to a curiosity about each other that had in time grown to an enduring friendship, and it was hard to imagine moving on to the next home without Maruman. He was grumpy, moody, and more than anything else rude-mannered, but I genuinely cared for him and sensed he felt the same, though he would have died rather than admit it. Once we had overcome our initial disbelief and pooled knowledge, Maruman revealed the astonishing fact that all beasts were capable of thinking together as we did, though not so deeply or intimately, sensing emotions and pictures as well as brief messages. He said animals had been able to do that in a limited form even before the holocaust, which, interestingly, he too called the Great White. Maruman said animals knew all about the Great White and the Beforetime.

I told him my one piece of knowledge about the link between animals and humans, gleaned from a Beforetime book my mother had read. It had claimed humans evolved from some hairy animals called apes, which no longer existed, but neither Maruman nor I could feel that was more than a fairy tale.

I had heard many stories about the Great White from my parents as a child, and from the Herders once I entered the orphan home system.

I remembered little from my childhood, but lessons about the Great White were driven into us during the daily rituals and prayers, exhorting us to seek purity of race and mind. The priest who dealt with such matters at Kinraide was old, with a sharp eye and a hard hand. His manner of preaching often reduced new orphans to screaming hysteria. He made the Beforetime sound like some terrifying concoction of Heaven and Hell, woven throughout with sloth, indulgence, and pride, the sins suffered by the Oldtimers. The holocaust itself was paraded as the wrath of Lud in all its terrible glory.

This exaggerated picture was tempered by the quiet stories one heard from other sources, gypsies and traveling jacks and potmenders, who presented the Oldtimers to us as men who flew through the air in golden machines, and could live and breathe beneath the sea. Those stories left little doubt that the Beforetime people had possessed some remarkable abilities, but it was obvious the stories were now completely fantasized and exaggerated.

Maruman had little to offer about the Beforetime, since what he knew had been passed on from generation to generation of his kind. He had more to say about the Great White. Unlike the Herder version, Maruman said it was believed by the beastworld that men had unleashed the Great White from things they called machines—powerful and violent inanimate creatures set deep under the ground, controlled and fed by men. Beasts called them glarsha.

I questioned him as to how inanimate things could be

violent or fed, but he could not explain this apparent paradox.

Maruman said he "remembered" the Great White, and though that was impossible, he wove remarkably frightening pictures of a world in terror. He spoke of the rains that burned whatever they touched, and of the charnel stench of the Great White. He spoke of the radiant heat that filled the skies and blotted out the night, of the thirst and the hunger and the screaming of those dying, of the invisible poisons that permeated the air and plants and waters of the world. And most of all, he spoke of the deaths of men, children, and women, and of the deaths of beasts, and when I listened, I wept with him, though I did not know if he had imagined it all or if he were somehow really able to remember back in time.

According to the Herder history of the Great White, the poisons were sent from Lud and only the righteous were spared.

But Maruman said those spared had the luck of living a long way from the center of destruction where the poisons had barely reached in their most terrible forms, and that was all. If he was right, then all that the Herders told us were lies, and the Council, supposedly devised by Lud, was man-made, too.

For the first time I began to understand what my parents had been fighting for with more than blind loyalty.

Maruman bit me, bored with my musings, then he licked the place as demanded by courtesy. I looked fondly at him, wondering where his wandering had taken him this time.

"Where have you been? I missed you," I told him.

He purred. "I am here now," he answered firmly, and I knew better than to question him further. He did not like to dwell on his travels, and when he did not want to talk, the worst course was to press him. He would become stubborn and one could get nothing from him. I noticed a few places where his fur had rubbed off and wondered that he had never caught the rotting disease. His way was not to tell everything at once. Gradually, over time, he would give me enough information to work out the rest. It was frustrating but that was Maruman. And since he had been to the Blacklands, he would almost certainly undergo another of his mad periods. I resolved to feed him because he did not eat at such times and was already too thin.

"She is coming," he said suddenly, and looking at his eyes, I saw that he was already half into a fey state and his words were probably only raving.

Nonetheless I asked, "Who is coming?"

"She. The darkOne," he answered.

I felt slightly disturbed, because of my own premonitions. Perhaps this was one of the times when Maruman's visions were right. "Who is she? Why is she coming?"

"She seeks you but does not know you," said Maruman. A thrill of fear coursed through me. His thoughts seemed to tally with my own deep unease and my persistent visions of being sought. "She comes soon. The whiteface smells of her." Maruman spat at the moon, which had risen in the day sky. It was full. I wondered again why he hated the moon so much. It had something to do with the coming of the Great White, I knew. He snapped at nothing above his injured ear, then yowled forlornly.

"When does she come?" I asked again, but Maruman seemed to have lost the thread of the conversation. I watched his mind drift into his eyes. He would be impossible now and I very much wanted to know what he meant. But Maruman growled and the hackles on his back rose. He shook his head as if to clear it of the fogs that sometimes floated there.

"When I was in the Oldplaces, I dreamed of the Old

One. She said I must follow you. It was my task. But I am . . . tired."

I gulped, for a horrible notion had come to me. "Where does the darkOne come from? Where will she take me?"

"To the mountains," Maruman answered. "To the mountains of shadow, where black wars with white, to the heart of darkness, to the eyrie above the clouds, to the chasm underearth. To the others." Suddenly he pitched sideways and a trickle of saliva came from his mouth.

I sat very still because none lived in the mountains save those at Obernewtyn.

A keeper from Obernewtyn would come; if Maruman was right, a woman who would find out the truth about me.

IV

Like every orphan, I had heard stories about Obernewtyn. It was used by parents as a sort of horror tale to make naughty children behave. But in truth very little was known about it.

An ancient institution in the wilds of the Western Mountains, it was ringed on all sides by Blacklands and savage peaks. In its early days the Council had been approached by Lukas Seraphim, who had built a huge holding in the mountains on land only just free of the Blacklands. He had offered his holding as a solution to the problem of where to send the worst afflicted Misfits and those who were too troublesome for use on the Councilfarms.

At first the Council had refused, for little was known of the man. He was thought to be slightly mad himself, but relatively harmless. In the end, an agreement had been made to send some Misfits to Obernewtyn where they would be put to work for their new master. Some said it was just like another Councilfarm, and that the master there had only sought labor for an area too remote to interest normal laborers. Others said Lukas Seraphim was himself afflicted in some way, and pitied the creatures, while still others claimed he was a doctor and wanted subjects to practice on.

Those Misfits taken there were never seen again, so none of these stories had ever been authenticated properly. But such was the legend of Obernewtyn, grown over the years because of its very mystery, that it was feared by all orphans, not least because in more modern times it sent out its own keepers to investigate the homes, seeking undisclosed Misfits among the inmates.

It was said these keepers were extraordinarily skillful at spotting aberrations, and that the resultant Council trial was a foregone conclusion.

If what I feared was true, Maruman's garbled predictions and my own premonitions could only add up to a visit by a keeper from Obernewtyn. In the past I had been fortunate enough never to have been present at a home under review by these keepers, but it was an occasion I had dreaded.

When official word of an Obernewtyn keeper's imminent arrival was circulated, my worst fears were realized and I felt a sense of dread of what was to come. All the omens implied disaster, and even Jes was worried enough to catch me alone in the garden and warn me to be careful.

His warning did not surprise me for my exposure would affect him too, but he looked scared and, oddly, that made him more approachable. Impulsively I told him of my premonition, but that only made him angry. "Don't start that business now," he begged. "This whole thing is enough of a mess. I have heard these keepers have an uncanny instinct for anything out of the ordinary."

I shuddered. "I'm afraid," I said in a small voice.

His eyes softened, and to my surprise, he took one of my hands in his and squeezed it reassuringly. "She can't possibly know what you are unless she is like you." I

stared because that was the first time in many ye.
had been able to talk about my powers without bitter.

He mistook my look. "Look, why do you think eve.
one finds out she's coming before she gets here? No on.
tell us anything, but everyone knows. They do it deliberately to scare people. If they're nervous, they're more
likely to give themselves away."

His unexpected kindness was almost my undoing, and
wanting badly to please him, I nodded in agreement. He
looked surprised and rather pleased. We had done nothing but argue for a long time. We smiled at each other,
hesitantly.

∽

The keeper arrived three days later and by then the
atmosphere in the home was electric. Even the guardians
were jumpy and the Herders' lectures grew longer and
more dogmatic. A keeper could not have wished for
more. My headpains had almost gone, though I had told
the guardians they had gone away some time ago because
I did not want to call attention to myself.

Like myself, many of the orphans had never seen one
of the Obernewtyn keepers. I was amazed to see how
beautiful she was, and not at all threatening. It was impossible to look at her petite, fashionably attired form and
credit the gothic horror stories that abounded in connection with Obernewtyn.

She was introduced to us at a special assembly as
Madam Vega. As the head keeper she would have ab-
solute say and a great deal of power in her own institution, and that frightened me all the more, although I saw
no particular sign of power or special perceptive abilities.
She only nodded and smiled when the head of Kinraide
said she would be observing us over the next few days;
then would talk to one or two of us individually before

she left. Everyone knew what that meant, but even this seemed a more rational possibility given her appearance.

The orphans she spoke to as she walked about and watched us spoke of her beauty and her sweetness and gentle manner. Nothing was as we had imagined, and I felt confused. In the normal course of things, a keeper would leave before her choices were announced, if there were any, later sending a carriage for those she had selected. These were taken to Sutrium and redesignated as Misfits.

Nothing happened in those few days to cast any suspicion on me. I was even able to convince myself that both Maruman and I must have been mistaken. Even so, I greeted the morning of her departure with a kind of relief.

At the farewell assembly, she thanked the Kinraide head for her kindness and all the guardians and orphans for their help. A few of us even clapped. Smiling sweetly she then bade us good-bye.

I was working in the kitchen when one of the guardians instructed me to prepare a tea tray for the head and her guest. It was an innocent enough request, but as I wheeled the laden tray to the front interviewing chamber, I felt uneasy. I took a deep breath to calm myself.

The Kinraide head was standing near the door when I entered, and gestured impatiently for me to transfer the tea things from the tray to a low table. I did this rather awkwardly, peering around trying to see where Madam Vega was. My mind was open and unguarded as I used my abilities to locate her. Sensing that she was up the other end of the room, I turned to see her standing with her back to the room, looking out over Kinraide's broad formal gardens.

Then, slowly, she turned around.

The room was a long one but never before had it seemed so long. At the farthest end was a desk and the purple-draped window. She stood to the left and when she turned it seemed to me she went on turning for an eternity, gradually showing more of herself. Struck with the dreadful curiosity of fear, unable to look away, I became convinced that when her movement was completed eons from now, I would be looking into the face of my most terrible nightmares.

Yet she was smiling at me, and her eyes were blue like the summer sky. She hastened to where I stood. "I hope I have not kept you waiting?"

I swallowed because it sounded like she meant me. I was too scared to say anything in case I was mistaken. The Kinraide head assured her the tea things had only just come. She gestured to me to pour the tea. My hands shook.

"My dear child," said Madam Vega, taking the teapot from me with her own lovely white hands, "you're trembling." Then she turned to the head with a faint look of reproach.

"She has been ill," the other woman said with a shrug. I prayed she would dismiss me but she was sugaring her tea.

The keeper looked at me. "I would swear you are frightened. Now why would that be, I wonder? Are you afraid?"

I shook my head but of course she did not believe me.

"You need not fear me. I know of all the silly stories. How they began, I really don't know. I am simply here to take away those children who are afflicted with mental problems. Obernewtyn is a beautiful place, though cold I admit," she added confidingly. "But there is nothing there to frighten anyone. And my good Lord Seraphim, the master there, seeks only to find a cure for such afflictions. He thinks it is possible to do this before the mind is full grown."

"A noble purpose," murmured the other woman pi-

ously. Madam Vega had been watching me very closely
as she spoke. I felt as if I were drowning in the extraordinary blueness of her eyes. There was something almost
hypnotic in them.

"I know a great deal about Misfits," she said.

I wanted to look away but I couldn't, and an urge grew
within me to find out what she was thinking. I let the
edge of my shield fade.

In an instant a dozen impressions pierced me like
blades, but beneath the blue compulsion of her eyes they
faded.

"Well, well," she said, and stepped away from me.

I stood for a moment half dazed.

"Well, go along then," said the Kinraide head impatiently.

I turned on shaking legs, willing myself not to run. As
I closed the door behind me, I heard Madam Vega's
sweet voice utter the words that spelled my doom. "What
did you say that girl was called?"

V

"Jes!"

I stumbled into the kitchen sending out a cloud of panic and urgency.

"Jes. Jes. Jes!"

I almost fell over the astonished Rosamunde who was working there. "Elspeth?" she said disbelievingly.

Jes charged through another door, his face contorted with fury. "What are you doing?" he shouted. Noticing Rosamunde, he stopped to stare at us in confusion.

"For Lud's sake, Jes, don't yell at her. It's one of her fainting fits again." Rosamunde looked uncertainly at me. "That water must have been tainted, despite what the Herder said."

"Water?" Jes whispered incredulously.

"Of course," she said sternly. "And stop glaring at her. She's just been in with the Obernewtyn keeper. I'll get a powder," she added, and departed.

"Is it true?" he asked, fear looking out of his eyes.

I nodded numbly.

"But why?"

"I think it was only chance. I don't know . . . perhaps it wasn't. She read the records. That might have made her wonder and ask for me. I had to serve tea. But she knows."

"How can you be sure?" he pressed. "You didn't . . ."

I shook my head emphatically. I wanted to explain how I knew, but now it all seemed too elusive. I thought of myself staring mesmerized into her eyes.

"What did you do? Tell me what they said," he asked urgently. "Did they speak of me?"

"They said nothing. But at the end, when I was leaving, she asked who I was," I said.

He gaped. "That's all?"

But I shook my head. There was no point in letting him hope. I knew. He saw that in my face and the light died in his eyes. He might despise my powers, but he did not doubt they existed.

"Even so, you could be wrong," he said, stroking his precious armband. "They might not know everything. If she just put things together from the records and then saw that you were scared . . .There must be some pretty queer comments about you in those papers. That must be what happened. I told you fear would be our undoing."

"Jes!" It was Rosamunde. She frowned at him and came onto the veranda. "Don't keep on at her like some idiot guardian. Help her into the kitchen porch. Some fresh air will soothe her."

"She's all right," Jes snapped, but he carried me onto the veranda and set me on a couch. Ignoring him, Rosamunde handed me a powder. I swallowed it without demur, hardly noticing its bitter aftertaste.

"I am sorry," I told Jes, suddenly remorseful.

He made no reply. His face was grim. I could not blame his hatred of my abilities. At that moment I hated them myself.

"It's all right," Rosamunde soothed me. But I knew nothing would ever be all right again.

She had noticed the look on Jes's face and sat on the couch beside him. "What is the matter? Tell me. You know you can trust me. I'll help if I can."

He looked at her, and to my astonishment, I could see that he did trust her. Lying to this girl would not come easily to him. I looked at her properly. She was a plain, sensitive-looking girl, pale as most orphans were, with a mop of brown curls neatly tied back. I wondered that I had been so blind as to miss the thawing of my self-sufficient brother.

Jes turned to face me. "Are you all right, Elf?" he asked. That had been his pet name for me in happier days, but he had not used it for a long time. How odd that it had taken a disaster to show me that there was still some bond of affection between us. His face was thoughtful and as often before, I wished I could read his mind. He was not like me, yet his was one of the rare minds that seemed to have a natural shield.

"I must think," he said to himself.

Rosamunde gazed at us both in consternation. She sensed something dreadful had happened. "Tell me, please," she urged.

"Elspeth. . . .Well, we think she will be declared a Misfit," Jes said tiredly.

"You poor thing," Rosamunde whispered. To her credit, she did not even wonder what was wrong with me.

"Elf . . . has begun to have unnatural dreams," Jes said slowly.

I stared at him. Occasionally I had dreamed true, but not often. Why was Jes lying?

His eyes were evasive and dismay filled my heart when he spoke.

"It was the tainted water that caused them," Jes said. "It has infected her."

I gaped openly now.

"But . . . surely that is not her fault really. Everyone knows that sometimes happens with tainted water. Surely she will not be declared Misfit because of that," Rosamund said incredulously. "She was normal before the accident and I am sure that will temper their judgment."

My own mind shied away from the tissue of lies Jes was weaving. It was obvious he wanted to make me look as blameless as possible, afflicted by accident rather than born a Misfit, to protect his own status. Fear was like ice in my blood and I tried to believe he lied only to protect us both from the consequences of the exposure of my true nature and not just to save himself.

"You could talk to them, try to explain," Rosamunde said eagerly.

Jes flicked an unreadable look at her.

"At least she might only go to the Councilfarms and you could petition for her once you have your own Certificate."

Then a look of concern passed over her features and for the first time she thought of Jes. If I were declared a born Misfit, he would be stripped of his armband and privileges and even his Certificate would be in doubt. If the Council judged that I had been affected by tainted water, made Misfit through misadventure, no blame would fall to Jes. Possibly the Obernewtyn keeper would not want me either. I thrust the memory of those piercing blue eyes from me. I looked at Jes. I had never known what motivated him. He had an oddly tortuous mind and even as a child had been inclined to secrecy. If I were right, I could not love this selfishness that motivated him. But perhaps he thought of me too. I found I could not bear to think so badly of him. It would go easier for me too if the Council thought I was a Misfit only by accident.

"Talk to them," Rosamunde urged Jes, but he shook his head.

"It would not help. They might even take me," he said, half to himself.

Rosamunde jumped to her feet. "You are no Misfit!" she cried.

"No," Jes agreed. He looked at me and his eyes were sad. He seemed to have forgotten his previous words. Now he seemed actually resigned. "Leave us," he said to Rosamunde gently.

She stared at him, then burst into noisy tears. "No. I will come too if they take you. I could pretend. . . ." But he would not listen and she faltered.

"Be wise," Jes said. "We don't know what will happen at Obernewtyn." He paused and I sensed a struggle taking place within him. "If things had been different . . ." he began, then stopped. He was silent then, his face troubled. I understood what stopped him for I felt it myself. Orphan life imposes shackles of silence that are not easy to throw aside at will. I liked him better in that moment than I had for many days.

Rosamunde seemed to understand and dried her tears. Her face was wretched with unhappiness. "They might not take you . . ." she said.

I looked at her and a plan came to me. I would have to be wary and delicate.

Carefully I directed my ability to manipulate thoughts into her turmoiled mind, seeking to create the chains of thought and action I needed, joining them carefully onto her own half-formed notions. I had not used my coercing ability so directly before, and I was curious to see how well the thoughts and decisions I had grafted hastily would hold.

"You must go," Jes told her. "I want you to go. Never speak of this or us again. It is bad enough that we have been seen together. I will not let you be dragged into this mess."

"Oh, Lud, no," she sobbed, and ran inside.

Jes and I looked at each other, neither of us having the slightest idea what the other thought.

∽

"Elspeth Gordie."

I trembled at the sound of my name, though I had been waiting for it. At that last moment, there was a flare of hope that I had been wrong after all.

I waited, still trembling, as those around me drew back. I could not blame them, for to be associated with a Misfit is a danger in itself. The head of Kinraide went on to say that I had been affected by tainted water and I knew my plan had worked. I looked at Jes and caught his amazed look. He did not understand what had happened. I prayed I knew him well enough to guess he would not speak out. My eyes sought out Rosamunde, who would not look at me, and I hoped she would not be too badly affected by what I had willed her to do. I felt a self-loathing for having burdened her with a betrayal she would never have contemplated undertaking without my coercing thought.

Her denouncement had come too late to stop the proceedings under which I would be bonded to Obernewtyn, but it had saved Jes from any trouble and had categorized me as a very ordinary sort of Misfit. I prayed the knowledge that she had saved Jes would be enough to salve Rosamunde. I did not want her to suffer.

An awful lethargy filled me while I sat in the punishment room, where I would stay until the Council coach came for me. I had overheard one of the guardians say it would come very early the next day.

Maruman came to my prison window that night. I tried to explain that I was going away but he was still under the sway of his fit and I could not tell how much he understood.

"The mountains have called at last," he observed wisely.

"Last night I dreamed of the oldOne again. She said your destiny is there."

"Oh don't," I begged, but Maruman was merciless in his fey state.

"I smell the white in the mountains," he told me with drifting eyes that reflected the moonlight. I found myself trembling after he had gone and wished that now, of all times, Maruman had been his grumpy sensible self, all too ready to scoff at my fears.

I slept fitfully until I heard movement at the door. It was still not dawn and I wondered if the carriage had arrived. But it was Jes.

"Forgive me," he said.

I gaped at him.

"I didn't tell them that business about the water. I swear. I . . . I thought of it, to save myself, but I didn't. I don't know how they came to know. I wouldn't blame you for thinking I had done it," he said wretchedly.

"It's better that they think I am only a Dreamer and not born a Misfit. It is better this way. You are normal," I said earnestly, hoping he would not confess his anguish to poor Rosamunde, who might blurt out her part in my denunciation.

"I was so scared when they read your name out," he said in a muffled voice. "I didn't even think of you. I was only scared for myself."

He was full of self-reproach now that it was too late, and I sensed his rigid nature would crumble completely if I allowed him to break down. He seemed to feel he had betrayed me simply because the thought had occurred to him. How confused he was underneath all his rigidity.

"Soon you will have your Certificate. Perhaps you will be able to petition for me," I said softly.

"But Obernewtyn does not let go of those it takes," he whispered and looked as though he would cry.

Hastily I took his hand. "Oh, Jes," I said. "You of all people afraid of monsters? You saw the keeper? Did she look so awful? I'm not frightened. And I would have hated the Councilfarms," I added with a smile.

Wanly he smiled back.

There was a movement outside and a voice called that the carriage was ready. I looked at Jes in sudden concern. It was dangerous for him to be here, but he shook his head, saying the Herder himself had given permission. I noticed he still wore the armband, Jes said he had asked to say prayers for my soul.

He leaned forward suddenly, his eyes fierce. "I will help you, I promise."

But you are only sixteen, I thought, *with two more long spans until you can even apply for your Certificate.* Yet I might have believed him, but instinct told me this would be our last parting. Impulsively I flung my arms around him. "Dear Jes, don't be sad. It really is best this way. You know that. And except for our parting, I am honestly glad it is done with. Believe me."

"Time now," said the guardian. Jes nodded. Suddenly aware that he was being watched, he said the last few chants of a prayer.

"Good-bye," I whispered in my thoughts.

He did not wait to see me bundled into the dark coach and I was glad. I had done my best for Jes and Rosa-munde.

I sat back into the stiff upholstery and wondered what destiny waited for me at Obernewtyn.

VI

There were few people around to see me arrive at the Councilcourt in Sutrium. Even at the busiest hour few tarried near those somber buildings. The white slate steps led up to the open double doors and for the second time in my life I ascended them, led by a soldierguard. The smell of wood polish made me vividly recollect my last visit. But then, Jes had been with me, squeezing my hand.

"Sit and wait till you are called," said the soldierguard, peering into my face as if to ascertain whether I was capable of understanding. I nodded dully and he went away. I wondered why I did not just run away.

Two men came through the front door. A soldier came up and spoke softly to the other of the pair, then pointed to a door. There was something unusual about them but I felt too numb at first to try to work out what it was. Then it came to me. They were very tanned, as if they had spent their whole life outdoors. Half-breed gypsies were that color but this pair wore plain brown working clothes and looked more like farmers. Perhaps that was what they were. I wondered why they were here.

The older man went through the door the soldierguard had indicated while the other looked around to find I was sitting on the only seat available. He hesitated, then sat beside me.

"Hello," he said.

I stared at him, amazed that he would speak to a complete stranger and here of all places. "Who are you?" I asked, suddenly suspicious.

He looked amused and his eyes crinkled in a nice sort of way. "Do I look like a spy?" He laughed. "My name is Daffyd," he added as I hesitated. "My uncle is petitioning the council for a permit to trade in the mountains."

"The mountains," I echoed.

"Well, not exactly the mountains. After all, whom would we trade with? I meant the high country," he explained. He smiled again and despite everything I found myself smiling back. "Why are you here?" he asked.

"I'm a Misfit, or soon to be one," I said bluntly. "I'm being sent to Obernewtyn."

But he didn't recoil. "So you will be going to the mountains." His expression was odd and impulsively I tried to read him. Like Jes, he had a natural block.

"You don't look like a Misfit to me," he said again, with that nice smile. "Well, if you are like me, you will find the mountains beautiful. I don't have much time for places like this," he added disparagingly, meaning the town.

"Aren't you afraid to be seen talking to a Misfit?" I asked. "It's not usually done lightly."

"Where I come from, they say Misfits are people who have been punished by Lud. But there are worse things," he answered.

"Oh yes?" I asked ironically. "What could be worse?"

"These people for one. This Luddamned Council," he said in a low, intense voice. I stared, for what he was saying was Sedition. Either he was mad or insanely careless.

Seeing my look, he only shrugged. "These fools think everyone who doesn't think and act as they do is evil.

"Are you afraid of Obernewtyn?" he asked.

I shrugged. "I heard some terrible stories, but then I met the Obernewtyn head keeper. . . . I don't know," I said honestly.

"It is a very large place and they have true farms. Not those things the Council calls a farm. Much better, with animals and crops and sowing and reaping. You might be sent to work there," he said reassuringly. He looked around the foyer.

"Have you . . . do you know it?" I asked.

His eyes were suddenly evasive and I did not press him. He bit his lip and seemed to be trying to make his mind up about something.

"I might escape," I told him, more for effect than because I meant it.

But he gave me a measured look. "If ever you do run away, you might seek out the Druid. I have heard he lives still in hiding. You could look. . . ." he said very quietly.

I wondered then if he was defective, because everyone knew the Druid was dead.

"I do not think he would love a Misfit but you need not tell him. . . ."

At the sound of footsteps we both looked up, and the boy stopped abruptly as the older man returned.

He looked at us sharply, then gestured to the boy. "Come, Daffyd," he said, his eyes skidding over me.

The boy rose at once. He said nothing to me but smiled when his uncle had turned.

I watched them go and wondered. The Druid had escaped with some of his followers after defying a Council directive to burn his precious collection of Oldtime books. That had been long years past and rumor was that he had died. Yet this boy implied the Druid was still

alive in the mountains. I shrugged. The boy was more
likely defective. He had been very careless in talking to
me at all.

A soldierguard stepped from one of the doors and
waved impatiently for me to enter. I went slowly, playing
the part of a dullwit. The trial room was quite small. At
the very front sat the Councilman seated at a high bench,
facing the rest of the room. Beside him at a lower table
were two Herders. The rows of seats facing the front were
occupied only by a few lounging soldierguards. They
were theoretically meant for interested members of the
community, but no one ever went there for fear of being
associated with whoever was on trial. No one looked up
as I came in, prodded to the front by the soldier on duty.
Feeling bitter, I looked up at the Councilman, wondering
what would happen to the daughter of such a person if
she were judged Misfit.

"Well now," said the Councilman in a brisk voice. "We
will begin this trial." His eyes passed over me with dis-
interest. I was less than nothing to him. "I understand
this is a routine affair with no defense?" he said to the
room. "You are Elspeth Gordie?" he asked in a perfunctory tone.

I nodded.

"Very well, you have been charged Misfit by Madam
Vega of Obernewtyn. Corsak, you will speak for the Master of Obernewtyn?"

A tall man in black walked forward and came to stand
near me. He did not look at me. "This is a Misfit who
has been exposed by the Obernewtyn head keeper," he
said. "She was also denounced by another orphan who
claimed the girl fell in tainted water and from that time
commenced to have unnatural dreams and fainting fits.
There are several other odd points. May I expand?"

The Councilman nodded.

"In her first home she was accused of laying a curse

on another orphan. She was also accused of giving an evil eye. Naturally we do not place too much credibility on these reports, but they do point to the possibility that she was already disturbed when this tainted water infected her."

The man in black had not once referred to notes. I was frightened by the amount of information he had. I had never imagined my report held so much. With such a report I would never have been issued a Certificate. I was relieved that Rosamunde had told them I was tainted by the water, for that seemed to have overshadowed the rest of the evidence.

"Your master feels there is some hope of a cure?" the Councilman asked.

"My master concentrates all his efforts on healing," the man in black answered somewhat defensively.

One of the Herders rose. "Misfits have minds which are inhabited by demons."

The man in black bowed. "My master feels the demons can be driven out and the mind healed if the subject is young."

The Herder grunted and looked at his companion, who also rose. "Driving away demons is Herder work," he said.

"My master's motives are good," said the Obernewtyn representative.

"Where are your successes?" asked the first Herder aggressively.

The Obernewtyn man cast an appealing look at the Councilman, who coughed. "You are well paid for these creatures," he said.

"That is not for discussion," snapped the Councilman coldly. He looked at the two Herders, who sat down.

The man in black looked nervous. "I beg pardon," he said eloquently. "You know we use these Misfits for labor, but my master diligently seeks a cure."

The Councilman eyed him thoughtfully. "We understand this from Madam Vega's reports. Even so, perhaps
it is time for us to visit your master and evaluate for
ourselves what Obernewtyn does."

His eyes flicked back momentarily to me as if he had
forgotten my presence. "Do you admit to harboring demons?" he asked in a bored tone.

I cringed and shook my head with what I hoped was
a convincingly vacant leer. The Councilman sighed as if
it were as much as he had expected before asking if anyone knew whether I was able to speak. No one answered
and the Councilman scowled impatiently.

"Very well, I pronounce her Misfit. Take her, Corsak,
and make arrangements to name her in the records when
you make the bond over. And we look forward to an
invitation to visit Obernewtyn," he added meaningfully.

Corsak nodded and indicated for me to follow him.

The Councilman forestalled him coldly. "If you please.
Is the scribe here?"

"Yes!" said a cheerful voice.

"Ensure this reaches the people. Misfits are a particularly foul and insidious threat to our community. They
often pass as normal for many years, since their defects
are not obvious to the eye. We know this because of the
efforts of our good and diligent Herders." The two Herders inclined their heads modestly. "They have lately in-
formed me that their researchers have revealed that
Misfits are the Lud's way of punishing our laxity. How
is it, the Lud asks us, that Misfits are permitted to roam
and breed among us for so long? The answer is that we
have failed in our duty of watchfulness. This attitude
threatens to hurl us back into the Age of Chaos and
worse. Therefore, it is the order and decree of this Councilcourt that penalties for aiding and concealing Misfits
and any other defective humans or beasts will increase.
Each man must watch his neighbor. . . ."

He went on to explain the various new rulings and penalties, and I shuddered at the effect this would have on the community. Each time the Council sought to tighten its control, a new wave of denunciations and burnings occurred. Oddly enough, I fancied a look of surprise had crossed the face of the younger priest at the mention of Herder researches.

VII

It took some time to reach the outskirts of Sutrium. I had not expected the city to be so big. The streets were completely deserted and it was well into the morning before we reached the end of the town's sprawling outer limits, but toward midday the city fell rapidly behind.

I had lived in urban orphan homes now for many years, but the curved road parting the soft folded hills and gullies brought back clear memories of my childhood, far from the towns and the ever present menace of the Council. I realized I had not lied to Jes when I told him I was almost glad. There was an odd sort of peace in having got the thing done at last. I thought of Head Keeper Madam Vega, and reflected that Obernewtyn was bound to be less terrible than the stories.

It was not hard to forget fear and to surrender myself to the peaceful solitude of the carriage. The morning burgeoned into a sun-filled day, and between naps, I watched the country unfold.

To the east of the road we passed the villages of Saithwold and Sawlney, and beyond them to the north were soft woodlands, where from the window I could see the downs sloping gently to Arandelft, set deep in the forest.

To the west of the road were the vast hazy moors of Glenelg.

The road curved down to pass on the farthermost outskirts of the village, where slate-gray buildings were framed by surrounding cultivated fields flanked by borders of bloodberry trees. More than twenty leagues away and closing the horizon were Aran Craggie and the Gelfort Ranges—Tor, Highfeld Gamorr, and Emerald Fel. They marked the border of the Highlands and as if to underline this, the road began gradually to incline upward.

We passed on the low western slopes of the Brown Haw Rises, hillocked and undulant—I was astounded to discover how much I knew of land I had never seen. My father had talked a good deal of these places. He had traveled much in the land before he bonded with my mother. Sometimes he had seated me on his knee and showed me colored pictures that he called maps. He would point to places, tell me their names, and explain what they were like. I thought he must have bequeathed his restless spirit to me.

We passed a small moor, wetter and more dense than Glenelg, and I peered through the leafy Eben trees along the roadside at the mist-wreathed expanse. There had been no moors in Rangorn but I recognized this from my father's descriptions. He had said the mists never went away but were always fed by some hissing subterranean source. He thought the moors were caused by some inner disturbance in the earth, yet another legacy of the Great White. I was astounded at my memories.

My mother had said good herbs always grew near the moors; she came from the high country and knew a great deal about herbal lore. I thought of the great, white-trunked trees that had stood on the hillside around our house. Were they still there, though the house had long ago been reduced to ashes? I remembered my mother making me listen to the whispering sounds of the trees, and of the rich, shadowed glades where we collected mushrooms and healing flowers and the summer brambles laden with fat berries dragging over the bank of our favored swimming pool. I thought of standing with my father and looking down from the hills to where the Ford of Rangorn met the onrush of the Suggredoon, and the distant grayish glint far in the distance where I knew there was a lake in the Blacklands.

And I remembered the burning of my mother and father, in the midst of all the beauty of Rangorn. Perhaps that was what Jes remembered most, what had made him so cold and strange in recent times. Yet in the end he had seemed genuinely distressed to see me go. What would happen to him now? It no longer angered me that he longed to become a Herder, though that could never be. I hoped he would be happy and safe, but he was already becoming a shadowy figure.

I had the fleeting impression something in me wanted to put the old life behind me and try to find something in this new life worth living for. It had been a long time since I had done more than live for the minute, preoccupied with fear of discovery and the desire to be free. I wondered if it would be possible for me to find a better existence in the mountains.

As the late afternoon sun slanted through the window of the carriage, we halted briefly at a wayside hostel and a new coachman came to take the place of the other. The hostel was just outside a village called Guanette and I felt a jolt at the name. It made me think of Maruman, and my regret at having to leave him. I wondered if he had understood that I really was going away for good. The name of the village would have intrigued him because of the dreams he claimed to have in which those birds appeared. I wondered how it had come to have thàt name. The way that word kept cropping up, I felt there ought to be some significance to it, though I could hardly see what. Resolutely putting Maruman and the tantalizing name of the place from me, I thought it would be pleasant to live there, if one could not live in Rangorn. But that was no longer even a distant possibility. As a Misfit, I would never be free. But perhaps I would find some compensations in the life that waited for me at Obernewtyn.

The village consisted mostly of small, stone-wrought hovels with shingled roofs. They looked ancient and had probably been established during the Age of Chaos. Their stolidness seemed a defense against the turmoiled past.

Laughter drifted in through the windows as we passed children scrabbling in pools of dust along the roadway. They looked up indifferently as we passed. I was once like them, I thought, rather bitterly, until the Council had taken a hand.

The carriage jerked suddenly to a halt and the coachman dismounted. We had stopped outside yet another hostel called "The Green Tree."

After a long time he came back, unlocked a window, and threw a soft parcel to me. "Supper," he grunted in a curious accent. Impulsively, I asked him if I could sit outside and eat.

He hesitated, then unlocked the door. "Out yer get then," he said.

Thanking him profusely, I did as he bade, and he relocked the carriage, muttering about children. I stood blinking at him. "Go round th' back. Ye can eat there. Mind ye don't wander." Thanking him again, I hastened away, thinking many of the late night callers at my father's house had spoken like this, slowly with a singsong lilt. They had looked like this man too, gnarled and brown with kind eyes.

There was a pretty, unkempt garden out the back of

the hostel and I scoured the porch for a spot under one of the trees.

"Least you could do is spare me some food," came a plaintive thought. I jumped to my feet in fright, dropping the food parcel. Maruman rushed forward and sniffed it tenderly. "Now look what you've done."

I stared at him in bewilderment, unable to believe my eyes. "What . . . how did you get here!" My mind reeled. Maruman gave me a sly cat look and fell to tearing at the parcel. I sat back down and unwrapped it for him, my own appetite forgotten.

"I came with you," he told me as he ate. I was so delighted to see him that I didn't know whether to laugh or cry.

"I came in the box with wheels, on the back. I am very clever," he added smugly and I burst out laughing, then I looked around in fright because my laughter sounded so loud.

"But why?" I asked, relieved at least that his fits were over.

"You regret my presence?" he asked. I shook my head emphatically and hugged him till he squeaked. "I had to come," he said when he had struggled free. "Innle must be protected."

I looked at his eyes but there was no sign of madness. "You won't be able to come all the way to Obernewtyn," I said. "The carriage goes over the Blacklands."

"Maruman knows that," he said haughtily. "I will stay here and you will come to me. I do not like the mountains. I smell the white there."

I shook my head impatiently. "I can't possibly come back. I told you, Obernewtyn is like a cage. I won't be allowed to do as I please." I forestalled a thought I saw forming in his mind. "And it's not at all like the orphan home so I won't be able to sneak off."

Unperturbed by my words, he began cleaning one of

his paws. "You will come," he said at last. "Maruman does not want to come to the mountains," he added reproachfully.

"Well, how will you live here?" I asked him. He gave me a very old look; Maruman had after all lived a good many years before meeting me. Just the same, I reflected, he was not a young cat, and then there were his fits of madness. He curled up in my lap and promptly went to sleep.

I thought of what I had said to Daffyd, the boy in the Councilcourt. I had not meant it then, but now I seriously considered escaping. I could run off; it would be far easier here than it would have been in Sutrium.

My mother once had bought a wild bird from an old man who caught the poor things. We hadn't much money but she had a soft heart and a sweet smile. He had given her the oldest bird, an ugly creature he had had for some time. She had opened the cage to let it fly away. But it was a poor half-starved thing and would not go even when prodded. It died there, huddled in the corner of the cage. My mother had said it had been caged for too long. Neither Jes nor I had understood then, but I wondered if, like that bird, I had been caged too long to contemplate freedom.

A voice called my name and Maruman woke and stepped from my knee. He melted into the shadows just as the coachman and a woman came onto the porch of the hostel. The old man blinked and I sensed he had seen Maruman, but he said nothing. The woman turned to him. "Just as well for you that she did not wander away." She flicked her hand at me. "Get into the carriage."

I followed them back to the road with an inward sigh, noticing the horses had been changed. I would have preferred to travel this last leg of the journey alone. The

woman climbed heavily into the seat and glared at me
as she settled herself.

Eventually she spoke. "I am guardian Hester."

I looked at her expectantly, but she seemed to feel it
was beneath her to say any more to me. She had a valise
with her and I thought she was returning to Obernewtyn,
possibly from a visit to the Lowlands. She yawned several
times and seemed bored. Eventually she took a small vial
from her pocket, uncorked it, and drank the contents. I
recognized the bitter odor of the sleep drug. In a very
short time, she was dozing.

Since leaving Guanette, the country had grown steadily steeper. The road was still well cobbled but it had
become progressively more narrow and winding. The
coachman maneuvered carefully around the bends, for
on one side was a sharp drop to a darkly wooded valley
extending as far as the eye could see. It was tough going,
and after about an hour, he pulled over to the edge and
poured water from a barrel into a bucket to water the
horses. I called out to him.

"Hey," he mimicked. "Is that my name then?"

"I'm sorry. No one tells us names. Can I ride up there
with you?"

I held little hope and predictably he shook his head,
peering in at the guardian's sleeping form. "If ye were
alone maybe I would let ye," he said slowly and softly.
"But if she were to waken an' see ye gone." He shook
his head in anticipation of the coals of wrath that would
be heaped on his head.

"But she won't wake for hours. She took some of that
sleep stuff." I poked her hard to show him I spoke the
truth.

He ruminated for a moment, then took out his keys.

"Oh thank you," I gasped, astounded at my luck.

"Well fine of me it is," he agreed. "But she better not
wake or I'll be in deep troubles." He finished watering

the horses while I capered in the crisp highland air. "Enoch," the coachman said suddenly.

"Pardon?" I said.

"Enoch, girl," he repeated. "That's my name." He
helped me up onto the seat beside him and I felt a thrill
as he clicked his tongue and the coach began to move.

"My name . . ." I began to say, then stopped. Perhaps
he wouldn't want to know my name. Misfits, after all,
weren't supposed to be quite human.

"Your name?" he said, and encouragèd, I told him.
He nodded and fell silent for a bit as if he didn't know
what else to say. Then he pointed to the valley. "That's
the White Valley."

I stared, thinking that Maruman would not like the
name. Enoch went on talking. "Many have gone to that
valley in search of hidin' but it ain't a friendly place.
Strange animals rove there an' they don't love men."

"I heard Henry Druid came to the mountains. Maybe
that's where he died," I said thoughtfully, but the old
man snorted with laughter.

"He's nowt dead," he said. He saw my quick look of
interest and his expression was bland. "Leastways, rumor
says his ghost wanders there, an' in th' mountains. That
valley goes on for fifty leagues in all directions. 'Tis said
this place was once part of the Blacklands but I dinna
think so."

I looked at the wood and reflected that twice in a very
short span, I had been told the Druid lived.

"That were a fine cat," the coachman said.

I jumped, but decided not to deny it. Instinctively I
guessed this man meant no harm.

"He'd been with us some way. I guess he just likes
ridin'," the old man said casually.

Still I said nothing.

"Some don't like cats. Reckon they're too haughty, but
I dinna think so. Either ye like cats or ye don't."

"He's not a very pretty cat," I said hesitantly.

The old man grinned. "All that's fine is nowt pretty. Look at me. As a matter of fact, I thought him a handsome creature." He looked at me again. "I've a good mind to have a bit of a look for him. Maybe he'd fancy living with me. Of course cats are queer creatures an' he might not take to me."

"Oh, he will!" I cried.

The coachman smiled and nodded slightly and we rode for some distance in companionable silence. Perhaps Enoch would find Maruman. I hoped so.

The valley was lost to sight at last as we wound into the mountains. "That stuff would kill a pig," said the coachman. He jerked his head back to where the guardian slept. "Now me mam gave us herbs when we couldn't sleep. Good natural things. That were good enough for us then."

"But herbal lore is banned," I said.

He looked taken aback. "An' so it is. Damned if I didn't forget fer a minute. But it weren't against th' law when I were a lad." He paused, seemingly struck by the oddness of something that had been a good thing in his youth but that had become evil since, in the eyes of the community. Finally he sighed as if the problem were unresolvable. "Things were different then," he said.

Looking around, he pointed again to where we had come back into the open; this time there was a broad plain on the other side of the road. The mountains hid the White Valley from us. "Th' land hereabout is Darthnor, and th' village of Darthnor is that way," Enoch said, nodding to the east. I stared but could see nothing. " 'Tis a strange place," he said, "an' I say so even though I were born there. None dwell in these parts but a few shepherds. Those at Darthnor are mostly miners but I reckon th' ground here is tainted so I dinna go under like me father did before me." He looked sad. "A few years under th' ground and the rotting sickness sets in, though it moves fearful slow." He looked ahead suddenly, then pulled to the edge of the road.

"Ye'll have to get in now. Soon we come to tainted ground an' the vapors are pure poison," he said.

I climbed down and held the horses while he watered them and tied rags around their noses and faces and bags on their hoofs.

"Won't *you* get sick?" I asked, but he shook his head saying Darthnor bred a hardy sort and that he would be all right for the short time we would be on tainted earth. Nonetheless he tied a scarf around his face before locking me back into the carriage.

Suddenly he gave a shout and pointed up. I looked but saw nothing.

"That were a Guanette bird," he shouted. "Ye missed it an' that's a shame for 'tis a rare sight."

"A Guanette bird?" I gaped, thinking I had misheard him. "I thought they were extinct."

Enoch shook his head slowly. "Nowt extinct, but I guess it might be better to be thought so. They're rare and rare things are hunted," he added darkly. "That village back there were named for the birds by the first Master of Obernewtyn, Sir Lukas Seraphim. He were the first to come to th' mountains, an' a grand queer man he must have been to make his home up there with the Blacklands all round. His grandson is master up there now."

There was a subtly different note in his voice at the mention of the present master of Obernewtyn.

"Have you seen him?" I asked, hoping to elicit further information.

"Never in me life," said the coachman. "All the time he's workin' on his treatments." A strange look crossed his face but it was so brief I thought I had imagined it. His mention of treatments made me uneasy.

"In yer go," he said, and moved to lock the window. He hesitated. "Look, if ye be special fond of animals, I've a friend of sorts up there. His name be Rushton. Tell him I said I'd vouch for ye an' maybe he'll find a job ye'll like."

But before I could thank him, he had locked me in.

VIII

I *dreamed.*

In my dream, I was somewhere cold and darkly quiet. I could hear water dripping and was afraid, though I didn't know why. I seemed to be waiting for something.

In the distance, there was a bright flash of light. A feeling of urgency made me hasten toward the light, stumbling over uneven ground I could not see. A high-pitched whining noise filled the air like a scream, but no one could scream for so long without stopping to breathe. I sensed danger, but the compulsion to find the light overrode my instincts. Again it flashed, apparently no closer than before. I could not tell what the source was, though it was obviously unnatural.

All at once, a voice spoke inside me. Shocked, I skidded to a halt, for it was a human voice. But that was impossible.

"Tell me," the voice said, "tell me."

There was a sharp pain behind my eyes and I flinched in astonishment that a voice was capable of hurting me, understanding at the same time that the crooning noise and the voice inside me were the same thing. I turned to run, at last obeying the urge to escape, then the ground under me burst into flames, and I screamed.

I woke and stared wildly about, my heart thundering even as the nightmare faded. I could feel perspiration on my hands and back. I lay back, trying to think what such a dream might mean. I rarely dreamed that intensely. I had slept for hours and it was dark. I wondered if we had already passed the tainted ground and did not know whether to be disappointed or not.

Bruised, purple clouds scudded across the sky making it appear later than it must have been. A distant cracking noise heralded the coming storm and within moments, a flash of lightning illuminated the barren landscape. There was a rumble of thunder and I pitied Enoch. There was another crack and this time the scent of charred wood drifted in through the window. I hoped Maruman was somewhere safe.

Despite the steep grade of the road, I sensed the unease of the animals and with each crash of thunder, their tension grew; yet I had the odd impression it was not the storm but something else that unnerved them. There was another loud crash, very close, and a log fell right alongside the carriage.

The horses' suppressed terror erupted and they plunged along the road at a mad pace, jerking the coach wildly after them like some doomed creature dragged to its death. I could hear Enoch's blasphemous thoughts as he fought to control the maddened team.

Holding tightly onto the window, I looked down at the guardian, who slept on. Branches scraped at the window and the road had suddenly narrowed and we were in the midst of a thick clump of gnarled trees. I hoped none would fall for they were big enough to crush the carriage.

A blinding gray rain began to fall, beating deep into the hard, cold earth as we passed from the trees out into the open again. I could see very little because of the rain and the darkness but the landscape looked barren and ugly. The rain stopped quite abruptly, like a tap had been turned off.

The silence that followed was so complete it was uncanny. The horses were under control again and I heard a tired snort from one. The sound almost echoed in the stillness. It had grown fractionally lighter and I could see sparse trees drooping wearily. This land must indeed be cursed with demons for the fury of nature to strike at it so mercilessly.

Then before my eyes, the land seemed to transform itself from a barren place to the bleakest, deadest piece of earth. Here was a place where it was impossible to imagine a single blade of grass or even the most stunted tree growing. A strange terrible burning smell penetrated the carriage, despite the locks and thick glass. I could see vapors rising sluggishly from the earth and writhing along like yellowish snakes. In some places, the ground was as smooth and shiny as glass.

This, then, was the tainted ground, but surely it could not long ago have been true Blacklands.

It was not a very great time·before we had passed over it, but it seemed to take an eternity. Now I understood the tension of the horses. It was not the storm they had feared, but the poisoned earth they must cross.

I heard a faint sound and looking around again, wondered what now. The noise arose almost from the hills themselves and I wondered if Obernewtyn was somewhere near. A small breeze rose in the trees and they moved sluggishly. The sky was lighter still but had the dull sheen of polished metal. It was colder now.

Then the storm burst over us again. This time there was no rain, just a fierce wind that tossed the cart around like a leaf. The long-suffering trees were bent almost double beneath this fresh onslaught and I began to understand their ragged appearance. They did well even to survive in this savage land. There seemed something primitive and destructive in the wind, an evil intent I could nearly feel.

Like the rain, it stopped suddenly and all at once I could hear only the slushy rattle of the wheels as they plowed through the new mud. The sound accomplished what nothing else had been able to do and woke the guardian.

With a grunt she sat up and blinked owlishly. "Have we passed the storms?" she asked.

I gaped "You mean . . . they're always like that?" I asked.

"If you went back there right now the storms would be going on," she said: "They're caused by the Blacklands." She saw the look on my face. "Obernewtyn is a way off yet."

I sighed with relief and looked out the windows again.

The last stretch of the journey seemed endless but it was as the guardian had said. Obernewtyn was some distance from real Blacklands and its belt of storms. The country grew more fertile and ordinary, though very jagged and uneven. It was still a wild sort of land but not so very different from the high country.

I had lost my sense of time many hours back, but I realized now that night must have given way to the early, morning, for its dense blackness had transmuted into a cold, dark blue.

"There it is," said the guardian suddenly and I saw a sign swinging between two posts. In dark lettering it read: OBERNEWTYN. KEEP OUT.

The sight of it chilled me more effectively than all the Blacklands in the land. Just beyond was an iron gate set into a high stone wall. The wall extended as far as I could see in both directions and I wondered how big Obernewtyn was. I half expected it to be a rambling building as most of the orphan homes were. Enoch pulled the horses up and unlocked the gate. He walked the weary team through, then relocked it from the other side. I wondered why they bothered—surely its remoteness barred the way more effectively than any locks. I tried to see the house, but thick, ornately clipped trees hid their secret well in the curving drive. Someone had gone to great lengths to keep Obernewtyn from prying eyes. What sort of person would make a home in such a place?

"Obernewtyn," whispered the guardian, looking out the other window. Her voice was low as if the sight of that sombre building quelled her as much as it did me. Even the horses seemed to walk softly.

It was a massive construction and outwardly more like a series of buildings than one single mansion. It was constructed of large rough-hewn blocks of gray stone streaked with flecks of darker stone. There was no grace in the outline and no effort had been made to make one section harmonize with the rest. In some places it was two and three stories high, each wall pocked with hundreds of slitlike holes that must have served as windows.

Impossible to tell exactly how big it was in the darkness, but what could be seen was immense enough to make me wonder how many hundreds of people lived here. There was something unnerving about the anonymity of all those windows. I had not imagined it would be so huge.

As we drew closer to the only obvious entrance, I noticed a tall pole rising from an ugly fountain set a few feet from the steps. At the top of the pole was a lantern whose flame flickered behind gleaming panels, making shadows dance and leap along the walls. I shivered, aware I was already letting the atmosphere work on me.

And there was an atmosphere about the place, for all its sprawling ugliness. It was a grim, gray place with an oddly secretive look because of the lack of doors and normal windows. I tried to tell myself the wind and the darkness and the hissing trees were creating their own sinister air, but I could not tear my eyes from the doors. The carriage drew up at the entrance and cold air gusted and made my hair and cloak flap violently. It was freezing cold outside and the branches of the trees were filled with the blustering wind.

At the top of broad low steps were two large, heavily carved front doors. The carving was an odd touch, since everything else about Obernewtyn was strictly utilitarian, at least outwardly. Looking more closely, I saw that the carvings were fantastical in nature, and completely inappropriate to the institution.

The guardian pressed a bell that sounded dimly within, and as we waited, I studied the carvings. Men and all manner of queer beasts were represented, many seeming half man and half beast. That struck me as blasphemous. Still, whoever had done the work was a true craftsman, for the expressions on the faces portrayed the essences of the emotions they bore. The doors were framed by a wide gilt border covered in exotic symbols. Those markings were so unusual I had the fantastic notion the doors were artifacts from the Beforetime, impossible though that was.

The doors opened to show a tall, thin woman holding a candelabrum. The light played over gaunt features, giving her face a curious fluid look and making it hard to tell exactly what she looked like. She bent closer and I wondered if she found me as indistinct in the light. I was too tired to pretend dullness, and hoped weariness would do as well.

"You'll get no sense out of her," said guardian Hester. "I thought Madam Vega said she didn't intend bringing up any more dreamers. She doesn't even look strong enough to be a good worker."

The other woman raised her eyebrows disdainfully. She was a cold-looking woman with her long face and severe bun. "Then it is fortunate for us you are not paid to think," she said. "If Madam brought this creature here, she will not have done so without purpose," she said very distinctly, and peered into my face in much the same way Madam Vega had at Kinraide, but without any of her hypnotic power.

"Elspeth, this is guardian Myrna."

"You may leave now," the other woman said abruptly.

"But . . . but I thought since it was so late . . ." She hesitated and faltered before the gaze of the other.

"It is not permitted for temporary guardians to stay in the main house. You know that. If our arrangement does not please you . . ."

Guardian Hester clasped her hands together. "Please. No. I . . . forgot. I'll go with the coachman," she begged.

Guardian Myrna inclined her head regally after a weighty pause. "You should hurry, I think they have put the dogs out," she said. The other woman paled and hastened to the door. Guardian Myrna watched her go with a smile, then she took some keys from her apron pocket. "Come with me," she said.

We went out a door leading off the circular entrance chamber and into a long hall pitted with heavy doors. Big, clumsy locks hung from each door. If this was an indication of the security at Obernewtyn, I would have no trouble getting away. Distantly, I heard the bark of a dog.

The guardian unlocked one of the doors. "Tonight you will sleep here and tomorrow you will be given a permanent room." She shut the door and bolted it.

I stood a moment in the total darkness, feeling the room out with my mind. I was alone. It was too cold to get undressed, so I slipped my shoes off and climbed into the nearest bed. Shivering, I wished I was anywhere but at Obernewtyn and drifted uneasily to sleep.

IX

The door banged violently open.

It was still not full light but I could see a young girl standing on the stone threshold with a candle in one hand. With her free hand she continued to hammer loudly at the open door with a peculiar fixed smile on her face.

"What is it?" I said.

She was some years younger than I, but very tall. She looked at me through lackluster eyes. "I have come . . . I have come . . ." She hesitated as though her feeble brain had lost the thread of whatever message she had come to impart. Then she frowned and her face seemed to change. "I have come to . . . to warn you." There was a glimmer in the depth of her muddy eyes and all at once I doubted my initial impression that she was defective.

"Warn me about what?" I asked warily, trying to decide if the approach was some sort of trick.

She made a warding-off movement with her free hand. "Them, you know."

I shook my head. "I don't know what you're talking about. Who are you?"

She jerked her head in a spasm of despair and a look

of anguish came over her face. "Nothing! I'm nothing anymore. . . ."

She looked across the room at me and started to laugh. "You should not have come here," she said at last.

"I didn't choose to come here or anywhere else. I was an orphan, and now I suppose I am a Misfit."

The other girl giggled. "I was no orphan, but I'm a Misfit. Oh sure I am." She laughed again.

Unable to make any sense out of her, I reached out with my thoughts. Her name was Selmar and her mind was a charred wreckage. Most of her thought links did not exist and little remained that was normal. Yet in that brief second, I saw the remnant of someone I could have liked. But whatever she had gone through, or suffered, there was little enough of that person left. All that remained of her past were half-remembered fragments. Here was a mind teetering on the brink of madness. She was a hair's-breadth from it now. It was impossible to know what she thought she was warning me about. I felt a rush of compassion for her.

Her eyes rolled back in panic and cursing my stupidity I realized she could feel me! She must have been one of those people with some fleeting ability. For an instant, her eyes rolled forward and the other girl looked out with a sort of puzzlement as if she were struggling to remember something of great importance. But all too quickly the muddiness in her eyes returned, and with it a pitiful cowering fear.

"I promise I don't know anything," she whispered. I stared in amazement. What was she talking about now? I had expected her to start screaming but she was behaving as if she were terrified. I climbed out of my bed onto the cold floor.

"Selmar," I began compassionately, then a childish voice interrupted my soft plea.

"Selmar, how is it that you take so long to wake one person?"

It was a sweet, piping voice, high-pitched and querulous. Not a voice to inspire fear, yet, if it were possible, Selmar paled even further as she turned to face the young boy behind her. No more than eleven or twelve years, he was as slender as a wand, with delicate curls, slim, girlish shoulders, and large, pale eyes. His lips were pressed tight with anger.

"Well, answer me," he screamed, and she swayed as if she would faint.

"I . . . I didn't do anything . . ." she gibbered. "It was her. She wouldn't wake up."

Ariel clicked his teeth. "You took too long," he said coldly as if he were pronouncing a judgment. "I see you will have to have a talk with Madam and then our master might want to see you again," he said with a cruel, thin smile. The malicious gleam in his beautiful face angered me.

"It is as she told you. I had trouble waking because we got here so late last night," I said.

He looked at Selmar and she nodded pathetically.

"Well, go on then," he conceded with a nasty smile. Selmar turned without another word and fled down the hall, her stumbling footsteps echoing after her. Chewing his underlip, the boy watched her departure with thoughtful eyes.

"What did she say to you?" he asked, turning back on me.

"Nothing," I answered flatly, wondering what right this boy had to interrogate me.

He frowned petulantly. "You're new. Before long you will find out things are different up here. You will learn," he said, his eyes flicking after the departed Selmar. "Get dressed and I will come back for you." He closed the door behind him.

Rummaging angrily through a chest of assorted clothes, I dressed myself. It was freezing within the stone walls and I wondered if the sun would warm the buildings at all when it rose. Yet I was heated in part by my temper. How dare that child behave like a guardian.

Forcing him from my thoughts, I looked around. I could not help thinking that Obernewtyn would be hellish in the wintertime. The pale, early morning light spilled in wanly from a high slitted window. There were no shutters and cold gusts of air swept freely through the opening. I had thought of looking outside, wondering what I would see, but the window was practically inaccessible, fashioned long and thin, reaching from above my head up to the ceiling. Cut deep into the ancient stone, it would show itself as the merest slit from the outside. Inside it was cut sharply away to admit the maximum light.

The door opened suddenly. "Come on then," Ariel snapped.

I controlled my irritation and suppressed a sudden fear that he was taking me to see the Master of Obernewtyn. If Selmar had shown such terror at the mention of him, what must he be like?

As we walked down the hall I noticed a good deal more than the previous night. The candle brackets I had seen along the wall were metal and shaped like gargoyles' heads with savage mouths. Cold, greenish drips of wax hung obscenely frozen from the gaping jaws. Whoever had built Obernewtyn had no desire for homely comfort.

We passed down the stairs and continued along a narrow walkway on the other side of the entrance hall.

"Are you taking me to the Head?" I asked.

The boy did not answer and presently we came to a double set of doors. He opened one of the doors with something of a flourish. The room it opened onto was a kitchen.

It was a long, rectangular room with two large side
arbors filled with bench seats and trestle tables. At the
very end of the kitchen almost an entire wall was taken
up with a cavernous fireplace. Above it was set an immense mantelshelf, laden with stone and iron pots. From
its underside hung a further selection of pans and pan-
nikins. A huge, blackened cauldron was suspended above
the flame and stirring the contents was a woman of
mountainous proportions to match the size of the giant
kitchen.

Her elbows, though bent, resembled large cured hams
and her legs were hidden beneath the voluminous folds
of her grown. A large, white bow sat incongruously on
her fat-cheeked hips and waggled whenever she moved.

The roaring heat of the fire had kept the noise of our
entrance from her. Tearing my eyes away, I saw that
there were several doors besides the one we had come
through and a great number of cupboards and benches.
A young girl was sitting at one of these. She had been
scraping vegetables and they sat in two mounds on either
side of her, scraped and unscraped. She had noticed our
entrance and now watched me from two startled curranty
eyes, buried in a slab-jowled face. The knife poised above
the potato glinted brightly.

"Ma!" she yelled, waving the knife in agitation, throwing its light at me.

The mountain of flesh at the stove trembled, then
turned with surprising grace. Her face was flushed from
the heat and distorted by too many chins, but there was
a definite resemblance between her and the girl. The
thick ladle in her hand dripped brown gravy unheeded.

"Ariel!" she cried in dulcet tones. Her accent was similar to Enoch's but less musical. "Dear Hinny, I have
nowt seen ye in an age. Ye have not deserted me have
ye, sweet boy?" I felt sick, but Ariel simply basked in her

fawning. "But ye know I don't mean anything by my scoldings. Come, I have a treat for ye."

She gathered him in a bone-crushing embrace and led him to one of the cupboards. She took a tin out and gave it to him.

"Why, Andra, thank you." Ariel's voice was muffled and amused as he looked inside the tin. He sounded pleased and I wondered what she had given him. I wondered why the cook treated him with such favor. He did not seem a commanding creature. Surely he was only a Misfit, but perhaps he was favored, or an informer. Yet he seemed too arrogant for the latter. Most informers were clinging and contemptible.

The girl with the knife giggled violently, the blade pressed across her plump cheek as though she fought to stifle her laughter by thrusting her fist down her neck. The knife flashed its silver light, and obscurely, I was reminded of the strange dream I had experienced in the carriage on the way to Obernewtyn. The girl exploded with laughter again and the older woman glared ferociously at her.

"Ye born noddy-headed thing. Shut yer carrying on an' get back to work." The girl's giggles ceased abruptly and she looked sullenly at me as if I were to blame. Again I noticed the similarity in the features and thought they must surely be mother and daughter.

"Now, Andra," Ariel was saying. "You recall how I promised you some extra help? Well, you know your Ariel does not lie. Anything I tell you will come to pass," he added with a vaguely fanatical gleam in his eyes. "Well, I have brought you a new helper," he announced, pointing unnecessarily to me. Responding with enthusiasm, the cook launched herself at him with much lipsmacking. I thought with suppressed glee that it served him right. He looked over her shoulder and caught the amusement on my face. He disentangled himself, and

with a vicious parting smile, ordered the cook to make
sure I worked hard as I was assuredly lazy and insolent.
Andra promised to work my fingers to the bone. "An' ye
come again to see me, lovey," she cooed as he departed
with a look of spiteful satisfaction.

Immediately the door closed, the daughter leaped toward me, brandishing her knife. "Misfit pig? What sort
of help will she be? Ye can see she don't have a brain' in
her," she sneered venomously, menacing me with the
knife. The syrupy smile dropped from the cook's face.
She crossed the floor in two steps and dealt her daughter
a resounding blow with the wooden spoon.

"If she has no brains then she'll be a good match for
thee, fool that ye are, Lila. Ninny of a girl. If Ariel gives
us th' gift of a fool, then ye mun show pleasure," the
cook snarled. "Oh th' trials of my life. Yer no good father
gives me a fool fer a daughter, then disappears. I have
to come to th' end of th' land so ye won't be declared
defective. I find a nice powerful boy to bond ye an' yer
so stupid I got to do th' charmin' fer ye. Lud knows ye've
little enough to offer without gollerin' an' gigglin' like a
regular loon," she added succinctly.

With some amusement, I realized that the cook desired
to bond her daughter to Ariel. But why did she say he
was powerful? What sort of power could such a young
boy possess?

With a final look of disgust at her daughter, the cook
turned to me. "As fer you, no doubt ye are a fool at that.
An' work ye hard I will, if that's what Ariel wants. Ye've
angered him somehow an' ye mun pay. He'll see ye do.
He ain't one to let petty angers gan away. Ye'll learn,"
she prophesied.

Turning to the sink, she explained that I was to wash
the mountain of dishes and then scour the pots. I looked
in dismay at the work ahead. In the orphan homes there
had been a great many of us and a share in duties was

always light. I nodded, my face dull. She pushed me toward the sink.

Lila watched this interchange with a sneering expression and I knew I would have trouble with her before long.

I had been working for hours when the cook announced that the easy work was over since it was nearly time for midmeal. I felt like weeping. Already I was exhausted, but I channeled my despair into fueling a growing hatred of Ariel, whom I regarded as the initiator of my woes. I was hungry, having missed breakfast, but I dared not complain. Lila moaned endlessly and received endless slaps for her pains. I judged it wiser to hold my tongue. Whenever Andra turned to the stove as we set the tables, Lila would torment me with sly pinches and slaps. By noon I loathed her thoroughly and at that moment my sole pleasure lay in devising the sort of tortures I could imagine inflicting on her.

Presently the cook began to ring a bell. Young people of varying ages came in through the double doors until all the tables were full. Lila and I proceeded to serve them. They did not look at us at all but ate with steady concentration. The meal consisted of chunks of freshly baked bread spread with toasted slabs of cheese, and a bowl of stew.

The food smells made me feel dizzy. In town, food had seldom been this good or this fresh, but we had never had to work so hard. Here it seemed everybody was expected to work and none of those eating lingered to talk once they had finished. When they rose, their place was taken by another who sat with a hand in the air until they were served. I wondered what they all did.

After a time, the people who came to eat were of a different sort. None of them put their hands up and they looked around them curiously. I judged them to be new to Obernewtyn like me and I wished bitterly that I could be with them instead of in the kitchen.

Throughout the long meal, Misfits would arrive and be given trays and pots and pies to take away. I supposed these must serve the favored Misfits, outside helpers and guardians, not to mention the Doctor and Madam Vega.

"Ye gan eat now," the cook said suddenly and thrust a plate into my hand. My stomach growled in appreciation. I sat in the nearest seat and devoured my food with relish. Only when I had finished the last morsel did I look up.

"Hello," said a voice at my elbow. I turned to look at the small girl alongside me. She smiled and I was astonished that anyone would ever want to condemn her. Even her ungainly clothes could not hide the delicacy of her features and her slender bones. Her hair was like cream silk. She looked about twelve and endured my examination without embarrassment. I looked away from her clear, naive gaze as I realized I was staring.

"I am Cameo," she whispered. I looked at her again and it was difficult not to respond to her smile, but Lila, seated at another table, was leering at me. Cameo did not seem aware of the attention she had focused on us.

"Really," I said in a repressive voice. I had not meant to hurt her and when the brightness of her face dimmed I wished I had not been so sharp. Obviously the girl was simple. Her smile was crooked, understanding and somehow accepting my rebuff without offense. She bent to finish her meal.

A sharp cuff on the side of my head signaled that my short respite was over. Stiffly I rose and began to clear plates. The afternoon was taken up with washing all the midmeal dishes and scrubbing the hard, jagged kitchen floor.

The nightmeal consisted of the remnants of the stew,

some crumbled biscuits rather than the bread, and more milk. I was too tired to be hungry.

Every bone ached and when I was taken by Ariel to my permanent bed, I was too exhausted to care that I was not alone. At that moment the Master of Obernewtyn could have been my roommate and met as little response.

X

My initial exhaustion wore off as I became accustomed to the hard physical labor, but that was replaced by a terrible mental despair. I could not endure the thought of going on in such a way forever, and yet there seemed no opportunity of finding Enoch's friend who might be able to help me move to the farms to work.

I had expected to be taken to the head keeper but apparently Madam Vega had not come back yet from her tour of the Lowlands. It would be some time before she returned.

I discovered the cook's temper was as precarious as her cooking. If she was in a bad mood, both Lila and I suffered from her weighty slaps and sharp tongue. I might have pitied Lila if I had not disliked her so much. She was not even a Misfit yet she had to work as hard as I did. Whenever the cook was not watching, she would be at me. It was terrible until I realized she was even more afraid of her mother than I. After that I gave as good as I got.

My sole hope was pinned on a conversation I had overheard at midmeal one day implying most of the house workers went down to work on the farms to prepare for the long wintertime. I prayed that I was right, and that I would be sent to work on the farms. There I might be able to contact Enoch's friend. But I had arrived at Obernewtyn in the spring and my calculations told me no extra workers would be required until at least the beginning of summer.

I shared my sleeping chamber with four other girls, including the strange disturbed girl I had seen on my first morning, Selmar, who now ignored me. Remembering the mess inside her mind, it would not be surprising if she had forgotten our meeting.

Sometimes Selmar would appear dazed and she was, I noticed, permitted to wander more freely than the rest of us. Quite often she did not come to her bed at all. Once I caught her watching me with a sly, speculative gaze that would have made me think she was an informer if I had not seen her mind.

There were surprisingly few guardians at all at Obernewtyn. Most responsibility seemed to be taken by senior and favored Misfits, though none was so favored as Ariel, who turned out to be a Misfit after all.

Altogether, life at Obernewtyn was a matter of grim endurance rather than terror. I had seen nothing of the mysterious master and had heard nothing of the "treatments." It seemed the rumors were, after all, just that.

I thought a good deal about Jes. I had imagined myself a loner, never needing anyone, but now I saw that I had never really experienced loneliness. In Rangorn there had always been my parents, and in the homes, there had been Jes and later Maruman. Before, I had discounted Jes, but now I often found myself longing to talk to him, even if we spoke of nothing important. I had mocked and sneered at him; perhaps I had driven him to the Herders. At least they did not laugh at him. The more I thought of it, the greater the wrong I felt I had done him. And I had even suspected him of plotting to kill me or denounce me. I hated the shallowness I now saw in myself. I only hoped he would find what he wanted in life.

One day, Ariel came to the kitchen to tell me I would be taken on a tour of the farms with some other Misfits. I was ecstatic and even Ariel did not mar the joy that met that day. I had not been outside for so long. All at once I wanted desperately to see the sky and feel the wind.

After the noon meal, Ariel had instructed me to go to the entrance hall. When I arrived, a boy took me down several halls and outside to a large courtyard. Three girls and a young boy stood waiting when I arrived, all of whom I recognized. The pretty girl who had spoken to me at my first meal smiled at me tentatively, but despite my growing loneliness, I did not smile in return. Beside her was a girl called Helga. Another was a girl I knew only vaguely as a face from the meal table. The last was one of my roommates, a lethargic girl of hulking proportions with a distinct lisp.

The boy who had brought me returned minutes later with twins, two big fair-haired Norselanders. I stared, wondering what was wrong with them. I could not sense any particular flaw in them, only that they each lacked a hand. My neck prickled and turning, I saw the slight, dark-haired boy was watching me closely. Frowning, I remembered that on the other occasions I had seen him in the kitchen, he had been watching me too. Then I had been too tired and depressed to see any significance in his stare, but now, noting the gleam of intelligence in his dark brown eyes, I wondered. He was very thin but there seemed to be nothing very much wrong with him. As most of Obernewtyn's inmates were Misfits, it was not easy to find out exactly what was wrong with a person.

Presently Ariel arrived with two more Misfits, and with rising astonishment, I felt the hatred rise from our party directed exclusively at him. I had no reason to like him, but there was something akin to fear in their hatred.

Oddly, I noticed that Cameo did not show any fear. Instead she smiled and, to my surprise, he smiled in return, though I thought it rather an unpleasant smile.

Briefly, he told us we were being taken on this tour in preparation for the harvest, when we would all be working there. Like the kitchen courtyard, this was roofed, but we went through a gate into another courtyard that was open to the air. The sun was shining brightly and I felt mesmerized by it. I breathed in the warm mountain air and tasted the coming summer days. I had expected a wan, sickly sunlight but had forgotten this season in Rangorn had been hot and bright, though briefer than on the coast.

Three sides of the courtyard were formed by the several-story–high walls of Obernewtyn. Windows pitted the gray expanse like hooded eyes. Above them the roof sloped steeply so that in wintertime the snow would slide off. Again I wondered what had led to the construction of Obernewtyn, so far from anywhere.

Ariel led us to the fourth wall, beyond which showed the tops of trees. There was no mortar between the bricks of the arch; rather, it was held up by perfect balance of positioning. Certainly someone had possessed an eye for beauty, remembering the carved front-door panels.

I thought the door would open right onto the farms, but it led into a dim shrubbery. Directly inside, a small grassy path led to the left and right of the gate. In front of us was a thick impenetrable wall of greenthorn. Peer as I might I could not tell what lay beyond it. Ariel steered us to the left and we followed the path a short way until it turned sharply to the right. We walked a few steps and came to a fork. Both ways looked exactly alike, bordered on either side by the towering greenthorn hedge. By now the powerful exotic odor of the greenthorn and the sameness had completely confused my sense of direction and I realized the shrubbery was actually a maze.

I had heard of mazes but had never seen one before. I could not even use my powers because they were befuddled by the heavy scent in the air. Crushed, the thorn provided a painkiller, but in such concentration, the scent alone seemed to have a numbing effect. If Ariel had left at that moment, I doubt whether we would have found our way out at all.

It was with some relief we came around a corner and back to the stone wall with its small arched door. But until we emerged from the maze, half-blinded by the strength of the sun after the diffused green light in the maze, we did not see that we had come right through the maze to the other side.

My eyes were dazzled by the brightness and I looked at the land around in amazement. Neat fields extended for leagues in all three directions and there were barns and fences and livestock everywhere. Dozens of Misfits were working, repairing fences or building them, herding and raking. To the far left was an orchard and there was the unmistakable scent of apples and plums. Ariel led us along one of the many dirt paths leading from the maze toward a group of buildings.

"The maze door is always locked and there are few at Obernewtyn who know the way through. To stray from the path means death," Ariel said as we walked. The thought that anyone would want to enter the fragrant green maze made me shudder. Ariel explained that the buildings we approached were where the animals were kept during the wintertime, and beyond them enormous storage silos.

"As far as you can see in all directions and much farther belongs to Obernewtyn," Ariel said. "We are almost completely self-sufficient here, as indeed we must be, for in wintertime we are completely blocked off from the

Lowlands by snow. During that season, everyone will work in the house, spinning and weaving and preparing goods for trading when the spring comes. This enables us to purchase what we cannot produce. Before the wintertime all the food in those silos must be transported to the main house."

We passed a massive shed, which smelled strongly of animals. Ariel wrinkled his nose delicately but I breathed in deeply because it reminded me of Rangorn.

"Those are the livestock storage houses. The grain and grasses in those must be enough to feed all the animals throughout the wintertime. One Misfit will remain down here and take care of them until spring. Some of the cows and poultry are transferred to the house courtyards for meat and eggs and milk."

There was no doubt that it was a highly efficient concern; and the surplus sold must more than cover the few things Obernewtyn wanted. I wondered what happened to the rest of the profits. No doubt some of it was used in purchasing more Misfits.

Far to the west, beyond the distant line of the wall around Obernewtyn, was a savage line of mountains. There were more mountains to the east. Busy with my own thoughts, I did not notice Ariel watching me.

"I see you are interested in the mountains beyond our borders," he sneered. "Look all you please, for you will never see them at less than a distance. Those mountains mean freedom and death for those who attempt to reach them."

A raucous squealing from behind us broke the tension. We followed Ariel toward a small shed, but before we reached it a man came out carrying a small pig. As he approached, it squealed lustily and I could see that he was not a full-grown man at all but a well-built youth of about nineteen. He set the pig down in a small pen and wiped his hands on his trousers before turning to us. His greeting to Ariel was amicable, yet there was a watchfulness in his manner that puzzled me. I was about to probe him when a strange thing happened.

He was telling Ariel about the pig he had just delivered when he broke off midsentence to stare at me with jade-green eyes. Some instinct of danger made me fear I had betrayed myself. I expected him to denounce me, but he seemed suddenly aware that he in turn was watched. He then let his eyes rove over our entire group, but I felt sure he did this only to cover the attention he had paid me.

Ariel's eyes passed from me to the youth thoughtfully. "This is Rushton," he said. "He is our farm overseer."

Startled, I realized this was Enoch's friend. The dark youth did not have the air of a Misfit, but Ariel did not choose to tell us his exact status. The overseer gave us a brief description of the farms and crops and the animals thereon, before leaving us to Ariel. His eyes flickered at me with some message too swift to comprehend as he departed.

That night my dreams were full of shadowed, green eyes conveying messages I could not understand. When I woke the following morning, Selmar and one of the other girls eyed me oddly and I knew I had talked in my sleep, though I could hardly have said much to incriminate myself.

The following day I returned with a leaden heart to the dim confines of the kitchen.

XI

One morning at the beginning of summer, while I was still working in the kitchens, I woke with the clammy feeling of apprehension that usually preceded some sort of premonition. My immediate fear was that Madam Vega had returned and that I would have to see the Master of Obernewtyn. The feeling passed and so did my fear, though an uneasiness persisted.

I was too bored and weary of the never-ending toil to dwell on anything for long. My only concern was that if ever I got out of the kitchen, I might not remember how to pay attention to the world around me. I had become so used to switching off.

My hands were cracked and red from the hot water and constant scrubbing. My hair was greasy and lank from the heat and cooking oil and I was pale and spotty from lack of fresh air. The silent war between Lila and myself had reached new heights that morning when she had ingeniously managed to spill hot grease down my leg. My shout of pain brought her a whack from Andra, but she grinned at me, knowing I had come off worse in that round. Biting my lip, I cast around for some method of revenge.

In the midst of these warlike cogitations, there was a

loud crash somewhere near. We all looked up, wondering
what it was. Another thunderous crash sounded and the
kitchen vibrated. Lila screamed in fright and I was
pleased to observe her mother slap her. The cook turned
to me, her expression irritated rather than frightened or
puzzled.

" 'Tis that damn roof. I told them th' posts were rotten
from damp." She waved her hand at the kitchen courtyard and I was fervently glad that I had not been out
there when it collapsed. "Ye better find Ariel. Or better
still, look for Matthew. I think he's up in th' house today."

I nodded and hastened away.

For once, the halls were completely deserted. I had not
been in them in the middle of the day before and wondered if they were always so astonishingly quiet then. I
searched and in the end even called out, but no one
answered. I had the odd feeling the whole place was
empty. Then I heard something approaching. It was Selmar and she stopped dead when she saw me. I had not
even opened my mouth to speak before she fell back and
cringed against the wall. Astonished, I could only stare.

"What is it? Are you hurt?" I asked gently. There was
something in that ravaged face that demanded pity.

"Don't hurt me," she said. "I don't know nothing."

She had not slept in her bed the night before or the
one before that.

"Of course I won't hurt you," I said, holding my hand
out to help her up. She shrank away, as if I held pure
whitestick. "What has happened? Are you sick?"

Her eyes stared into mine and she would not speak.
Her pupils were pinpoint small and the white showed all
around them. It occurred to me she might have taken
too much of the freely available sleep potion. But why
was she so afraid? I looked around nervously, hoping no
one would catch me with her. I did not even dare read

her since the last attempt. She was crying now and I touched her hand.

"If you are sick I'll get someone, perhaps Ariel . . ."

She uttered a thin scream and clawed against the wall as if she were trying to be absorbed by it. Startled, I wondered if Ariel had hurt her. That would explain her reaction to his name.

"Please, I don't know where it is. I swear," she moaned. I stood up and looked down at her helplessly, for truly she seemed beyond any sort of help. I heard footsteps and looked up in fright.

Unexpectedly, it was Rushton, the overseer I had seen on my trip to the farms. He looked less surprised to see me and his eyes fell to the huddled form of Selmar. Quickly, he knelt beside her speaking to her softly and very gently. She crawled into his arms.

"Oh, Selmar," he whispered tiredly. Then he tenderly helped her to her feet. She was still weeping, but the ragged terror that had so unnerved me before was no longer there.

He looked up at last with accusation in his eyes and I drew myself up indignantly. "I did nothing to her. She was like this when I found her," I said coldly.

"What are you doing alone in the halls?" he asked. I frowned and wished I understood more about the power structure at Obernewtyn. Twice now I had been questioned by people who seemed to have no right but behaved as though they did. Rushton was even more arrogant than Ariel. But I was too afraid not to answer. I told him about the courtyard roof. As he listened, his hand stroked Selmar's bent head softly and it was hard to reconcile the cold disbelieving look on his face with that hand.

I stammered to a halt, aware my muttered tale sounded unlikely. "You had better find Matthew then. Go back that way and you will find yourself in the right

section. And see you don't wander about like this again.
This part of the house is forbidden," he said.

I dutifully went where he had directed. What a nasty,
haughty character he was. Not at all the sort of person I
had thought Enoch's friend would be. He hadn't liked
me, that was clear. I sighed, thinking I would not now
ask if I might work with animals on the farm.

I heard voices and followed them, to find a group of
Misfits whitewashing a stone wall. To my surprise, they
were being directed by the thin, sharp-eyed boy who had
stared so hard at me during the farm visit. I saw recog-
nition flare in the boy's eyes. Going up to him, I asked
for Matthew and he said that was him.

I told him about the damage to the kitchen courtyard
and he agreed to come after giving orders to the others
to continue until he returned. Like Enoch's voice, Matthew's had an attractive lilting accent. As we walked back
to the kitchen, I noticed again the pronounced limp that
I had seen on our tour of the farms. In the manner of
orphans and Misfits generally, we made no casual conversation. I felt the boy glance at me but refused to return
his look, uneasy at this apparent interest in me. I was
determined to avoid all of the struggles and stresses of
life at Obernewtyn in the same way I had kept to myself
at Kinraide. It was much lonelier here, but it was safer.

After makeshift repairs to the courtyard had been ef-
fected, and the fallen timber cleared away, the cook told
me I would be working on the farms the next day. Ecstatic and full of excitement, I could not keep my happiness from her. But she was in a good mood and only
smiled.

" 'Tis hard work there too, mind. But see ye dinna get
on th' wrong side of anybody an' ye'll be set," she said

kindly, obliquely referring to Ariel's dislike of me. I vowed to myself that I would, but I gloomily remembered the look on the farm overseer's face.

Once in bed, I couldn't sleep. Selmar came in quite late but there was no sign of the hysterical terror of the afternoon.

It had been a strange, unsettling day. First there had been the roof collapsing and the burn on my leg, then the queer incident with Rushton and Selmar.

I shook my head and hoped fervently my time on the farms would be less mysterious and confusing. But then I reflected that nothing could be as bad as the kitchens.

Nothing.

Part II

Heart of the Darkness

XII

The next day I had my first glimpse of a Guanette bird. It was a surprising start to a surprising day.

I had been standing quite alone, in the courtyard outside the maze waiting for Ariel to return, when the bird flew straight up from behind the wall into the silver-streaked, dawn-gray sky.

Uttering a long, lonely call, it flew in a graceful arc toward the northwest. I recognized the bird, though I had never seen a picture of one, by its massive wingspan and the brilliant red of its underbelly. As it crossed the line where the far mountains touched the sky, the sun rose in fiery splendor as if to welcome it. It crossed the face of the sun, shimmered and seemed to dissolve.

"Fair mazer it is," said a familiar voice behind me. I turned to face the boy I now knew as Matthew. He was not looking at me, for once, and his face was touched with the pink dawn light as he watched the sun rise. Behind him was an older boy with a tall, angular body, a rather big nose, and a million freckles struggling to cover his face. His eyes were fixed on me with peculiar intensity, and though I sought to hold his gaze, my own eyes dropped first. Catching my discomfort, the younger boy grinned.

"Can't ye feel how uncomfortable she is?" he asked his companion. He turned to me. "Dinna worry about Dameon gawkin' at ye. He's as blind as a bat," he told me cheerfully. Horribly embarrassed, I was shamed to think of the icy look I had given him and was thankful he could not see me.

He grinned apologetically. "I'm Dameon. I'm sorry if I seemed to stare," he said disarmingly and held his hand out. Startled, I took his hand and wondered at his elegant manner.

"An' I'm Matthew, as ye know," said Matthew. "An' you're Elspeth." I did not know what to say. I didn't want to get involved but Dameon's blindness had confused me.

"What were you both admiring?" Dameon asked.

Matthew answered. "We saw a Guanette bird an' ye know how rare those are. It came from near th' maze. Queer to see one here though. They dinna usually come down from the high country. Ye know, they say it was one of th' few creatures to survive the Great White."

I was thinking about what I had heard of Matthew since I last saw him. He came from the Highlands not too far from Guanette, and his village had denounced him as a Misfit not long after his mother died. He had lived alone in her shack poaching and fishing and generally living close to the bone, and developed a reputation of being odd. A group of village boys constantly tormented him. Finally several of the ringleaders in the gang came to harm. One fell from a roof and another ate poisoned fish. The village called in the Council and claimed Matthew was dangerous. No one could explain how Matthew, with his lame foot, had hurt the boys, but somehow the Council had been convinced and he was declared Misfit.

The other courtyard door opened and a group of other Misfits arrived, most of those who had come on the earlier tour. Ariel came last, with Cameo in tow. He unlocked the maze door, then relocked it when we had gone through. I moved to follow Cameo, but Matthew restrained me and others went past, looking at us curiously. Furious, I shook his hand off and followed them. He came directly behind with the blind boy and I could feel his eyes boring into my back. I wished then that I had completely ignored him to begin with.

We walked in silence for a bit, then Cameo began to chatter to Ariel. With her masking prattle, the twins, who were also in front, began to talk in low, intense voices. Curiosity made me send out a probe. They were planning some sort of escape so I withdrew smartly. I didn't even want to think of escapes, planned or otherwise. I noticed Matthew had hurried his pace and was now almost abreast of me.

I gave him a cross look. "We are supposed to go single file," I said, determined to snub him until he left me alone.

"I know about you," said a voice in my thoughts. Shocked, I tried to stay calm, but my dismay had been obvious.

Matthew put his hand on my arm again. "I thought so," he said in a low voice. I could only stare and half-heartedly pretend not to know what he meant. But there was no mistake. He had read my mind! "I heard you 'listening' to the twins. But I suspected ye before that." He was positively delighted.

I could only feel numb. I had never really thought there would be anybody else like me. "I . . . I don't understand," I said doggedly, trying to make my mind take it in so that I could work out what to do.

The boy smiled again in an impish, knowing way. "Before I come here, I thought I was alone. I suppose you did too. I expect it's a shock. I knew someone else was about. Me mam was th' same but I thought there was only us. So I knew what it was when I felt ye. I started to keep a watch to try and figure out who it was. It came to you in the end, *Elf*," he added. I shivered at the added proof of Jes's nickname for me. That knowledge could only have come from my own mind.

"I tried to reach ye but ye had a powerful shield. I knew if I couldn't get in, ye must be stronger than me. So I bided my time, I knew sooner or later, ye'd show yerself. An' I was pretty certain ye wouldn't be all that careful because ye'd think there was no one else like ye. An' in the end, I sensed ye send a probe out to th' twins, and I was even able to read some of th' thoughts on th' outside of yer mind," he added smugly. I heard his added reflection that I was a lot stronger than I realized.

"I know how strong I am," I said. There was no point in pretending. He might be weaker than me, but he knew. It was too late to be cautious and probably impossible. But could he be trusted? I reached into his mind some little way. Before I could learn what I wanted to know, Matthew's eyes narrowed and I sensed a slight withdrawal in him.

"There now. Ye've just deep probed me. Now I couldn't do that to you. Not only do ye have th' ability to farseek, ye can do that too." He looked suddenly pensive. "Now that I think of it, I can almost understand why those idiots from the village were afraid of me. 'Tis a queer thing to know yer thoughts are on show. Dameon here has some power too, but I can't quite make out what it is. It's nothing like us. It's something to do with being able to feel what people are feeling." Matthew shrugged as if he did not think it a very useful ability.

My mind was reeling with the things he had said. In one moment he had changed my life. Not only were there others like me, but there were people who had different sorts of abilities. Surely that would mean we were not isolated Misfits. I realized I had been rude to dip into his mind. It was different when they did not know. I would have to be more considerate. I knew then that I had decided to trust the boy and his blind companion. In one sense I had no choice, but my sudden desire not to invade the thoughts of another person was new, and told me that I had accepted something I had previously thought impossible. I was no longer alone.

"We'll manage canny between us," Matthew was saying, still in that barely audible voice. "I'd be pleased though if ye'd show me how to shield so well," he added humbly. I looked into his funny boyish face and bright eyes and it was as if some wall in me crumbled.

I smiled and it felt like I had taken off a layer of skin. "I will teach you," was all I said, but he beamed, seeming to understand the momentousness of sharing for the first time. Just then he reminded me of Jes and I wished Jes could know what I had discovered.

"And Dameon friend?" Matthew asked anxiously, breaking into thought speech.

I turned slightly to watch Dameon's graceful progress and sent out a gentle probe. He flinched and stumbled and I withdrew hurriedly.

"I'm sorry," I whispered, but he shook his head.

"I was just surprised. It's different from Matthew," he said, and he smiled. "I can feel your curiosity." He laughed. "It's almost as bad as his. I call my own ability empathy."

"He does that all th' time," Matthew reassured me. "He picks up th' weirdest things. No words though, an' he's deaf as a doorpost to other things."

"Quiet back there!" Ariel shouted, effectively silencing the entire group. I hoped Matthew would be careful and to my relief he said nothing more and dropped back. He sent a silent promise that we would meet again soon, when it was safe.

I made a mental note to ask him about Selmar. The incident in the hall nagged at me. I thought about what had just happened and the ease with which I had broken a dozen of my own rules. I hardly knew Matthew or Dameon, and already I was treating them as trusted friends. And, I saw that if there were three of us, then there would surely be more. I wished we were somewhere so that we could talk at length. If only we were free. All at once the walls of Obernewtyn were too close. If I could just get away, perhaps Matthew . . .

I stopped myself ruthlessly. I knew nothing about him, and even less about Dameon. Even if I could trust them, escape was another thing entirely. Unbidden, I remembered Daffyd, the boy I had met in Sutrium. He had said the Druid lived and I might find a refuge with him. I shook my head resolutely. It was all happening too fast. Busy with my thoughts, I cannoned into the person in front of me. We had reached the end of the maze. It had seemed a remarkably long trip.

Ariel let us all out and told us to wait by the gate until Rushton came to collect us. Matthew and Dameon made no move to join me so I took their cue and stared vacantly around me. The sun had risen quite high now and though the grass was still dew-soaked and the shadows long, the air smelled delicious with the mingled farm smells.

As the tall figure of Rushton detached itself from the shadows around the sheds, I determined to give him no reason to remember me. I caught Matthew's sober expression and felt an unaccountable desire to make a face. I was amazed at the warmth of my feelings, but as the farm overseer approached, I felt a moment of apprehension. There was a strange aura of power about him. I was reminded of something Maruman had once said about wild animals—that even the most gentle was not quite safe. That was how Rushton was—as if one might run a great risk in simply knowing him. Yet when he came among us and began assigning tasks, his apparent boredom reassured me.

Some of us followed him over to the buildings. He stopped again, pointed out a large building that he called the drying shed, and sent a group to wait for him there. Dameon and Matthew were among them. Cameo and two others were sent across to the orchards and only two of us remained. The other girl was sent to feed the pigs. She went with a wry grin. I, Rushton said, was to clean out the stables.

I stood while he told the other girl what to feed the pigs and where it was. I did not like his bold green eyes, nor the expressionless looks he gave me. The girl mixed up his instructions when he asked her to repeat them and impatiently he told me to wait and went away with her.

A large dog came in when they left. He fixed me briefly in his eyes before turning away to settle in a pile of hay.

I looked into his eyes. "Greetings," I thought.

He looked around before deciding I was the only one there. "Did you speak, funaga?" he asked with mild surprise.

I nodded, projecting assurance and friendship. "I am Elspeth," I said.

"I am called Sharna here," he said. "What manner of funaga are you?"

"I am a funaga like other funagas," I replied formally. "But now that I look at you, you do not seem to be an ordinary dog." In fact, I wondered if he might be a wild dog. He was very shaggy.

"And you do not seem to be an ordinary funaga," the dog answered with some humor.

"So," I grinned, "you are wary. That is good. But I am curious. I did not imagine there would be pets at Obernewtyn."

The dog growled. "I am no nannyhammer to the funaga. I come where I please. I think I will leave," he

added, obviously offended. But when he made no move
to disturb himself, I perceived that his curiosity out-
weighed his dignity.

"I did not mean to call you that. It is simply that I
wonder why you are here. Are there no better places for
a dog to be?" His reaction to being called a pet made
me more than sure he was, or had been, wild.

"There are at that," he said with a sad sigh. "I have
heard your name before," he said unexpectedly. "A cat
spoke it."

"Maruman!" I projected a picture with the name but
Sharna was unresponsive.

"I did not see this mad cat who seeks a funaga. I heard
it from a beast who had it from another."

"Do you know if the cat was here?" I asked excitedly.

"Who knows where a cat goes?" he said philosophi-
cally. "It was only told to me as a curiosity. Whoever
heard of a cat looking for a funaga? I thought it a riddle."

I heard a movement and looked up to see Rushton
enter. Sensing my withdrawal, the dog settled back into
his corner. Rushton looked about sharply, sensing something amiss, then tersely told me to follow him.

If he had shown a peculiar interest in me at our first
meeting, this time he seemed at pains to assure me of his
total lack of interest. "The stables have to be cleaned
every second day," he said in a bored voice as we entered. A rich loamy smell rushed out to greet me. I
watched as he showed me how to catch hold of the
horse's halter and lead him out. The horses were to be
released into the yard leading off the stables, their halter
detached and hung on a hook. Rushton gave me a
broom, a rake, and a pan, taking up a long-handled fork
himself.

"You have to lift the manure out in clumps and drop
it in the pan, along with the dirtiest hay." Deftly he slid

the prongs of the fork under some manure and threw it neatly into the pan. "When you've done all that, rake the rest of the hay to one side, then fork in some fresh stuff." He forked hay from a nearby pile onto the floor with economical movements. It looked easy.

"You lay the old hay over the new because if you don't the horse will eat it." He handed the fork to me. "There are twelve stables in this lot so you'd better get on with it. Call me if you have any trouble getting the horses out." I nodded and briefly those inscrutable eyes probed mine, then he turned on his heel and left.

I turned and surveyed the stables.

"You would do well to mindspeak to them first," Sharna commented from his corner. Taking his advice I approached the nearest box and greeted its occupant, a dappled mare with a large comfortable rear. She flicked her tail and turned to face me.

"Who are you?" she asked with evident amusement. "I have spoken to many odd creatures in my time but never one of you. I suppose you are behind this," she directed the latter thought to Sharna, who had come to watch. She leaned her long nose close to my face and snorted rudely. "I suppose you want to put me out? Well, I'm not having that thing on my head. Just open the door and I'll walk out."

Fearfully, I did as she asked, hoping Rushton would not come back and find me. Sharna muttered about her but I ignored him and concentrated on trying to copy Rushton's movements.

Except for a big nasty black horse whom Sharna said had been badly mistreated by a previous master, the rest of the horses walked easily to the field. I had finished and was leaning on a post watching them graze when Rushton returned.

"You have been uncommonly fast," Rushton said. The

smile fell from my face and I realized I had been stupid.
Of course I had been too swift.

"Too quick to believe, even if Enoch did recommend
you," he added reflectively.

And as I looked into his hard face, I was afraid.

XIII

"Well?" Rushton inquired grimly.

"I . . . my father kept horses," I lied, hoping he did not know how young I had been made an orphan. There was a speculative gleam in his eyes but he nodded.

"All right. There are packages of food from the kitchen for midmeal out by the barn. I'll find something else for the afternoon," he said mildly.

I left as fast as I could to escape those curious watchful eyes. Rushton seemed to hold a special place at Obernewtyn. I did not think he was a Misfit, yet he had been wary around Ariel, who was one. And there was that strange business with Selmar in the hall.

The packages were on the ground next to a large bucket of milk covered with a piece of gauze. I scooped up a cup of milk but avoided the squashy packages I recognized from my days in the kitchen as bread and dripping. Propping myself up against a rain barrel in the sun, I admitted that I had been stupid working so quickly. I could have been with Sharna and the horses all day but instead Rushton was sure to give me some horrible job. I sighed, thinking that no one ever needed to get me in trouble—I could do that well enough myself.

I turned my thoughts to Maruman and wondered if

he had really been here. I could not think so. He would not have crossed the tainted ground on foot and I did not think the carriage had returned since he brought me because I had noticed no new faces at meals. Yet he had been oddly defiant when he said he did not want to come to Obernewtyn, as if he felt guilty. His dreams had told him to follow me. I hoped he had not had another fit and decided to come anyway. I decided to ask Sharna to see if he could find out the origin of the story of a cat who searched for a funaga.

I was so deep in thought I did not see Matthew approach and jumped as his shadow fell across my lap.

"Dreamin' again?" he asked. He sat himself down beside me and called to Dameon, who joined us. In the past this casual intrusion would have annoyed me, but I found I did not resent the company of this odd pair.

Nevertheless, I felt bound to point out to them that groupings of people were invariably dangerous. "I'm not saying I don't want your company but maybe it's not a good idea to be so obvious," I ventured, looking around doubtfully.

Matthew shrugged. "Elspeth, yer thinkin' like an orphan. We are Misfits now. What more could they do?"

Burn us, I thought, but did not say it for that seemed unlikely now. And he was right. I *was* thinking like an orphan. The two boys unwrapped their lunches. Dameon rewrapped his with a grimace but Matthew ate his with a bored expression.

"Have ye come across old Larkin yet?" Matthew asked presently. I shrugged, saying I hadn't seen anyone but Rushton. "Nivver mind." Matthew laughed. "Yer bound to see him soon. Ye'll know when ye do. He's not th' sort ye could easily forget."

"Who is he, a guardian?" I asked curiously.

"There are only three permanent guardians up here," Dameon explained. "The others could come and go.

They don't last long though. I suppose they think it is too unfriendly." I thought of guardian Myrna's treatment of the hapless Hester and did not wonder.

"Strictly speakin' Larkin is a Misfit, but he's much older than all the rest," Matthew said. "Do you notice how there are no older Misfits? I think they probably send them back to th' Councilfarms. But Larkin has been here practically since this place was built. I don't know why they keep him on. But he's a queer, fey old codger, an' rude as they come. I'm not even sure I like him exactly. At first I thought he must have been an informer and maybe that's why they kept him here. He'd a nasty glint in his eye and a sly air. But when I talked to him, I stopped thinkin' that. He hates Ariel and Vega and he even swears at the guardians!"

"You make him sound awful." I laughed.

"In a way he is," Matthew said seriously. "But if ye can get him talkin', he has some interesting ideas."

"I don't suppose half of it is true," Dameon scoffed.

But Matthew refused to be drawn. "No doubt. I daresay he does make a lot of it up. But he knows a lot too. An' there's no harm in hearin' ideas, whoever tells them. Especially ideas about th' Beforetime."

"And who mentioned the Beforetime?" Dameon inquired smartly.

"He did," Matthew said defensively. Their talk proceeded as if they had had this argument before, but it was new to me and I was becoming interested in this Larkin. "Sure a lot of what he says is just stories. But nothing comes from nothing. An' some of th' things he says makes a lot more sense than the rubbish the Herders put about. There's no harm in it . . . unless ye happen to be blind in more ways than one," he added with an oblique glance at Dameon. I thought it rather a tactless jibe but Dameon only laughed.

"Well, where is he, then?" I asked crossly, somehow envious of their casual friendship.

"Well, he's nowt a man to blow th' whistle an' bang th' drum. In fact I sometimes think he'd like to be invisible. He works on th' farms. Ye'll meet him soon enough, doubtless," Matthew said.

I thought of something else. "Tell me, that farm master, Rushton. Is he a Misfit or what?"

"Nobody really seems to know," Matthew said. "I asked Larkin once an' he told me to mind my business."

Dameon nodded. "He might work for pay, like the temporary guardians. But I don't know. Whenever I'm near him, I sense a command, a rare completeness in him. I sense a purpose and drive."

I stared, again wondering about his curious ability.

"What about Ariel, then?" I asked.

"I hate him," Matthew said with cold venom. I was taken aback at his vehemence and Dameon actually flinched.

"I'm sorry," Matthew said contritely. He looked at me. "Ye have to be careful about what ye feel. Sometimes things hurt him."

"Burns," mumbled Dameon. "Hate always burns."

I thought that was true enough.

"Ariel is a Misfit but he has great authority here. He seems to be Madam Vega's personal assistant. Perhaps he started off as an informer and proved especially good at it."

"Do you ... I mean, what do you feel when you're near him?" I asked.

"Lots of things. Not nice. I don't really know. It's like being near something that smells sweet and then you realize it's that sweet smell that rotten things sometimes get," he said, then he sighed as if annoyed by his vague explanation. But I found it a curiously apt description.

"And you say Larkin has been here for a long time?"

I said, changing the subject because Dameon was looking pale. His powers seemed to demand more of him than mine did of me.

"Forever, practically," Matthew said extravagantly. "An' if ye want to know about people . . ."

I shook my head hastily. "Oh it wasn't so much people as Obernewtyn I was thinking about. It seems such an odd place. Why would anyone build here in the first place? And when did it become a home for Misfits, and why? There is some kind of secret here, I sense it. I don't know why I should care. The world is full of secrets, but this nags at me."

"I feel that too," Matthew said eagerly. "As if something is going on underneath all these everyday things."

"It makes me cold to listen to you two," Dameon said suddenly. "I don't deny that I have felt something too. Not the way you two do, and not by using any power. A blind person develops an instinct for such things and mine tells me there is some mystery here, something big.

"But some things are better left unknown." His words were grim and I found myself looking around nervously.

Dameon went on. "Sometimes I am afraid for people like you who have to know things. And there's no point in my even warning you that finding out can sometimes be a dangerous thing. Your kind will dig and hunt and worry at it until one day you will find what is hidden, waiting for you."

I shivered violently.

"Curiosity killed th' cat," Matthew said. I looked up startled, thinking of Maruman. "That's what Larkin told me once. He said it was an Oldtime saying."

"And how would he know Oldtime sayings?" I asked, throwing off the chill cast over me by Dameon's words.

"In books," Matthew said calmly. "He keeps them hidden, but I've seen them in his cottage."

"It seems like a silly sort of saying to me," I said.

"Well, sayin' it cleared the ice out of me blood." Matthew looked at Dameon, who seemed preoccupied with his own thoughts since he had uttered his chilling little speech. "Ye fair give me th' creeps talkin' that way," he added.

"Do you know, I was just thinking," Dameon said. Matthew gave me a "not again" look. "I once thought it was the end of the world to be sent here, the end of everything. But here I sit, happy, safe, and with two friends, and I wonder."

"I know what ye mean," Matthew agreed. "I near died of fright when Madam Vega picked me to come here. I thought I would be going to th' Councilfarms. But now I sit here an' I sometimes get th' funny feeling that this, all along, was where I was meant to come."

I said nothing but thought of Maruman saying that my destiny waited for me in the mountains.

"Yet it is not freedom," Dameon added, softly, and we both stared at him. The bell to end midmeal rang, seeming to underline his words.

"Ah well. Back to work," Matthew said glumly, and pulled Dameon to his feet. With a sketchy wave they went back across the fields.

Rushton came to stand beside me as I watched them go. "I see you accomplish many things quickly," he sneered. "You choose companions as easily as you muck out a stable. I should have thought the orphan life would have taught you more caution."

I said nothing.

"Well, this afternoon you can show me your talents at milking. I don't suppose your father had cows as well as horses?" he added.

I sighed and fell into step behind him, hoping he was not to be my teacher for the afternoon. I was beginning to ache from the morning's work. We went to a big barn that Rushton said was the dairy. A bearded man sat on a barrel near the entrance.

"Louis, this is Elspeth Gordie," Rushton told the man. "You can have her for the afternoon." The old man's deeply weathered face twitched, but it was too wrinkled to tell if he smiled or not.

"I hope she's quicker than th' last," the old man said abruptly.

"Oh, she's quick all right," Rushton said pointedly as I went after the old man. I turned, expecting to see his departing back, but he stood there watching me.

Louis turned out to be something of an enigma. He instructed me thoroughly and at such length that I began to wonder if he thought me a half-wit. I understood what he meant long before he completed his explanations.

He reminded me of a tortoise. That is not to suggest, however, that there was anything foolish or absurd about him; tortoises, though slow, are dignified and self-sufficient. On the other hand, I had the distinct but unfounded impression that his thoughts were not nearly as slow as his appearance would have me believe. He grunted his satisfaction when I demonstrated that I could milk the cow. Then he gave me terse instructions about emptying the bucket into the right section of a separation vat.

"Nowt like it," he said suddenly and I jumped because so far the only words he had spoken had been orders. He pointed to the milk and I nodded, wondering if he was slightly unbalanced. "Ye don't gan milk like that in th' towns. Watery pale stuff tasting of drainpipes," he said, patting the cow's rump complacently.

"Ye mun call me Larkin," he said suddenly.

"Oh," I said.

"Well, ye gan on with the cows in that shed. I've done most of them. Dinna mix th' vats up," he cautioned me.

So that was Louis Larkin. Odd that we should meet

so soon after Matthew had spoken of him. Remembering that earlier conversation, I wondered if permission to use his last name was a good or bad sign. It was hard to be sure with that beard and his leathery face, I took the opportunity to question the cows about him. Like most cows they were slow, amiable creatures without much brain. But they were fond of Louis and that disposed me to like him, for animals have an infallible instinct about funaga.

"Niver gan done that way!" Louis snapped and jumped. I had been leaning my head on the cow's warm velvety flank, sensing the odd pleasure it got from having its udder relieved. Louis pulled a box up and sat on the wrong end, scraping at a pipe.

"I suppose you've been here a long time," I ventured. He nodded, still busy with his pipe. "I suppose you would know just about everybody here. . . ." I looked up quickly but he seemed unperturbed by my questions. Perhaps he was used to them. "Where did you come from . . . before?" I asked daringly.

Louis chewed the end of his pipe and looked at me thoughtfully. "I were born in th' Highlands," he said. I stared but he did not elaborate. "Then they put me in here," he added, looking at me with a smile that was both sly and childishly transparent. "Them smart town folk think they know everything. They think they can keep things th' same forever. But change comes an' things have gone too far to drag 'em back to what they was. Every year there be more Misfits an' Seditioners an' one day that Council will find there's more in th' prisons than out." He chuckled. "It's too late to undo what's been done," he added, almost to himself. His eyes slid away from the curiosity in mine, suddenly evasive.

What people, I wondered? People like me and Matthew and Dameon? Matthew had been right about the old man's fascination. I wondered how I could get him to talk about Obernewtyn. "This place . . . it's been here a long time," I said.

He shrugged. "I been here a long time too, an' I know practically everybody who lives here," he said.

I decided to try another tack. "Do you know Ariel? And Selmar?" I asked.

He nodded but his eyes had grown wary and I wondered which name had produced the change. "Oh, aye. I know them all, an' more. Selmar's a poor sad thing now. Ye'd nowt know her if ye could see how she were when she first came. An' she were th' hope of Obernewtyn . . ." he said bitterly.

I frowned in puzzlement. I had assumed Selmar had always been the way she was now. She must have degenerated. Some Misfits did.

I started to ask him about Ariel but he stood up and ordered me tersely to get on with the work. He grunted and stomped off and did not come back.

When I had finished the milking and washed the buckets, I sat outside the barn forlornly, thinking I had a bad habit of annoying the worst people.

"Don't tell me you are tired?" came Rushton's mocking voice. I looked up at him with open dislike.

Suddenly I could not stop myself from saying what I was thinking. "People like you are the worst sort," I said in a low, furious voice that seemed to surprise him with its intensity. "You make everything so much worse with your sneering and snide comments. I do my work. Why don't you just leave me alone?"

For a moment he looked taken aback, then he shrugged. "I hardly think the opinions of one stupid Misfit will worry me too much," he said.

This time I did not reply. The weariness in my body had somehow crept into my spirit and I felt too old and tired for anger. Matthew and Dameon had returned in one of the earlier groups to the house so I waited silently at the gate, not speaking to the others standing there. I felt isolated and dispirited from the encounter with the farm overseer. He had taken a complete and irrational dislike to me. Again I thought how unlike Enoch he was. What a strange pair they were, to claim friendship. I wished I had thought to ask the old coachman more about him while I had the chance.

Thinking of Enoch made me think of Maruman and wonder again where the story of a cat searching for a funaga had originated. If only he were safe with the friendly old coachman.

But if he was not, then what was he doing in the mountains?

XIV

I *was in one of the tower rooms at Obernewtyn, a room I had not*
seen before. It was very small and round. There was a
small window and a door.

I heard voices and realized Louis Larkin was outside.
I was afraid he would catch me. I was hiding.

Then I heard a strange keening noise, a grinding sound
like metal against metal, only more musical. There was
a note in the noise not unlike a scream.

As I drifted awake, the noise seemed to carry on into
my waking state. It was a tantalizingly familiar sound.
Not something that I had ever heard in my life but a
sound that sometimes came to me in dreams.

Thunder rolled in the air.

I opened my eyes unwillingly to see Cameo hasten into
the room. I looked around but we were alone.

"Are you all right?" Cameo said. "You yelled out and
I was passing. . . ." She faltered, unsure of her welcome.

I smiled. "It was just a dream," I said yawning, and
got out of bed. "I can't even remember what it was about
now."

Uninvited, Cameo sat on the edge and watched me
dress. She seemed very pale. "I have dreams," she said

in a strange, grave tone. I stared at her curiously for she
did not mean ordinary dreams.

"Nightmares," I suggested gently, thinking she had lost
weight. She looked very small and pathetic and I saw a
tear slide down her nose and drip onto clasped hands.

"I have always dreamed," she said. "The things I
dreamed . . .sometimes came true. That's why they sent
me here. But they are getting worse. I dream something
is trying to get me, something horrible and evil. And it's
a true dream!" She wept.

"Perhaps you were mixed up. It probably wasn't true
at all. I have heard it's hard to tell," I said.

She looked up and a wave of exhaustion crossed her
features making her look suddenly much older and wiser.
"I get so tired," she said. "I try not to go to sleep because
I'm scared."

I hugged her and thought she reminded me of Maruman in one of his fits. He had sometimes frightened me
and for a minute, I had been frightened by what Cameo
was saying. My neck prickled and I looked up to see Ariel
watching us from the open doorway. He had a peculiar
expression on his face and he was watching Cameo.

"What is going on here?" he asked sharply, but I had
the impression he had been there for some time, and
already knew. Cameo looked at her feet. In the early
days, her liking of Ariel had puzzled me. But now she
seemed uncertain. She would not look at him and I wondered if he had appeared in her nightmares.

"What's meant to be going on?" I asked insolently,
hoping to draw his attention from her. I did not like the
way he was watching her, like a hunter before he shot
the killing arrow. But he only told us to hurry up since
we had already missed firstmeal.

∽

Thunder rumbled all morning over the farms but no rain fell. The sky was a thick congested gray with streaks of milky white cloud strung low in fibers from east to west. I ate midmeal with little appetite, despite having missed firstmeal. A foreboding feeling filled me. I could not talk to Dameon and Matthew because two other boys sat near and engaged them in conversation.

Before we went back to work, Matthew did manage to tell me quickly that the boys he had been talking to were special friends of Rushton's. He said he thought they were up to something and had been his most friendly to put them off.

"He might be some sort of informer," Matthew said softly of Rushton. "He's been watching me quite a bit today, and Dameon. We'd better be careful. I wouldn't like anyone to find out about us. I can just imagine the Doctor wanting to try his treatments on us."

I wanted to ask him about the treatments, but there was no chance, for Rushton had come out and was looking pointedly at us.

Since my outburst in the milking sheds, he had been curt and cold in manner, but he did not say anything to me apart from giving me instructions. I had expected some punishment, but nothing happened. That afternoon I was to spend with Louis Larkin learning how to make butter. By now I had been working on the farms for several weeks. I spent quite a lot of time with Louis and was looking after the horses and some goats. Best of all I liked the time I spent alone with the horses. Sharna, whom I had found lived with Louis, usually spent that time with me.

Midmeals I spent with Dameon and Matthew, and when it was safe, we talked, insatiably curious about the very different lives each of us had lived. Astonishingly, Dameon was the son of a Councilman, who had died leaving him vast properties. A nephew of the Councilman had conspired to have him declared Misfit. I was amazed at Dameon's lack of resentment. But he said he had never really felt like a Councilman's son. Because of his ability, he had always felt less than certain about his future. "And after all, ironically, I *am* a Misfit," he had laughed.

Cameo sometimes came to work on the farms too, and sat with us at midmeal.

Matthew was very protective of her and was quickly coming to be fond of her. I wondered what Dameon felt of this. It must be odd always to be feeling what other people felt. I wonder how he could tell the difference between other people's feelings and his.

Midway through one afternoon later that week, Matthew came to the milking shed with a message for Louis and stayed on talking. Usually Louis discouraged gossip during work time but that day he seemed inclined to conversation.

"Any news?" Matthew asked casually.

Louis was a fountain of Highland news. It was hard to tell where he got it from, since he appeared to hate almost everyone. I suspected some of it came via Enoch, who was certain to know the old Misfit.

"Nowt much," he said.

Matthew grinned at me and waited, and presently the old man went on. "Rumor says something is gannin on in th' Highlands." Our interest quickened as he took his pipe out for it was a sure sign he was in an expansive mood.

"I've known for an age, something was up. It was in th' air. Lots of strangers up in the high country, sayin' they lived out a way when it was a lie. 'Tis nowt enough just to listen to what people tells ye. Ye have to look in their eyes an' watch what they do. An' them folk belongs to th' towns."

I exchanged a puzzled look with Matthew as Louis relit

his pipe. I wished we could get him to talk about Obernewtyn but he always shied away from that.

"Ye don't believe they live up here?" Matthew prompted.

"Think, boy," Louis retorted with sudden scorn. "What would town folk be doin' up here? They're up to some mischief."

I had an odd thought. "I heard Henry Druid lived up there still; that he wasn't dead. Maybe it's the Council looking for him in secret," I suggested.

The old man looked at me sharply. " 'Tis nowt th' Council, I'll say that straight. They stay away from th' mountains. They get paid to stay out, mostly."

"I thought he was dead," Matthew said, looking at me curiously. I had not told them about Daffyd, the boy I had met in the Councilcourt. I remembered him quite clearly, not handsome but with a nice smile and a face full of character. Odd that a relative stranger should have made such an indelible impression on me.

"He might be alive at that," Louis said.

Matthew looked at me, sending a quick thought that trouble in the Highlands would detract attention from any escapes. We had spoken of escape but not with any real intention.

"Do you think it is him, then?" I asked.

"I dinna know," Louis said, disappointingly.

Matthew persisted. "Th' last really big battle was his defection, wasn't it?"

Louis frowned. "Aye. That'd be some ten years now. A long time ago," he said after a pause.

"Well, he could be planning to take over the Council," Matthew said.

But this time Louis shook his head definitely. "No. I dinna think that's it. Henry Druid must be over forty now. Not a hothead any more. He was smart, I heard, and smart turns into cunning when ye get old. He'd

never win in an outright battle against th' soldierguards.
He'd find some other way. His son an' his daughters was
killed in th' troubles. He would hate th' Council enough,
to be sure," Louis added.

"What was it all over, anyway?" asked Matthew.

"Nobody knows for sure what started it," Louis answered. "Ye'll hear th' Council say he was a seditious
rebel settin' to take over an' drag the land back into the
Age of Chaos, but that's only one side to th' story an'
Henry Druid ain't here to talk in his defense. But he was
a scholar an' a Herder, not a soldier. I dinna think he
would even consider war. Not unless he were sure of
winnin'."

"I heard he was a Herder," I said. "No wonder there
was such a fuss. It was all over forbidden books, wasn't
it?"

Louis nodded his head approvingly. "Aye. That's what
began it. The Council decided to burn all Oldtime books.
Henry Druid had a huge collection of books, an' he
looked after th' Herder library too. The Herders agreed
but Henry Druid refused. He was a popular man an' he
called on friends to help him. I dinna think he had any
idea of what would happen. The soldiers killed some of
his friends and burned his whole house down, books an'
all. The Herder Faction disowned him and they were
plannin' to execute Henry Druid as an example. But he
escaped with some followers an' no one's seen them since.
Leastways, no one who's talkin'," he added craftily.

"It seemed a good idea at th' time, to burn all th' books
that had caused th' Oldtimes to go wrong. But now . . .
I ain't so sure." Louis's eyes were troubled as if he re-
called some long past battle with himself.

"He should have been able to keep th' books," Matthew declared, ever the advocate of the Beforetime.

"I dinna know about that either," Louis said sternly.
"There's none alive to say whether th' books were th'

cause or nowt. An' maybe Henry Druid only wanted a
look at th' past an' had no mind to seek trouble. Then
again, maybe he was after some of th' power th' Oldtimers had. Time was when everyone wanted that
an' I reckon th' Council had th' right idea in sayin' th'
Oldtimers had gone th' wrong way. It seemed like a
good idea that people kept from startin' it all again. But
then th' Council changed . . ." He sighed. "Everything
changed."

"How do you mean changed?" Matthew asked.

"Everything was changed by the Great White," Louis
told him, almost gently. "Even th' seasons have changed.
Once they were all a similar length. Nothing is like it was
in th' Beforetime. The Great White killed th' Beforetime,
an' it woke lots of queer things. It ain't th' same world
now."

"I don't believe people have changed," Matthew said
defiantly, obviously taking Louis's words for criticism of
the past.

"People," Louis said with great contempt. "They've
changed all right. Pity is in some ways they're still as they
were—greedy, grasping, selfish. They're th' things ye
have to stamp out if ye want th' world to be better. No,
'tis in other ways people have changed, an' who's to say
if that's to the good, either."

"How do you mean changed?" I asked, very carefully.
But Louis would not answer.

"You mean th' magic is gone?" Matthew asked.

"Magic! Pah!" Louis scoffed. "I dinna think for one
moment they was any more magic than thee. Not th' sort
of magic ye find in fairy stories anyhow. Some of th'
things they could do might seem like magic to us now.
But 'tis my feeling they was just mighty clever people—
too clever for their own good."

"Well, I think they were magic!" Matthew said stubbornly. "An' I think Lud never destroyed them at all."

That was as close as you could get to outright Sedition, and to Louis, who we all agreed was interesting but probably not to be trusted.

But the old man only puffed at his pipe for a minute. "Boy," he said finally. "Ye mun be careful of what ye say. It ain't safe to be blatherin' out every crazy notion. As to what ye said, well, ye could be right. But if ye are, then who made th' Great White? Yer wonderful Beforetimers, that's who."

Matthew's face was stricken and he did not answer.

"Do you think the Beforetime is all gone?" I asked, voicing some inner longing of my own.

"I dinna know," Louis said. "Seems so, an' excepting a few wild tales, it might be so. Sure enough th' people are gone. But maybe they left some things hidden, even from each other, so th' Great White didn't destroy them, an' th' Council didn't find them. Maybe there might be something left, but just in case Matthew is right an' th' holocaust were man-made, it might be better to leave that stuff hidden. After all, we dinna want to be finding out how they did it."

"But we wouldn't have to use the magic like they did," Matthew said at last.

Louis shook his head. "Dinna say it, lad. Ye dinna know what ye'd do. Power has a way of . . . changin' a person. In th' end, what would all that power do to yer good intentions?"

XV

Thoughts of escape began to plague me.

It might have been partly discovering I was no freak
that hardened the notion that life seemed worth more
than just endurance. Obernewtyn hadn't turned out as
badly as I had thought, but any way you looked at it the
place was still a prison and I wanted to be free. I wanted
to find Maruman and make a home for us.

Then something happened to make me determined to
go. I had begun having nightmares. Dreams so full of
horror and fear that, like Cameo, I was afraid to sleep.
One day I had a terrible premonition. As usual it did not
seem to be connected to anything, but coupled with the
dreams which, though not true dreams, were somehow
significant, I sensed trouble ahead.

Later that same day the promise of rain was fulfilled
with a vengeance. The raindrops were big and forceful.
Everyone took shelter and glumly watched them pelt
down. Those in the orchards ran for the nearest buildings
and even the cows and horses came under cover. It was
impossible to work or go back to the main house, so we
just sat there. I milked the few cows remaining and listened to the thunderous noise the rain made on the tin
roof. The day's disquiet left me and I felt soothed. The

downpour stopped obligingly just before we were due to go back through the maze.

I was waiting for Louis to come and start the separator as the others made their way to the maze gate. Ariel was waiting by the time I ran to join the others. I was surprised by the air of gloom among them all. Then one of the girls leaned near and whispered, "Madam Vega has returned. Ariel just told us." Her eyes were frightened and I felt that old fluttery terror come back into my stomach.

It wasn't as if anything had really changed, but all at once I realized what had struck me about the atmosphere at Obernewtyn since I had come here. It had been waiting. . . .

XVI

I *had thought* I *would be interviewed by* Madam Vega *at once.* But as the days passed much as before I wondered whether I could have been wrong about the premonition.

Then I discovered something that drove my nagging worry over the head keeper to the back of my thoughts. Dameon told me he heard Cameo had been receiving "treatments" since Madam Vega's return. Questioning Matthew and Dameon, I found none of us knew what the treatments were, except that they were supposed to be helping Misfits to become normal. Dameon said he had heard a rumor they were some sort of shock intended to stimulate the mind. He said the treatments were supposed to be terribly harsh. I found it odd and rather frightening that so little was known of the treatments given to so many. I resolved to keep my ears open.

Strangest of all was Cameo's reaction when I asked about her visits to the Doctor's chamber. She just stared at me in surprise and said she didn't know what I was talking about. With anyone else I might have thought they were lying, but not Cameo. She was not made for guile. I thought Dameon's informant must have been mistaken.

Then someone else told me they had seen Cameo being taken by Ariel to the Doctor's chamber. That might explain her change in attitude to the boy. Perhaps she had true dreamed of him taking her there. Again I asked her about it, but she was so obviously confused that I did not go on. She was definitely telling what she thought was the truth. Somehow she was blocking the rest from her conscious mind.

I wondered why the Doctor would want to treat Cameo. Everyone seemed to think he was only interested in unusual cases. Apart from her mental simplicity, and a tendency to true dream, which almost all Misfits have, she was quite ordinary.

I was even more surprised to hear that no one seemed to know what the mysterious Dr. Seraphim looked like. Dameon said he had never seen the Master of Obernewtyn. He said he thought those who had been to the Doctor had been prevented from talking about what they saw or the treatments they received. I could not imagine why there was any need for the Master of Obernewtyn to keep his practices secret, unless they were so horrible that it would create trouble among the Misfits.

The whole idea of treatments to make us like ordinary people was irrational anyway. There must be something more behind it, and the passion for secrecy of the Master of Obernewtyn. Who ever heard of a master that never appeared? Remembering the comments of the Councilman in Sutrium, I knew I was not alone in wondering what really went on at Obernewtyn.

As to Cameo's apparent ignorance of what happened to her, Dameon told me he thought it might have something to do with an Oldtime technique called hypnosis, which sounded to me like coercing. I had not outlined my ability in that area to Dameon or Matthew, feeling they might react uncomfortably to a companion capable of tampering with their minds. Dameon went on to say he believed someone had made it impossible for Cameo to remember what had happened to her using this hypnosis, since I would have been able to detect a lie or evasion. And that suggested that all those who had visited the Doctor and received treatments had been similarly made to forget.

That was extraordinary and apparently senseless.

"More and more, I am beginning to feel this mysterious Doctor doesn't exist. Nobody has seen him, no one speaks of him. All the commands come through Madam Vega and Ariel." Dameon hesitated. "And . . . I have heard, though it may be nothing, that there is someone else, I don't know, a man." He shook his head, ever impatient with his inability to explain things fully.

I tended to the belief that the man Dameon had heard mentioned was probably the Doctor himself, and that there was some more sinister purpose behind his absence. One day I tried probing Cameo, in an attempt to find out what was happening to her. Her mind was maze of blocks and it was immediately obvious she had been tampered with, though clumsily. I could have done a far more delicate job with my abilities, so I was inclined to believe in Dameon's theory of hypnosis. I could have forced my way through the blocks and walls roughly established, but that would have caused irreparable damage to Cameo. Removal of the blocks would be a long, painful process. I withdrew, feeling confused and helpless.

Why would anyone bother to do such a thing to the mind of a feeble little Misfit? It just didn't make sense.

A week later, I saw Cameo again and she looked terrible. Matthew went nearly as white when he saw her. We were all too frightened to ask her what was happening. She said she had been ill, and resting in a place where they kept sick Misfits. She talked and laughed but her smile was brittle and her laughter had jagged edges. She wandered off after a moment and Matthew and I looked at each other worriedly. His eyes were anguished.

"What are they doin' to her?" he asked, but no one knew. He begged me to deep probe her, to force my way in if I had to.

"No," I told him firmly. "She's hurt enough. If I force my way in it will be very painful for us both. I'll try later."

I did try again, but if anything the block was deeper. Even so, I suspected I would be able to force it. But as I had told Matthew, the pain would be awful for her, and with our minds linked, I would feel everything. I might not even be able to get out again.

That night I had another nightmare, and again the following night.

Cameo's awful dream about being pursued haunted me, and when at last I told Matthew, he admitted he had been having nightmares too, though in his dreams someone else was always being chased, while he stood by helpless.

Dameon said nothing but it was obvious from the shadows under his eyes he was sleeping badly, too. I asked him once, when we were alone, if he could use his own powers to find out what was wrong with Cameo. He told me he had already tried.

"I don't see things like you do. It's much hazier. Feelings are not so precise. On the surface, there is nothing. Deeper down there is a block, and below that fear for herself and fear of something else less personal."

"Some*one* else, don't you mean?" I asked.

But he frowned. "No, it's not a person. It's something else," he said. "And then sometimes when she is near me, I sense another person, someone completely different from Cameo." He shook his head in frustration. Neither of us said any of this to Matthew, who was already beside himself.

Without warning, Cameo was moved into my room and an extra bed put in to accommodate her. New Misfits were coming and extensive repairs were being carried out in some areas of Obernewtyn before wintertime. This meant we would be more crowded. I was glad of the opportunity to spend more time with Cameo, hoping to have better luck in discovering what was happening to her. It might even be simpler to probe her while she slept if it was true that hypnotism was the mind working against itself.

But from the first it did not proceed as I had hoped. At first I could not get a moment alone with her; then I fell into a restless sleep only to be woken by Cameo's screams. I looked in astonishment at the others who were all still soundly asleep. Then I realized what I had heard had been a mental scream. I probed the others lightly to make sure they were asleep before getting out and padding across the cold floor.

Cameo was lying with her back to me, moaning and whimpering very softly. The moon fell across the pillow and gleamed whitely in the light. She was murmuring to herself in a funny, deep voice. It didn't sound like her. I reached out to touch her but she began to shudder convulsively. I pulled my hand away as if it had been burned and stared at her frail back with the sudden crazy idea that it wasn't Cameo there at all.

I sat that way for ages, too scared to turn her over, but unwilling to leave her. Finally, of course, she rolled over and I could see it was her. I nearly wept with relief, sagging against the side of the bed and grinning like an idiot at my stupid fright. I glanced at her face and my grin froze when I saw her eyes were wide open and she was staring at me.

My heart missed a beat. Those eyes, looking out of Cameo's face, were the wrong color! They weren't even the same shape. They were a hot, sick ochre hue and full of amusement.

"You'll never find it," she rasped in a weird, deep voice. If it had been possible I would have grown more frightened, but I seemed to have reached a threshold. Part of calming down was seeing she wasn't really looking at me at all. Cameo was in a trance. Impulsively, I decided to try to talk to her. Maybe this was the result of the hypnosis. Now she might tell me the truth.

"Tell me about the Doctor's chamber?" I asked after checking to see that the others still slept.

"Find it if you can. I'll not show you," said the voice. She cackled with laughter like an old woman, and shuddering, I hoped she would not wake anyone.

"Cameo, tell me what happens when Ariel takes you to the Doctor."

"You'll never find it. It's my secret . . ."

I frowned. I was getting nowhere. It was worse than when she was awake. Looking at her staring eyes, I wondered if somehow a demon had gotten into her. Louis said there were no such things, but I wasn't so sure. Presently she closed her eyes and dropped into a sound sleep and I pinched myself to make sure I hadn't dreamed the whole thing.

Shivering, back in my own bed, I wondered if Dameon would think me mad.

⧢

The next night, Cameo woke me again with her nightmares and again I tried to get through to her. She raved about wolves and hidden power and birds. I even debated waking her, except that I had once heard it was dangerous to wake someone who was dreaming. I didn't know if this was a dream or not. In the end I told Dameon because I was so worried.

"Poor Cameo," he said. "I'm afraid whatever is being done isn't helping her much."

"She looks terrible," I agreed. "Pale and lifeless. But I don't know what to do. What about sleep drugs?"

Dameon said he did not think they were the answer. "I think she would still dream," he said. "We have to find out why she's dreaming."

In the midst of this there were rumors that someone had tried to escape. Later I heard the Norselander twins had been involved but had been locked up. That did not surprise me. Everyone knew they thought of nothing but getting away. But the rumors said someone else had been with them.

That night I managed to get Cameo alone. Once more I asked her about the Doctor. Once again she said she didn't understand, but this time I sensed her fear and I wondered if the block was beginning to topple. It was much harder to keep a block when you were tired. I asked her if she had been having any nightmares and she burst into tears.

Relieved to have managed to break through her control, I put my arms about her.

"I'm so scared," she whispered. "It didn't seem so awful at all when I came here. Not like I expected. But now I keep dreaming of things chasing me, and of an old lady laughing." That sounded like the persona that I had seen during her nightmares. I debated whether to ask her about the Doctor again but decided against it because she looked so ill.

Suddenly I decided I would deep-probe Ariel. I wondered why I had not thought of it before. Probably because of what Dameon said about him being rotten. I thought his mind would be like stepping on something dead. But I would do it. I would find out once and for all what they were doing to Cameo.

But I forgot about that when, at the nightmeal, I heard someone ask if Selmar had been caught yet. She had been missing from her bed for more than a week. I had seen her once from a distance at midmeal and assumed she had been moved to another room, or had been wandering at night. Now a horrible notion formed.

"Caught?" I asked shakily, remembering the rumor that the Norselander twins had not been alone in their escape attempt. Was it possible the other person hinted at had been Selmar? Common sense said she would not be capable, but everything about Selmar was odd.

"Haven't you heard? She was with the twins when they tried to get away," said the girl beside me, confirming my worst fears. Looking up blindly, my eyes focused on Cameo, whose face was the color of dirty soap. Why would the news of Selmar cause such a look of horror in her? Looking down at my own meal, I determined to talk to Louis about Selmar. What he said about her being different had intrigued me. But now a terrible idea was forming in my mind, yet I dared not voice it even to myself until I was certain.

I asked Louis about her the next day, but he would not answer and flew into a rage. He was so angry he told me to go away, he didn't want me there anymore. Upset, but aware he probably didn't mean it, I did not mind helping cut some grain for the goats. I wondered why he reacted so strongly whenever Selmar's name was mentioned. He said she had degenerated. I wondered what she had been like in the beginning. Perhaps she had been nearly normal and Louis had grown fond of her.

No one knew whether or not Selmar had been caught and there was talk that the twins would be sent to one of the remote Councilfarms that dealt with whitestick. Ariel no longer came to take us to the farm or pick us up. Some of the others said he had gone after Selmar. They said he always chased anyone who ran off. And he always caught them. Remembering Selmar's reaction to Ariel, I pitied her.

I decided to try probing Rushton instead, though I did not think it would be as revealing as reading Ariel.

He came to the maze gate to collect three of us. It was

my day for cleaning out the stables so he went off with
the other two saying he would be back just before midmeal. I decided to practice.

I loosened my thoughts and let them fly and hover. It
felt odd since I had kept them under constraint for so
long. I felt almost lightheaded; waves of thought and impressions washed over me. They came from everywhere,
flitting like butterflies, drifting like peat smoke. Idle
thoughts about how to saddle a horse that had not been
ridden or what to do with a fevered mare, a fleeting
thought about a bitter wintertime when hundreds of animals had died. The barn was alive with memories now
that I had opened myself to receive the imprints they had
made. There was no telling how long the impression of
a thought might last. It depended on the thinker and the
time and the place and a dozen other things. But right
then I was not trying to analyze the thoughts, I simply
wanted to be sure my touch was as light as I could make
it for the delicate task of probing Rushton.

I pushed my thoughts further afield, reaching out to
where Misfits were picking fruit, and beyond where livestock grazed in far fields, into every corner of the farms.
I was ranging too widely now to receive any individual
thoughts. It was like traveling through a pool and getting
deeper and deeper without ever touching the bottom.

I went out beyond Obernewtyn, wondering suddenly.
how far I could go. If it were possible to go beyond the
mountains, I might be able to reach Maruman. It seemed
incredible but I could think of no reason why I would
not be able. Yet it would be very hard to sort out one
thought stream in all that distance.

All at once something squirmed beneath my touch. I
recoiled, but curiosity made me withdraw only a little
way. Foolishly I ventured near again, and again my
thoughts brushed something. The stirring grew stronger
and suddenly I was afraid. I began to withdraw but some-

thing immensely strong rose up and reached for me. Frantically I pulled back, but whatever I had disturbed clutched me and began to slide down my own probe. Dimly I registered that I had fallen to my knees.

Terror assailed me and I pulled madly in an effort to free myself. I felt as if I were being forcibly pulled from my body. Inexorably the force drew nearer. It was close enough for me to sense that whatever held me had no real life of its own. It was not human and I was certain it was no beast. Possibly, I thought, it was a spirit from the Oldtime.

A drumming sounded in my ears and a wave of new fright washed over me when I realized it had begun to call me.

With a sob, I felt my legs tremble and stand.

"No!" I screamed at it.

Then I sensed someone else. "O reaching girlmind . . . who?"

This mind was far stronger than Matthew's and almost as strong as my own, but there was something disjointed in it, as if the same voice were speaking in an echo chamber. It was an odd, disconcerting effect like a chorus of voices, each voice slightly displaced from the timing of the others. I felt the cool probe tendrils mesh gently with mine and instinctively, I fought free of its embrace, knowing that such a connection would reveal me utterly to that unknown mind.

"Who are you?" I asked, as I felt it hover near again.

"Trust me, little sistermind. I would like to know you, but not now. My friends and I have sensed you. Tell me what you are called?"

I struggled for a moment in the viselike grip of the other force and realized I was walking toward the open door.

"No!" I cried to the other.

"Perhaps if we help you will trust. You are strong.

Maybe even stronger than any of us. The machine that holds you is very strong too, but together we will be stronger. Mesh with me and when I signal, pull away as hard as you can. The machine has no mind to make a decision. It will try to hold us both. To divide is to conquer."

"I can't mesh," I said desperately, fearing the revelation that must come almost as much as I feared the terrible force that drew me. But I was beginning to panic and before long I would be out in the open.

"You must," said the othermind urgently. "I will not read you, I promise."

I was right in the doorway now. My terror gave me extra strength and I swayed uncertainly, neither moving forward nor back.

"All right," I agreed because I had no choice. The othermind moved forward at once and I felt a great desire to simply surrender to those soft tendrils, but the othermind held itself rigidly away from the center of my thoughts, thus keeping its promise.

"Now!" it called and we began a terrific tug-of-war. As predicted, the machine, if such it was, tried to keep us both but did not have the strength. The moment it slid off me, I slammed a shield into place.

I opened my eyes. I was outside the door and shakily I stepped back inside the stables, appalled to discover the extent of my weakness. My face dripped with perspiration and I wiped it hastily on my sleeve.

A machine able to deal with thought. I was astounded and frightened. That meant someone was using a forbidden machine. But what sort of machine could do that? Had the Oldtimers known about telepathy? And who was the othermind? A man, I thought, but difficult to tell because of the subtle distortion of the probe.

I did not know where he came from or how old he was. But without his help I would have been exposed.

Returning to my work, I cursed the stupidity that had led me to farseek. I would not dare attempt it again. In fact I was now too frightened to use any but the most basic powers. Who knew what would alert the machine?

From that moment, I was determined to get away from Obernewtyn and all of its mysteries and dangers. Cameo must come, and Dameon and Matthew. I knew of no other I cared to trust. Four people. Fleetingly I thought of my rescuer, but there was no way to contact him without arousing the machine. Yet he seemed smart and strong enough to take care of himself. Besides, he had spoken of friends, so he was not alone.

But Matthew disagreed. "If we really are going to escape, yer bound to take him too," he argued.

"Impossible," I told him bluntly and explained my fear that the machine might trap us if we used too much power.

"There must be some way," Matthew insisted, entranced with the idea of my gallant rescuer.

I was less romantic. "He might not even want to leave. We don't even know that he is a Misfit. I'm not even really sure it's a he. And the whole thing might have been a trap. He wanted to mesh with me. And he said he had been looking for me!"

"Ungrateful Elspethelf," Matthew sputtered into thought. "He had the right to ask who you were. He saved you!"

"Yes, he did," I conceded hastily, forestalling one of Matthew's emotive lectures. "So I'm not going to throw my life away. That would be really ungrateful."

"He would not have helped ye if he were an enemy," Matthew said angrily.

"But he didn't know who I was, so how could he know what I was?" I said.

That stumped Matthew and he subsided.

"Speaking of help," Dameon interjected quietly, "I

have been thinking. If you really intend to escape, you should not take me. I would slow you down. You know I want to come and to be free. But it is not so bad for me here."

"Of course yer comin' with us!" Matthew said firmly. "We've taken yer blindness into account."

Dameon smiled at his friend sadly. "Sometimes I think you have more heart than sense. Most times," he corrected comically and we all laughed. Then Dameon grew serious again. "Well, if I am to come, then I will speak. This is a dead quest from the start if it is not planned carefully. Have you thought what will happen if we do get away? We have no Certificates and we will stand out wherever we go." I stared at him. I had not thought beyond getting away. We had to plan everything, otherwise it would end like the last escape. We still didn't know what had happened to Selmar.

"What about dressing up as gypsies?" Dameon said. "With some brown stain and a carriage with bells we could pass for half-breeds."

"Wonderful!" I cried and he blushed.

"It seems nearly real when we talk about it like this," Matthew said with a funny chirp of delight. Suddenly he stiffened. "Look out. It is our surly friend the overseer."

"He takes an interest in us," Dameon said. "He does not like what he sees."

"Maybe he's only interested in one of us," Matthew said with a sly glance in my direction.

Catching the gist of his thoughts, I scowled. "Don't be an idiot," I snapped. Rushton made no pretense of his dislike and I did not like him either. But it was true that he seemed to watch us. I had abandoned my plan to read him since my encounter with the machine.

"He's coming," Matthew said, and we all munched our food casually.

"You! Elspeth, come with me," Rushton said. I looked

up but could not make out his expression because the
sun was behind him. I stood up and followed him back
into the barn.

"You are foolhardy to make your friendships so bla-
tant," he said. I stared at him in astonishment. What
could he care? He shook his head. "But I did not call
you to say that. The girl Selmar, when did you last see
her?"

"She sleeps in my room, but she wanders at night," I
said, wondering where this was leading.

"Did she sleep there the night before she disappeared?" he queried.

"I don't know. I can't remember," I said, completely
dumbfounded. "Why do you want to know?"

"You have no right to ask me questions," he said
haughtily.

I saw red. "And what right have you to ask them of
me?" I snapped.

"I belong here," he said icily. I did not dare speak, he
was so angry. "Fool of a girl," he snarled. "Go back to
your cows."

It was too late to join the others, so I went on to the
dairy. Once more I tried to ask Louis about Selmar.

This time he did not fly into a rage. "She were a good
girl," he said sadly. I frowned because he spoke as if she
were dead. "She's nowt escaped," he added.

"Where do you think she is then?" I asked him very
softly.

"With that devil-spawned brat," Louis snapped. So he
thought she was somewhere with Ariel. "That Doctor will
be treatin' her again," he added.

With a flash of awareness, I admitted to myself what
I had begun to suspect since Selmar's disappearance.
Louis had spoken of Selmar being different on her arrival
in the mountains. He had called her the hope of Obernewtyn. I did not know what he meant by the latter, but

it was blindingly obvious now that Selmar's mind had
been destroyed by the Doctor's treatments.

"He never meant it to be so, th' first master didn't,"
Louis said, unaware of the violent conflicts in my mind.
I found it hard to make sense of what he was talking
about. Instinct kept me silent as he went on. "He were a
good man an' he built this place because he thought th'
mountain air were a healin' thing. Two sons an' a wife
he had buried already from the rotting sickness an' another burned. He wanted to make this place a sanctuary,
then he took another wife. He died an' his son was too
weak to fight against the yellow-eyed bitch. Then th'
other two came, an' that were th' end."

The old man was talking about the past, but I understood a little of his musings. He had spoken of the first
Master of Obernewtyn. That would be Sir Lukas Seraphim, who had moved to the mountains after his family
died. That explained why Obernewtyn had been built in
the mountains. He had married again—someone Louis
called a "yellow-eyed bitch," who had borne a son. That
would have been Michael Seraphim, the second Master
of Obernewtyn. The rest was inexplicable. Dr. Seraphim
was the third Master of Obernewtyn and obviously the
son of Michael Seraphim. I wondered what had happened to Michael, and to the mother of the present Doctor.

An icy shroud fell over my skin as another thought
occurred to me. Cameo was now receiving treatments. If
what I suspected were true, she was in terrible danger.

That night, I learned she was not the only one. I was
told the Doctor wished to interview me the next day.

XVII

Matthew came to the kitchen early the following morning. Not many people were up yet and as it was some time before first-meal we were able to sit alone. Our rooms were always unlocked in the morning by one of the Misfits and it was the only time you could really do as you pleased, depending on how early you got up.

The cook was in the kitchen, but apart from her hunger to bond Lila to Ariel, she was completely indifferent to the subtleties and undercurrents at Obernewtyn. Usually Ariel was up at this time too, but since his mysterious absence, we felt able to talk privately.

We talked about him for a while, and Selmar's disappearance. I told Matthew that neither Rushton nor Louis seemed to think she had escaped, whatever anyone else said. But we could not imagine where Ariel was, if he wasn't looking for Selmar. When I told Matthew that I was to see Madam Vega and the Doctor, he reassured me that a lot of Misfits only went to see him once. A shadow fled across his face and I knew he was thinking of Cameo.

"You know she has not been taken again for a few days now," I said reassuringly. "Maybe he's finished with her."

I could not bring myself to tell him just then what Louis had told me about Selmar and what I suspected was the end result of the Doctor's treatments.

"That murderous bastard," Matthew said forcefully, as if he saw what was in my mind. "Do ye know Louis once warned me to watch out for him? He said there was a dragon in the Doctor's chamber. What does that mean?"

"I might find out soon enough," I said, and he looked at me with quick sympathy. I changed the subject. "Louis told me something odd yesterday. He said the first master here opened the place to Misfits because he thought the clear mountain air would help them."

Matthew laughed. "Now I bet that's a story." He grinned.

"I don't know. He thinks it's true. He seemed to think it went wrong because of Lukas Seraphim's wife. He really hated her." I did not really know why I was repeating Louis's nonsense, except that it took my mind off Cameo.

Matthew shrugged. "What happened yesterday when you went with Master Mucky-muck?"

"Oh, Rushton was his usual friendly self. That was when he asked me about Selmar."

The door opened and one of the Misfits entered with a stranger.

"Who is *that*?" Matthew whispered.

I shrugged but something about the stranger seemed familiar. He sat at one of the tables and Andra gave him something to eat. He was very tall and tanned and the knees of his pants were sturdily patched.

"So where do ye come from?" asked the boy who had come in with him. Matthew had nicknamed him Sly Willie because he was an informer.

"From a village in th' East. I had to cross badlands to get here. No one warned me," the man grumbled.

"We don't get many visitors up here," Willie said.

The stranger shrugged. "I repair things. I go where

there is work. I heard nobody comes here so I figured there would be plenty to do. Potmetal is my specialty."

Hearing this, Andra came forward. Most of the kitchen pots were in need of repair. Watching the man's face, I was more than ever convinced that I had seen it before. But where? It seemed important for me to remember.

Willie hung around the man until the cook cuffed him and sent him about his business. He came over to us. "Ariel said you're to help me repair some stairs," he said.

Matthew stood at once. We could not talk while he was there. "I'll come now," he said and followed Willie out.

I stayed in the kitchen when the others left to go down to the farms. The man repaired some pots, then went away to fix some of the farm implements. Still I could not recall where I had seen him before. Willie came back just before midmeal saying he was to take me to Madam Vega. I was glad to go, for the waiting had made a wreck of me. My stomach churned nervously. We went back to the entrance hall, then through a doorway on the other side leading into a windowless hall. The way was lit by pale green candles that flickered and hissed as we passed.

At the end of the hall was a small room, obviously a waiting room adjoining a larger chamber. Willie made me wait. He knocked on the door to the inner chamber before entering. I had not been to this part of Obernewtyn before and reflected that in its own way, the complex was like the maze with its halls and endless doors. There were strict rules about where one could go, and I wondered what went on in the forbidden sections.

Willie returned, disrupting my reverie and my calm as he gestured for me to go in.

Taking a deep breath outside the door, I pushed it open resolutely, determined to stay calm no matter what happened. My first impression on entering was of heat. A quick look around revealed the source—a fire burning brightly in an open fireplace. Spare wood was piled high on one side of the fire, and two fat, comfortable-looking armchairs were drawn up facing the hearth. The stone floor was covered by a brightly colored woven rug and there were a number of attractive hangings on the walls. It was a pleasant, lavish room compared to the rest of Obernewtyn.

Against the back wall of the room was a desk and behind this a wide window with a magnificent view of the cold arching sky and the jagged mountains. I stared, mesmerized, thinking how much better the view was from this height. Madam Vega stepped abruptly into my line of sight, with the same vivid blue eyes and the same stylish attractive figure that I remembered. But her expression was no longer the coy, girlish one she had worn during her visit at Kinraide. Her blue eyes were cold and calculating, and her lips, though beautifully curved, did not look like they smiled much. Even so, I found it difficult to be intimidated by her, though I had reason enough to know this was an effective ruse calculated to lower defenses.

She waved impatiently at a chair. I walked forward, and choosing a hard upright chair, I sat down.

"It pleases me to see you looking happier than at our last meeting," she said briskly as if she did not really care. "You should have told me you were a dreamer and that you had been in tainted water. I thought ...." She hesitated. I saw she was angry at her mistake and wondered why. A strange smell seemed to emanate from the fireplace and I felt slightly sickened by it. "I told you there was no need to fear Obernewtyn. You don't fear it now, do you?" That was easy, I shook my head eagerly, concentrating on keeping my eyes clear and unhesitant.

"Well then," she said sweetly. She sat back in her seat and watched me through narrowed eyes. "I hear you have even made some friends," she said.

I thought of Rushton and damned him. It seemed he was an informer after all. "I only eat with them at meals," I said hastily. "I won't do it again."

Irritation flicked over her features. "There is nothing wrong in making friends here. As a matter of fact, you could help me. I need someone bright like you to ... keep an eye out for me."

I stared. "I couldn't be an informer," I said with honest disgust. I would pretend stupidity but not that.

"Of course I would not ask you for that. No," she said so kindly that I was filled with suspicion. "All I want you to do is keep a watch out for any Misfits who seem ... different. I am concerned that some do not tell us the full extent of their ... mutancy. It is most unfortunate because we want to help them." She did this beautifully and I even saw a hint of tears in her eyes. But what she had said terrified me too much for me to be taken in by her wiles.

My heart was thumping so hard that I was certain she must hear it. What did she mean by Misfits who were different?

"I do not want to hear anything of petty misdeeds. I want to know of anyone with unusual or undisclosed deviations of the mind," she said. She regarded me closely and I could do no more than nod.

She sighed, and launched into an oft-repeated lecture on Obernewtyn. "As for your stay here, you must not cherish any hope of leaving this place. Escape and death are the only ways. I do not imagine you want to die, and, as for escape, the nearest settlement is Darthnor, some leagues from here and off the main road—a mining town. And of course there is the tainted ground which the highlanders prefer to call badlands. I'm sure you noticed them in your journey here. On all sides of Obernewtyn lies the wilderness. Do not imagine that you have seen wilderness before, perhaps even roamed in it, for this is true wild country, untamed by men. The forests are filled with wolves of the most savage kind and there are still bears living in the heights. Even stranger things dwell in these shadow-pocked high mountains.

"The wintertime alone is more dangerous than either wilderness or beast, and when the snows come we are completely cut off from the Lowlands. That is why we need few guardians. In wintertime all the guardians but Myrna go back to the Lowlands. You must accept this life here and put freedom from your thoughts."

While speaking she had gradually circled the desk, her eyes on a black beetle that had come out of the wood and set off on a trek across the rug. An odd glitter came into her eyes as she reached out a dainty foot and crushed the squat creature.

I repressed a shudder of revulsion.

"Now. I am sure you will be of much help to me," she purred. "Cameo tells me you are her friend?" she added.

I felt the snakelike coil of fear in my belly. "She is defective," I said with a shrug, but I wondered how much Cameo had said.

"Have you ever noticed anything . . . unusual about her?" Madam Vega asked, so casually I knew it was important.

"She has true dreams sometimes," I said, knowing she must know that already.

"Very well," she said with sudden impatience. "I am going to take you to the Doctor's chamber now," she added, coming toward me, her satin dress whispering to the rug. She walked behind me and I felt her breath stir my hair. A moment of blind terror made me want to turn where I could see her but I forced myself to be still.

"Come," she said, and I followed. One of the panels alongside the fireplace was an ornate door, so intricately worked I had not even known it for a door. It opened into a narrow dark hall, which smelled of damp. There was a candle on either side of a door at the end of the short hall, and this had obviously been carved by the same hand that had carved the front doors. It had the same theme too—of cavorting man-beasts. The only human figure in the picture was chained to a tree. As Madam Vega unlocked the door, a great wave of heat rushed out.

The Doctor's chamber was an enormous circular room with no windows, but there was a huge skylight in the center of the roof. A fireplace almost as big as the one in the kitchen provided the heat. There were books everywhere, not only of recent origin, easily recognizable by their coarse workmanship and purple Council stamp of approval, but also hundreds of books from the Old-time. The walls were lined with bookshelves, each full to overflowing. There were tables everywhere and these, too, were piled with books and papers and maps.

"Dr. Seraphim?" called Madam Vega. There was a flurry of movement and a rotund man emerged smiling from a dim corner. If this was the Doctor, he looked completely different from what I had expected. Certainly I had not imagined a smile, but when I looked at him more closely, there was something not quite right about his face.

"Another Misfit," he sighed. He peered shortsightedly into my face. He giggled suddenly and slapped his leg. He had a high-pitched, almost hysterical laugh. I had the sudden mad notion that he was defective.

"You are a cool one," he gurgled coyly. I did not know what to say and I glanced helplessly at Madam Vega, who was looking around with a frown. She walked away.

"You don't look like a Misfit," the Doctor said. "But the taint rarely shows. Vega tells me you are a dreamer and that tainted water caused your dreams. I have not seen anyone affected so by water, who lived," he said. That at least explained why he wanted to see me. How ironic that a lie meant to protect me from curiosity should arouse interest for its own sake. "I do not have a great deal of time at the present but I am going to write your name down for future research." He began to look for a pencil and I glanced around, wondering where Madam Vega had gone. I had seen no other door. There was a portrait of a woman hanging in a small alcove. I felt instantly repelled by the painted face.

"I see you are looking at my dear grandmama," said the Doctor. "Her name was Marisa," he whispered.

I saw the chance to ingratiate myself. "She is beautiful," I said admiringly, though I thought the face too sharp and cold for beauty. There was a fiery gleaming intelligence in the eyes.

"She is that," said the Doctor rather sadly. "It was such a shame she had to die." I stared at him, but he had discovered a pencil at last. "Elspeth Gordie, wasn't it?"

I nodded, thinking that this was the woman Louis had called a meddling yellow-eyed bitch.

"Misfits are not always what they appear to be. Often there are more demons which the treatment reveals."

I looked at my feet, afraid the cold hatred in my heart would show in my eyes. The only demons in people's minds were the ones put there by treatments. Blind to my lack of response, he had stopped pacing and was now staring blankly at the ground between us as if he had fallen into a trance.

Presently he spoke again. "I treated a girl once who harbored amazing demons. Selmar was her name. My treatments rendered her quite docile in the end. Presently, I am treating another who may be hiding demons."

I gaped openly, wondering if I had gone mad. Surely this could not really be the terrible, powerful Dr. Seraphim. And was it really possible fear of him had reduced Selmar to the timid, shivering half-wit I had met that first day at Obernewtyn? I could hardly credit it. He seemed so completely ineffectual.

"Doctor, I do not think you should discuss such matters with a Misfit," said a voice as rich and smooth as undiluted honey.

"Alexi," said the Doctor, looking over my shoulder with a furtive, almost guilty expression. I turned slowly and there, half-concealed by a shelf, stood a tall beautiful man with shining white hair. His skin was pale and soft like that of a child and his eyes were the coldest and darkest I had ever seen. As he stepped closer, I felt an overpowering urge to step away. I forced myself to be calm, but a mad fear was barely leashed inside me.

"Of course you're right. I was forgetting," said the Doctor, talking too quickly. He seemed afraid of the other man. Alexi flicked his weird eyes over me.

"Alexi is my assistant," the Doctor said and I gaped. "Would you like to examine her? The tainted water . . ."

"I am sick of this," Alexi snarled, cutting the Doctor off. "She is of no use to me. I do not need another dreamer. Get rid of her. Where is Vega?" he asked imperiously.

The Doctor looked around, as if he expected her to pop up in answer to her name. "She was here . . . a moment ago," he stammered.

The blond man turned his shadow-dark eyes on me. The colored section seemed to be much larger than usual, with very little white visible around them. "Well, sit down. I might as well see if there is any use in you."

The Doctor rushed away and brought back two seats. Alexi sat down to face me and I wondered who he was to order the Master of Obernewtyn around like a servant.

"Her name is Elspeth," said the Doctor nervously.

"That is of no consequence," said Alexi coldly. He fixed me in his frigid black stare.

"Your family were Seditioners?" he asked.

I did not know if he was asking or telling me so I nodded slightly.

"They were burned by the Herders?"

I nodded again.

"You dream true?" he asked.

"Sometimes," I said firmly, but my voice came out as a croak.

"Are you able to know what people feel or think before they tell you?" he asked.

My heart almost stopped but I managed to shake my head.

"Can you sometimes sense things that have happened before, in rooms or . . . or from some object?"

I shook my head again.

"What was the crime of your parents?" he asked. "For what were they charged?"

"I don't know," I said truthfully.

He stared at me, then jumped to his feet growling with frustrated anger. "This is impossible. When will the right one be found?" he snarled.

"That blond girl . . ." the Doctor began, but Alexi shut him up with a poisonous look.

"My dear Alexi," said Madam Vega suddenly. I realized there must be rooms behind some of the shelves. "I have been looking for you."

Alexi stalked over to her. "This one is impossibly stupid. I cannot tolerate fools. Why did you bring her here?"

"I already told you what happened. You are too hasty and Stephen wanted to see her," Madam Vega added in a soft but steely voice. I stared, wondering if they were bonded. He seemed to have some regard for her where he had none for his master. "Does it not occur to you that stupidity is easily feigned? The one we seek would be clever. Have a care, someday you will make a fatal error in your impatience."

She glanced at me. "I admit, that one was a mistake, but there are others," she added calmly.

"That last fiasco had better not . . ." Alexi began, but Vega soothed him.

"We will speak of this matter later," she said, her eyes sliding pointedly to where I sat. She moved closer, her expression vaguely threatening.

"It is not wise to speak of visits to the Doctor, Elspeth. See that you remember to mind your own affairs, and keep to yourself. You will be most regretful if I hear that you have spoken of this visit." Her voice was ice cold and I felt a chill at the underlying menace of her tone. I did not doubt for one moment that she would carry out the implied threat. So this was how they prevented talk.

The Doctor had not spoken and stood crouched beside me like a third-rate Councilman's official. He was, I thought suddenly, a ridiculous figure, and obviously intimidated by the other two. Abruptly I remembered Dameon's notion that there was no such person as the Doctor. This man was so timid and ineffectual, despite the treatments he meted out, that I wondered who did control Obernewtyn.

Dismissed and returned to the anteroom adjoining Madam Vega's domain to wait for Willie, I was lost in reflections and seemingly mad speculations. I was certain, though, of two things. Selmar had been to the Doctor's chamber since her supposed disappearance, and the mysterious Dr. Seraphim was defective. No wonder those who saw him were not permitted to talk about the experience. But some greater influence than a mere threat must be used to make those subjected to treatments keep quiet. The great Doctor appeared to be little more than a simpleton.

So who was the real Master of Obernewtyn?

XVIII

The morning dawned warm and the air was full of butterflies. Harvest time in the mountains was not the event it had been in the Lowlands with local fairs and festivals. Few of the hardy mountain bushes flowered or retained their leaves so the mountains became gaunt-looking, the bones of dark rock showing through the foliage like the skeleton of a half-starved creature. And yet, there was a special promise in the air, a sort of sweetness you could almost taste, that marked the final days before wintertime began in earnest, for that season came far earlier to the mountains than to the coast.

Between mouthfuls, Matthew had told me Ariel was back. Nothing had been said officially of his absence and it seemed where he had been would remain a mystery. There was still no sign of Selmar.

In the fields we all toiled, baling and packing the rest of the harvest. Every spare Misfit was on the farms and each of the sections was alive with activity. Some of the boys were already transporting the stores to the main house. There was one final field to bale before midmeal, and to my delight, Matthew and I were sent out with a group of others. Baling is a two-person job, so whenever we were at the far end of our row, we were able to talk.

"Where is Dameon?" I asked.

"In th' dryin' rooms. Everyone is busy today. It was like this last year. It seems like a big fuss but wintertime is really a killer. You know that stranger we saw in th' kitchen yesterday?" Matthew said suddenly. I nodded, again struck by the teasing feeling that I had seen him somewhere before. "I saw him talking to Rushton later in th' day."

"It was probably because of the plow. I remember someone saying it was broken," I said.

Matthew looked disappointed, but there were enough mysteries around Obernewtyn without looking for them.

"So what happened in th' Doctor's chamber, or don't you remember?" he asked anxiously.

We had not had the chance to talk since my visit to the Doctor's chamber.

"Madam Vega made it very clear that there would be unpleasant consequences if it got back to her that I had talked about my visit. I think that must be how they shut up people who only go there once. As for others, well, I think Dameon is right about hypnosis."

"So, what else?" Matthew urged.

"Not much . . . on the surface. But Madam Vega asked me to keep a watch out for Misfits who were unusual," I said meaningfully.

Matthew paled. "Us?" he gasped.

"I think so. I'm sure she didn't suspect me. My being here at all was a mistake, according to her." I had already told Dameon and Matthew about the tainted water and the denouncement. But I had not said I forced Rosamunde to denounce me. "The Doctor only wanted to see me because he was curious about the effect of tainted water."

Matthew laughed incredulously. "What is he like?" he asked.

I frowned. "If I didn't know better, I would think he was defective," I said.

Matthew stopped work and gave me a look of disbelief. "He can't be. It's agin' th' lore fer a defective to run a place like this. I dinna think defectives can even inherit."

It was now my turn to gape.

"Of course," I whispered fiercely. "*That's* why he's kept out of sight. So that the Council won't come to hear about him, and take over Obernewtyn." It was so obvious that I was amazed I had not seen it at once.

"But . . . then who is runnin' Obernewtyn, and what are the treatments?" Matthew pondered.

I bit my lip, for it was obvious from Madam Vega's words that the Doctor had something to do with treatments. That didn't make sense. A fantastic notion occurred to me. "Maybe the . . . the Misfits given to him are just something to keep him occupied. He thinks he's a doctor and is quite content being locked away conducting his 'researches,' so they give him a few patients."

Matthew grimaced in horror. "It can't be true."

My mind raced. "And as to who runs this place, of course Madam Vega and this Alexi must do. The Doctor actually seemed afraid of Alexi, though he called him his assistant."

"Alexi?" Matthew asked with confusion.

I nodded impatiently, telling him quickly about the pale-haired assistant.

"But why?" Matthew asked, and my mind stumbled to a halt, for I could not answer that question. Possibly it could be for power, but what glory was there in controlling a remote institution supposedly aimed at rehabilitating Misfits? No, there must be more to it than that, and I was convinced the Doctor could not have made Selmar what she had become. There was something missing, some unseen element.

Soberly I looked up. "I don't know what it's all for,

but from what Madam Vega said, and from the sort of questions Alexi asked, I am certain it has something to do with us, or people like us." I remembered something else.

"Do you know, before I came to Obernewtyn, I heard a rumor this place was only interested in unconventional types of Misfits; ones who varied from the usual sort." Matthew gave me a quick frightened look and we fell silent as the couple working along the next row passed us.

"If only we knew what they were up to," he said, and I knew he was thinking of Cameo. He looked up, a fire in his eyes. "We have to get away from here."

We had spoken often of escape in a philosophical and practical way, but nothing had ever been seriously planned.

I bit my lip and thought for a while. "We have to do something positive to get us moving," I said, lowering my voice as another pair of workers passed us. "I want to have a proper look at that room. I could steal a map maybe . . ." I said. But I thought to myself that I would also try to find out what they were up to.

"Yer daft," Matthew said. "Ye'd never get through all th' locks. An' what if someone was in there." I explained to him about my ability to pick locks mentally. He was mildly impressed but still worried about the idea. The bell for midmeal rang and we joined Dameon.

Matthew went to collect our food and returned practically stuttering with excitement. "Ye'll never guess!" he cried. "Selmar's back."

"When? Where?" we asked together.

Matthew didn't know, but Sly Willie had told him. He had also said a new Misfit had arrived, sent by the Council.

"Was he telling the truth?" I asked cautiously.

"Oh, yes, I think so. He said she was defective."

"Selmar?" I asked puzzled.

Matthew shook his head. "The new Misfit."

"I meant was he telling the truth about Selmar?" I asked patiently.

"He just said he saw her, that's all," Matthew said. "I wonder where she's been all this time."

I looked up suddenly and saw Cameo, standing in the shadows and watching us. "Come and have something to eat," I said gently, bringing her over to sit down. She looked awful. Then I saw her eyes clearly. She was in some sort of trance.

"Elspeth, we have to get away. Something-terrible is going to happen," she whispered. She leaned very close and looked straight in my eyes. "They want you. They want the power . . ." She slumped forward in a dead faint.

"Oh, Cam . . ." Matthew whispered and gathered her up into his arms. I looked at his stricken face but could feel nothing.

There was no doubt in my mind that Cameo's peculiar warning was connected to whatever Alexi and Madam Vega were doing. I remembered, too, vividly, what Maruman had said about the things that waited for me in the mountains. Somehow, he had seen in his dreams a little of what I would encounter.

Dameon shuddered violently and I realized some of my feelings had reached him.

"I'm sorry," I said, forcing myself to calm down.

Dameon looked pale. "It cannot be helped. You are in danger?"

"I think we are all in danger," I said, quelling ripples of fear that ran down my spine. "Whatever Madam Vega and Alexi are doing at Obernewtyn, it is linked with people like us, with forbidden mental abilities. I can't imagine how they know we exist. But I don't believe they suspect any of us yet, except Cameo."

"Cameo! But that's absurd," Matthew exploded. "Anyway, I thought th' Doctor was treatin' her."

I shook my head briskly. "I think those treatments are a cover for something else that has nothing to do with Dr. Seraphim," I said stonily.

Dameon's face took on a determined look. "We must get away from here before it is too late," he said. "Cameo will be better too, if we go."

I told him that I wanted to go to the Doctor's chamber and find a map. "Maybe there is a way through the mountains that would avoid our having to cross tainted ground and keep us off the main road."

"Ye cannot go. Who will lead us if yer caught?" Matthew interjected.

I nodded. "The time has come for us to decide on a leader. It cannot be me. There are those made to lead and those to follow. There are also those who go a lone path, to scout the way ahead. I am a scout at heart. I do not lead or follow very well. We need someone smart and steady to lead. I think Dameon is the best choice."

"But I am blind," Dameon said, truly astonished.

"You are not blind when trueseeing is wanted," I said. "You will lead us with those cautious instincts of yours and not be led astray by false paths."

"O wise and tricky Elspethelf," Matthew laughed. Cameo stirred in his arms and he looked down at her with quick concern until she settled. "Ye know I'd follow either of ye, so maybe I am a follower. But if Dameon is leader an' says ye mun nowt go to th' Doctor's chamber, ye mun obey him," he added so slyly I had to smile.

"Well?" I asked Dameon, somewhat defiantly.

Dameon shook his head slowly. "I will accept your decision for now, but I will not lead when we go. It would be stupid. As for the other, I wish you had not given me the power of veto, Matthew, for I must disappoint you. If Elspeth can find a map it would be worth some risk.

Also you might look out for an arrowcase. Do you know what that is?"

I nodded solemnly. "A thing to point the direction. In the Old time it was called compass," I said.

"Bad will come of this," Matthew said darkly as Cameo woke. She struggled from his arms and stood up, seemingly unaware of her collapse or her words prior to that. Matthew watched her go sadly.

I worked alone that afternoon, cleaning and oiling bridles and saddles and other equipment for storage. I was glad of the chance to think. Things seemed to be moving too quickly. If the rumors were true, both Selmar and Ariel had come back.

I had discovered a few important things about what was happening at Obernewtyn. No wonder guardians weren't allowed to stay at the main house, and official visitors were discouraged. I wondered what would happen if a visiting party of Councilmen from the Lowlands did come up, for they rarely traveled without soldiers. And again I racked my brain, trying to fathom what Alexi and Madam Vega intended.

I thought of Cameo's warning. Maruman had been right; my destiny did await me in the mountains. But where would it lead? Suddenly I wanted very much not to know the answer to that question. I would go to the Doctor's chamber, find a map, and we would escape. Nothing else mattered.

That night I saw Selmar. Nothing could have prepared me for the look of her. Completely drained of blood, she resembled a walking corpse. Even her lips were white, and her eyes stared blankly around the room as if she were blind. Ariel had led her in, sat her down, and put food in front of her. The room was utterly silent. She did not eat or drink. She only sat, staring at nothing.

I glanced across the table at Cameo, but she was staring at Selmar. She looked terrified.

XIX

The walls were chill and silent as I slipped along them in stocking feet. The locks on some of the doors were very old and more complex than any I had encountered before, but none would keep me out. I was absolutely determined to find a map. The sight of Selmar had only increased my resolve.

I crossed silently through the entrance hall, reflecting that I had not crossed that hall since the first day I entered Obernewtyn. Slipping quickly into a hall on the other side, I hoped my sense of direction was accurate, for I could not recall the way Sly Willie had brought me to Madam Vega. The halls were very dark, for no windows opened into them. All but a few candles had been allowed to die, and I hurried past the pools of light they made.

At one point I detected someone approaching, and concealed myself quickly in one of the numerous alcoves along the halls until guardian Myrna had gone. I was using a very slight amount of power to warn me when anyone approached. When she had gone I continued, following the way Willie had brought me only days before. I passed through the outer room of Madam Vega's chamber, making sure no one was inside before I unlocked her door. The air was cold and smelled of stale smoke.

Searching, I eventually found the snib that worked the door alongside the fireplace. I left it ajar behind me to show the way down the musty hall. I searched ahead, very carefully probing the Doctor's chamber, but there was no sign of life. I hoped no one slept in there; it was much harder to sense a sleeping presence unless you knew the person. The lock was very difficult and for a while I despaired of opening it. At last I heard a faint click and the door slid open.

The enormous fire had burned low and only a few orange embers remained. I closed the door and walked softly across to the fireplace. Looking around, I wondered where to start. It was a matter of too much rather than too little. I tried to remember where I had seen maps when I was there before. Though it was quite dark, the dim coals threw an orange light over everything. The painting of Marisa Seraphim caught my eye and I crossed to look at it.

In that light she did not look so sharp and detached. There was a gleam akin to amusement in her secretive yellow eyes. The artist had caught a faint hint of cruelty in her mouth and heavily lidded eyes. She seemed to be watching me with those brilliant eyes, almost laughing. Even when I turned away, those painted eyes bored into my spine.

Scanning the room quickly, I tried to remember where I had spotted the maps, but I was distracted by the sight of so many books. Of course, most were forbidden, but up in the mountains who would care? Impulsively, I reached out and took a thick tome from the shelves. In the manner of Oldtime books, the pages were as thin as leaves and the scribing perfect. Who could guess how long it had taken priests to perfect that style?

The book itself was uninteresting, filled with diagrams,

symbols, and words that made no sense to me. On the book's spine I read *Basic Computer Programming* without comprehension. The next book was exactly the same, except that the diagrams were beautifully colored.

Faintly disappointed, I moved to another section of the shelves and took out a book. This time some of the words made sense, but these were sprinkled with terms that meant nothing. Interestingly, someone had written copious notes in the margins of the book. Pulling others out at random, I discovered many were notated and underlined as if someone were trying to decipher them. They were a long way from the Oldtime story books and fictions my mother had read.

Changing my method, I took out a couple of modern books, finding them to be filled with incantations and magic spells. Snorting with contempt, I laid these aside. I had grown up to share my parents' scorn for the Black Arts.

Turning around, I remembered seeing a pile of maps on the table near the fire. Fortunately, my memory proved accurate, but the maps were of little use, being Beforetime maps, and badly tattered. The spaces on them were covered in small faded ink notes and I wondered why someone would study with old maps. Everyone knew the shape of the world had been changed forever by the Great White.

One would not bother with such maps unless they wanted to locate an Oldtime place, but that was forbidden.

Wide-eyed, I stared into the fire wondering if I had stumbled on Alexi and Madam Vega's plan.

Could it be that they wanted something from the Beforetime? They had already broken the lore by not burning the Oldtime books, and by concealing the mental state of Stephen Seraphim. They would not then be stopped by fear of the consequences of searching the past.

And yet that was considered by the Council to be the worst sort of Sedition. They would certainly burn if that were known.

So what did they search for that was worth risking such a terrible death?

Thinking of the Council made me think of the stranger in the kitchen and suddenly I remembered where I had seen him before. He had been with Daffyd, the boy I had met at the Sutrium Councilcourt. It was too much to believe that he was here by chance. What was he up to?

I shook my head. It was no time to be pondering. I must find a modern map. Sometimes maps came in books. I took out a few of the modern volumes and flicked one open. An inscription inside read: "To Marisa."

Marisa! Impulsively, I opened the others, only to find many of the inscribed books were Oldtime books. Those with inscriptions had all been given to Marisa Seraphim! Amazed, I understood that all of the books in this room belonged to her; therefore, whatever search had been conducted was hers, at least to begin with. The same handwriting had made all the notes. I turned back to the painting and Marisa's eyes mocked me.

My instincts were telling me I had already been there too long, but I ignored them. With Marisa dead, perhaps Alexi was carrying on her research. But that still didn't tell me what he was after.

I went around one of the shelves to the semicircular room behind it. In a corner was a shiny, square steel box. It was a cupboard with a lock built into the door. Curiously, I worked the tumblers and the door clicked open.

There were only two shelves and these were stuffed full of old papers and letters. Why were such worthless paraphernalia locked away? On top was a partly completed letter.

My darling,
I have bitterly thought this over and I have decided
we cannot meet again. Mine is a strange family,
tainted with madness. I do not want you to be part
of it. I am the Master of Obernewtyn and I belong
here. Forget what has passed between us. My mother
has arranged a marriage. This is best. The lady in
question does not love me. Lud knows I do not love
her. She bonds for gold and I for convenience.

The letter ended suddenly halfway down the page.
Which Master of Obernewtyn had penned it? Not the
first, but perhaps the second. I wondered why the letter
had not been completed.

I found two more letters, unsealed but replaced neatly
in their envelopes. One was a note from Lukas Seraphim
to his wife Marisa, and the other was addressed to Michael Seraphim. I guessed it was the latter who had written the letter to his lover. I had no chance to read either
through, because I heard noises that told me someone
was approaching the room.

I slammed the door on the cabinet, the forgotten letters
falling from my lap. I thrust them in the narrow space
under the cabinet and crept to the opening of the shelf.
No one was there. I moved through the rest of the chamber and listened at the outer door.

I heard muffled voices.

I was trapped!

My heart only began to beat properly again when I
realized the voices came from outside the Doctor's chamber. I could not tell whom they belonged to. After a long
time, they receded and there was silence, but it took me
several minutes to raise enough courage to leave the small
side room. All I could think of was the terrible dead look
in Selmar's eyes. Whatever had been done to her could
happen to me. I was too frightened to stay in the Doctor's

chamber any longer. Trying to regain the sense of calmness I had carried on my arrival, I returned to my own
room, praying none of the others had wakened and noticed my empty bed. I thanked fortune that fate had seen
fit to make my roommates dull-witted creatures who slept
like logs.

I slept, too tired even to think of what I had learned.
Right through the next day I had no chance to see either
Matthew or Dameon. I took the chance to have a short
sleep at midmeal but felt worse than ever when I woke.

At nightmeal, Matthew leaned across the table and
whispered into my ear that the new Misfit had come into
the hall. I shrugged, too tired to care, but I looked where
he had indicated and my exhaustion fell away in my
shock, for I knew that face.

It was Rosamunde! She seemed to sense my gaze and
looked up. She was thinner than I remembered. As I had
expected, she recognized me. What I did not expect was
the look of cold bitterness she gave me.

XX

It *was several days before* I *had the opportunity to speak to her.*

After the first meal, Rosamunde did not come at the same sitting. I saw her from a distance on the farms once or twice, then one midmeal I saw her come out of a barn to collect her lunch. I went over to her, ignoring Matthew's perplexed look for I had not told him that I knew her. I could not waste the chance to talk to her.

"What do you want?" she asked listlessly. I sat down by her, wondering at the change in her. She had always been vivacious, friendly, and gentle.

"You know me," I said in a low voice.

She stared at me blankly and I wondered what on earth was the matter with her.

I leaned closer. "Is it Jes?" I asked bluntly. "Where is he? Is he all right?"

Those were not the sort of questions orphans or Misfits generally asked one another but the dull apathy in her face made me want to shock her.

"I don't want to talk to you," she said dully.

I bit my lip and suppressed an urge to shake her. "He was .my brother. I have a right to know. He would not have let you come here alone. He cared about you," I said. Her face trembled with some feeling. "You must tell me if he's all right."

Again an expression, too quick to be read, came over her features and I began to feel frightened.

"Leave me alone," she whispered. Something in her eyes made me want to shudder.

"You denounced me," I said, desperate to have some response from her. Perhaps I could use her guilt.

Her face paled a little. "You know? Of course. I should have guessed it," she said. I was more confused than ever.

"I don't understand," I said.

"He could do it too. Read my mind. But he promised not to. I was scared he would find out I had denounced you," she said colorlessly.

My mind grappled with what she was saying. "*Jes* could read your mind?" I said at last.

She shook her head slowly as if she was too tired to talk anymore. I was baffled more than frightened now.

"I made you tell them about me," I said to her, trying again to make her react.

She did not seem very surprised or interested. "I don't want to hear about that. I knew you were different. Everyone did. It was better after you went. He wasn't so worried and closed up." Her voice was bitter and I felt anger stir in me. She looked up and saw my expression. I thought she would say no more, then she shrugged, again with that queer exhausted air.

"All right. I might as well tell you, then you'll leave me alone. It doesn't matter now anyway. Though I wonder why you don't just read my mind," she said.

"It was his fault in a way. He should have told me. He knew I cared. It would have made no difference." She looked up at me with sudden pathetic appeal. I saw a ghost of the old Rosamunde.

"We were happy in the beginning. It didn't matter about us being orphans because soon that would all be over. We were going to live far away from any home. Then a boy came." The deadness returned to her features.

"He was different too. Nobody liked him much because he stood out. You could see at once he would never get a Certificate. Jes said he made people feel uncomfortable. Then all of a sudden they were the greatest friends. I couldn't understand it. I didn't like him and I knew Jes hadn't either. But when I asked about it, he just changed the subject. He became secretive and evasive after that. I did not see him so often and there was a barrier between us. An awkwardness. I don't mean he stopped caring about me," she said slowly, "but something had come between us.

"Then one day, he told me. He said, 'I am a Misfit.' I thought he was joking and I laughed. But he wasn't. He wasn't!" This last was almost a sob. "He said he was different and so was that boy. He said there were others too. I asked him how he was different and he said . . . he said he could talk to people inside their minds. He said sometimes he could know what people were thinking. He said that boy had shown him what he was. A group of people like him were meeting secretly. He kept saying you were right about having to use the powers once you knew they were there."

"Then he showed me." Her voice cracked. She was too absorbed in her memories to notice she was attracting curiosity. I was too enthralled to care.

"He said he had not meant for a rift to grow between us," she went on. "He said the others had not wanted me to be told, but that he trusted me with his life. I was terrified he would read my mind and know what I had done to you. I made him promise . . . I was frightened of his friends. Jes started to talk about escaping. He wanted to run away with these new friends and live somewhere where no one would find us. If he had said just the two of us, I might even have gone. But all of us. There would have been a massive search. But he didn't care. He said the Council had guessed about some of them and that the Herders wanted to know more about his sort of Misfit. He said the Council was frightened of them. Some of his friends did not even come from our home. He said the boy could talk to them over great distances."

She fell silent for a while, but I did not prompt her. Now that she had begun, I knew she would say it all.

"Jes told me then that a group of his people from Beldon had been uncovered and betrayed. They had been taken to the Councilcourt and were being interrogated by the Herders. He said he and some others were going to try and help them. He wanted me to come. I thought I was going mad. It was a nightmare. What could a handful of orphans do against the Council and the Herders? It was madness.

"He said I would never understand." She paused with deep sadness in her eyes. "I guess I knew then what I had really known since the whole thing started. Jes had changed. He loved me, but it was as if I came from another race. I would always be found wanting. I said I would not come. I think he was relieved but he said he would come back for me, when it was safe. I knew he wouldn't. In some ways Jes was hard like a stone. He told me he had rejected you because you were different. He regretted that, yet now he did the same to me, because I was different.

"The night he went, he came to say good-bye. I loved him so much. He asked me again to come with him and I almost said yes. But I refused, and he climbed out the window to meet that boy." She paused. "That was when the soldierguards got him."

My heart froze but her voice was calm. She had probably replayed this scene a hundred times.

"I don't really know what happened. One of the others

had talked maybe. The Herder would have made them. They shot Jes with an arrow. He tried to run. They had already killed the other boy. One of the soldierguards went over to Jes. The arrow was sticking out of his side. He told Jes the others were dead. He said the Herders would be pleased to hear they had a live one. I heard him cry out when he heard his friends had been killed. That was when Jes . . . he did something. The man just stopped laughing and fell over. He was dead. Then one of the other soldierguards fell down screaming. One of them shot Jes. He died."

Her voice was like cold death and I wondered numbly if that was the end, but she went on. "I wanted to die too. At first they thought I was like Jes. The Herder asked and asked, but in the end they . . . showed me what they had done to his friends. I told them everything. They wanted to know all about Jes. Everything he could do. They wanted me burned, but in the end they decided to send me here, in case they needed to talk to me again. They told me to say nothing of Jes or the others or else I would die."

She saw the question in my eyes and shook her head. "I didn't tell them about you. Not because I was trying to save you. I just forgot. I would have told them if they asked. But I think they will find out in the end. Jes was right. They were badly frightened by him and the others. That's why they were so violent." Two tears rolled slowly down her cheeks and she did not wipe them away. "They will come for you," she said again.

I stood up without a word and walked stiffly into the barn. I could not bear to talk to anyone, not even Dameon and Matthew.

Oh, Jes, I wept silently in the privacy of my thoughts. I cried for the pity of his end and for the irony of his late discovery and my needless loneliness. I cried for Rosamunde and for Jes's friends. I remembered my premonition on the day we had parted at Kinraide. I had imagined I would never see him again, but foolishly I had imagined the loss to be his, not mine.

And lying in the sweet-scented hay, the tears fell and I did not try to stop them. They flowed steadily, splashing my wrist and running down my throat. Their warm wetness made me feel like I was bleeding to death.

I sensed Sharna nearby, seeking entrance to my thoughts. "Sharna," I wept bitterly, "why is life so full of pain and hurting? There seems no end to it. When are the moments of happiness to come?"

"It would take a truer wisdom than mine to answer that," he answered, nuzzling my arm for comfort and blessedly not asking any questions.

"Then teach me to be wise, for I cannot bear this pain," I thought, and looked into his sad shaggy face. He told me with compassion that wisdom was not something one could teach, but a thing each person must discover for himself. I let him see into my thoughts and oddly, I felt that he really did understand what I felt.

"Death is known to the wildbeast," he spoke. "All who live, not only beasts, live with death riding on their back. But beasts do not regard it as a burden. The funaga think death is evil. It is nature. Evil exists only in life. There is so much good and evil allotted to each life, and there is much that is neither good nor bad. Death is such a thing. As for the rest, you can only weigh up how much good or bad there is and decide yourself what adds up to evil." He licked me roughly, then left me alone with my grief.

My heart was tight with pain and I felt as if I would cry forever.

"What is it?" came Rushton's voice.

I thought of him telling Madam Vega about my friends and my pain became a raging fury.

"Nothing that you should feel compelled to report," I shouted rashly. "I am not planning to kill anyone, or burn down your precious farms. There is no dire plot in hand. Nothing . . . of any importance has happened. I have just heard my brother has been murdered by that filthy Council." My rage died as quickly as it had begun and I lay my head down and wept.

Rushton knelt in the hay beside me and touched my arm as gently as he had ever touched a hurt animal. "I suppose you will not believe it, but I am no informant for Vega. I am sorry about the death of your brother. You must think badly of me to imagine I have no compassion. I have only a half brother and there is nothing between us. I could almost envy your affection, though now it brings you much pain. I have cared for few since the death of my mother. My life has been filled only with anger and cold purpose. . . ."

His voice faded and I looked up. For a long moment he said nothing, only staring into my eyes with his searching green gaze. Then he bent closer until his breath fanned my face, his eyes probing.

"Why do you plague me?" he whispered, as if I were a dream or a wraith.

I shook my head and he sat back abruptly.

"Come now. You must return to work," he said gruffly but not unkindly. "It is not wise to grieve too long; though I am no tattletale, there are many who are."

He was brisk as ever, but strangely his manner no longer offended me. I rose, feeling empty of all emotion. Rushton sent me to a distant field alone to check the foot of a horse he said might be going lame.

That night my slumber was surprisingly peaceful. I was too tired to dream, yet when I woke I had a sharp picture of Rushton's expression as he asked why I plagued him.

His behavior in the barn made it less easy for me to focus my fears and frustrations on him. Strangely, I believed him when he said he was not an informant. Any number of Misfits knew of my friendships; Rushton had only warned me that it was dangerous to make friends too openly.

I still felt he was mixed up in whatever was going on at Obernewtyn. His words had seemed to confirm he was no Misfit and he had said there was some purpose in his life.

But now I saw that dislike had made me attribute him with black motives. Once the hate was gone, I saw that there was little to base it on. Still, I did not trust him as I did Dameon and Matthew, and I determined to be as careful as ever.

Remembering that he was Enoch's friend, I considered asking him about Maruman. I had grown steadily more concerned about the old cat, and I missed him badly, despite my relationship with Cameo and the two boys. I was frightened he would take it into his head to come to Obernewtyn—if he had not already tried, I reflected, remembering the mysterious rumor of a cat searching for a funaga.

If I had dared to farseek, I would have tried to reach across the mountains, though I had never tried communicating over such a distance.

For a moment I seemed to see his tawny gold eyes, staring at the mountains. . . .

XXI

The final weeks of harvest passed swiftly as we worked hard to complete preparations for Obernewtyn's long bitter wintertime. In the Lowlands, the season of rains would have begun. Jes's death faded too quickly; it was as if a memory had died rather than a person, because I had already accepted that I would never see him again. I was nervous that Rosamunde would reveal all to Madam Vega but whatever story the Council had sent, the girl did not arouse any interest.

Rosamunde and I had no more to do with each other. She did not want it and had retreated into a shadowy world of memories and regrets. I told Matthew and Dameon what had happened to Jes, but they, like me, felt the final incident was too unbelievable. What could Jes have done? We thought the horror and fear of the moment had made her misjudge what she was seeing and dismissed the matter.

More important was the way the Council had reacted to the discovery of people like us. There was no doubt in our minds now that we would be interrogated and burned if we were discovered. Their reaction also proved they would go to great lengths to have one of us; and if they did discover my existence, and looked at my records in light of what had happened with Jes, they might guess I had similar powers.

My biggest fear was that I would be forced to tell them about Matthew and Dameon. I had seen the horror on Rosamunde's face when she spoke of what had been done to Jes's friends in the course of an "interrogation." I did not doubt that they would be able to make me talk. I had no illusions about my courage or my ability to bear pain.

Matthew tried to argue that I would never betray them, but in the end, I think he was as worried as Dameon and myself.

"If we organize our escape to coincide with the end of wintertime, just before the pass thaws, they will have no way to contact the soldierguards," Dameon said. "We will only have Ariel and his wolves to contend with. Madam Vega won't be too concerned over our disappearance since they think we are ordinary Misfits, and they will think we are trapped. They might not even bother sending Ariel out at once. Of course when the pass thaws, there is every chance the Council will send someone up looking for you, Elspeth, to find out if you are like Jes. Alexi would hunger for you then, but if we can find a way through the mountains that avoids the main road, or even some place to hide for a time, he and the Council will have a cold trail to follow."

"If they lost Henry Druid with dozens of soldierguards after him, they can lose us," Matthew said eagerly.

They would not listen to my protests that having me with them would endanger them far more than if they went alone. Dameon closed the matter by saying as our appointed leader, he refused to accept my withdrawal. They would take the risk of having me with them, for it would not in any case be an immediate risk.

I thought them foolish, but deep down I was touched by their steadfast loyalty. Yet I promised myself that if by chance the Council did send someone after me before wintertime cut us off from the rest of the Land, I would go at once, and alone.

I had intended to return quite soon to the Doctor's chamber to find the map and arrowcase, but something had happened that seemed to make it impossible. A rumor had spread that someone had broken into Madam Vega's chamber. Nothing was said of the Doctor's chamber but they would know of that break-in if they knew of the other. Where had I slipped up? They must have found the letters I shoved under the steel cabinet.

Selmar moved about Obernewtyn like a gray wraith, unsmiling, silent, and pale. Nobody took much notice of her and, as before, she was permitted to wander freely. The Norselander twins had disappeared, their mysterious escape attempt forgotten. We would never know what really happened.

Preparations had begun for the escape; we were stealing and hiding whatever we managed to find under a hole concealed by a loose board in one of the barns. We had two good knives and some coats and blankets.

According to Louis, things were increasingly unsettled in the Highlands. He told us there were even rumors that the ghosts of the Oldtimers had been stirring restlessly on the Beforetime ruins at the edge of the Blacklands. That made me nervous because our escape plan would take us very near to Blacklands. I would almost rather face the Council than a ghostly Beforetimer.

Cameo still disappeared occasionally at night, but as the incidents were becoming isolated, we hoped Alexi and the Doctor were losing interest in her. A shy relationship had begun to develop between Cameo and Matthew that gave us all delight.

Perhaps the strangest thing of all, though, was the relationship that arose between Rushton and myself. I could not like him exactly, but his gentleness about Jes's death made me wonder why I had ever thought him a sinister figure. I had even found out from Louis that he was a paid overseer who had been given the job by Madam Vega when he came to the mountains after his mother died. But what was the purpose he had spoken of so fiercely?

On his part, Rushton no longer sneered at me whenever the opportunity arose and he even stopped warning me about associating with Dameon and Matthew. I no longer felt any real urge to probe his mind.

Ariel was another matter entirely. There was something frighteningly unstable about him. He had a queer mania that made him hurt people and see them cringe—as though he wanted proof of his superiority. As the days shortened, his temper increased and everyone stayed out of his way as much as they could.

Yet it was a tranquil end to the good weather and my fears that the Council would come soon faded. I even began to hope they might not find out about me.

But the tranquillity was shattered as the wintertime began in earnest. Cameo's nightmares recommenced and once more, she was often absent from her bed at night. I was still unable to get through to her and did not force it, in fear of the machine that had caught me before. Matthew tortured himself with what they were doing. He could not bear even to look at Selmar, now that he had heard what she had once been like.

One night, Cameo woke me with her mental cries, but when I went over to her she was wide-eyed.

"You'll never find where I hid the map," she whispered, her eyes again that strange color. Somehow, Cameo was mixed up in Vega and Alexi's search for the maps. All at once I remembered that Selmar had muttered something about a map that day in the hall. But what map?

"Lukas said it was dangerous, but I found it. You won't

find it. I hid the map," said Cameo. I looked into her eyes and realized whom Cameo's altered eyes reminded me of—Marisa Seraphim. Was Cameo possessed by a ghost? She suddenly fell back into a natural sleep.

The next day I told the others what had happened.

"It could be something she overheard them talking about. If she was being hypnotized at the time she would be very suggestible," said Dameon.

That sounded plausible enough, but I reminded them of her eyes. "You didn't see her face," I insisted. "It didn't even look like her. And her eyes looked yellow!"

"Are ye tryin' to say she's being haunted by the shade of a long-dead mistress of Obernewtyn?" Matthew asked bluntly. I stared at him, knowing that this was exactly what I did think.

"I don't know. It sounds ridiculous. But I've seen her. You'd know why if you saw her when this happens. But whatever it is they're doing, it's got something to do with some map Marisa Seraphim hid."

"A map to what?" Matthew wondered.

I looked at him helplessly.

Cameo's decline accelerated rapidly after that, and she lost weight and color. It was impossible to talk to Matthew about it because he was too emotionally involved. Both Matthew and Dameon thought I was wrong about her being possessed. Dameon was afraid Matthew would do something desperate.

But one day Matthew said, "Every time we talk about Cam, ye shake yer heads an' look worried. But we're nowt doing anything. I say we should get away from Obernewtyn now, before the wintertime sets in proper. If we don't, we'll be stuck here for the whole season. It might be too late for Cam by thaw, an' maybe for all of us."

His words heightened an unease we all seemed to feel but had feared to express. Deep down, I had felt a grow-

ing urgency to get away. The only time I felt safe was
when we were talking about the escape.

∽

I decided to risk another trip to the Doctor's chamber.
It had been some time since the last. If we did decide to
go suddenly, we would need the arrowcase and the map
for the wintertime snows. Matthew had begun to press
seriously for Dameon to bring the escape forward, but
Dameon opposed the notion of an early escape.

"If we go now, wintertime will catch us even before
we get to the mountains. The wolves will be growing
hungry and daring, and Lud knows what other beasts
would be on the prowl. We would be up against the cold,
the snow, hunger, wild animals, not to mention pursuit.
The mountains themselves would be nearly frozen solid
and the snow would keep us from being able to tell where
the ground was tainted."

I was of two minds. On the one hand, I had a growing
fear that it would be too late for us to get away if we
delayed, but what Dameon said made sense. There was
no point in flying from one dangerous situation into another.

Unlike him, though, I could not just wait and see what
happened. I had to do something, and this and my desire
to understand what it was Madam Vega and Alexi were
after prompted me to return to the Doctor's chamber.

Somewhere there, I was convinced, I would find the
answers to all my questions.

XXII

The next day there was a story circulating that someone had tried to break into Obernewtyn. One of Ariel's wolves had been shot and someone had been wounded. No one had any idea, though, who the attackers were. It seemed incredible and insane. Whoever would want to attack a home for Misfits? Surely there was not enough of value to entice robbers over the badlands.

I asked Louis about this that afternoon, but he was unusually reticent. I was sure he knew more than he said, but one always felt that with him. Someone told Matthew the attackers had been the Druid's men. I thought of Daffyd and his uncle's visit. Was it possible that the two events were connected?

That night, I ventured out into the halls. It was freezing cold now and though I was shivering violently, I dared not hurry. I relocked my bedchamber door, having this time taken the precaution of arranging my bed as if I were in it. Cameo was inside, sleeping normally for once, and the other girls slept as soundly, one snoring loudly. Yet again, I was lucky I had such indolent roommates. It would have been far more dangerous if they had been light sleepers, or informers anxious to gain favor from Ariel.

I had gone right into the circular entrance hall before I noticed a strange pungent smell in the air. I had just about reached Madam Vega's outer chamber when I stumbled clumsily, and realized the smoke contained some insidious new kind of sleep potion. My eyes felt leaden and I stumbled again.

Stopping, I dredged up the merest bit of power to hold on to my consciousness. I probed ahead, then entered Madam Vega's room, farseeking to be sure the way was clear before letting myself into the dark hall and finally into the Doctor's chamber.

Fortunately, the smell had lessened in the hall and there was no sign of it in the Doctor's chamber. I was relieved because it took some effort to fight off its effect. Obviously Obernewtyn used it as a security backup when the temporary guardians went back to their homes in wintertime. The fire was burning quite brightly. Someone had been here not long ago, and I hoped they wouldn't return.

This time I ignored the books. There were simply too many of them. Working on the assumption that Alexi would need modern maps with which to compare the Beforetime ones in an attempt to orient them, I was convinced he must have some somewhere. I decided to work methodically from left to right, checking all the tables and drawers.

In the second drawer I found a pile of arrowcases. There were some very old and some quite modern ones. Quite a few were useless and full of the red-metal decay. I chose a very small one with a cracked case, thinking it would not be missed. Heartened, I slipped it into my pocket and began to search anew, not letting myself become as distracted this time.

Finally I went back to the table and took one of the maps. There were dozens of them, and unless I was unlucky, its absence shouldn't be noticed for some time. I folded the map carefully and turned to go.

Impulsively, I crossed to the hinged shelf and went into the small arbor containing the cabinet of old papers. Kneeling, I reached under—and pulled out the two letters I had thrust there in a panic.

I sat back on my heels, confused but relieved that I had not given myself away. But if the report about someone breaking in had not been caused by the letters, then what? There was nothing else. Was it possible that someone else had broken in on the same night? I remembered the voices and wondered now if they had belonged to other intruders.

I chewed at my lip but no answer came. It would be safer to go on assuming I had given myself away. It was just too much to think that someone else had been sneaking around that same night. Looking down at the letters, I decided to read them. I had not been in the chamber long and there was something about the history of Obernewtyn and its masters that nagged at me. I felt certain the answers to the mystery of Obernewtyn were entrenched in the past, particularly in Marisa Seraphim's life.

The letter from Marisa was brief and cold, a perfunctory inquiry after her husband's health, then a request for certain books and a long list of scientific materials. The other letter was only one page, but I gaped as I read it.

> *My friend,*
> *I wish you would reconsider your notion to adopt young Alexi. Marisa finds him sly and I fear I must for once agree with her. She is a strange creature, and too preoccupied with books, but she is still your mother. I think she knows that you never loved Manda and regrets your unhappiness. Now that she is dead, you must make another life. What of the vil-*

lage girl you loved as a youth? Can you not seek her out?

The page ended abruptly but there was no second sheet. Irritated, I thrust the letter back in its sleeve and replaced them both in the cabinet, my mind occupied with the revelation that Alexi was the adopted son of Michael Seraphim. I wondered why the melancholy writer of the letter to his lover had decided to adopt the child at all. A slight scraping sound alerted me and I slid quickly from the arbor, where there was no place to hide, and under a table in the darkest corner of the chamber.

There was another scraping sound, then to my utter amazement, the entire huge fireplace suddenly swung open to reveal steps going down. A moment later, four people came out of the hidden passage. From where I was hidden, I could only see legs and hands, but I could guess whom they belonged to.

They were warmly dressed and snow fell from their cloaks, so the passage obviously led outside. The fireplace swung back into place, and when they spoke, my guess was confirmed.

"I could have sworn I heard something," said Ariel, rubbing his hands together.

"Don't be a fool," came Alexi's deep voice. "How could anyone come through all the candles?"

"Thank Lud we banked up the fire. It gets colder every time we go out," said Madam Vega. The fourth person, a woman, said nothing and I had no idea who she was.

"What are you going to do about Druid?" Ariel asked. I gasped out loud, then bit my tongue so hard it bled, but fortunately no one had heard me.

"He won't be any more trouble. You can put that body out for the wolves. If the Druid's men see it well and good. I don't know what he hopes to achieve. This place is like a fortress," Vega said sharply.

Alexi laughed. "I expect they hope to achieve the same things we hope for. He always was fascinated by the past. Not a good hobby for a Herder," he added.

"We don't know for sure if the old man is even alive. It could be his followers," Vega said.

"That's not what his man said. And I think he was too afraid to lie by the time I had done with him." Ariel laughed unpleasantly. "It's a pity we can't call the Council in to clear them up."

"Impossible," Alexi said coldly. "Soldierguards up here would make our search impossible, and imagine if they found out what we planned. It is hard enough to keep those nosy Herders out."

"Well, tonight was a waste of time," Ariel said. "I told you she would be useless."

"I did not think to achieve anything. I merely wanted to try out that new machine. I don't want to ruin Cameo like this one," he added. I understood that the silent fourth must be poor Selmar.

"I'm sick of these idiots," Ariel said petulantly.

"They keep Stephen happy, and when the time comes to dig, they will be good labor. Marisa once told me she thought the things we seek would be buried and I have no intention of digging them up like a common farmer. It's just fortunate the Zebkrahn machine is as close as it is to Obernewtyn. I loathe walking. Besides it would have been impossible to suddenly stop purchasing Misfits without the Council wondering what was going on. And you must admit, the business of searching the orphan homes makes the perfect cover for our search for the right Misfit."

Madam Vega paused thoughtfully. "You really think it was Cameo who set the machine off that day?"

"It would have taken a high level of power to engage the machine, and then to escape it," said Alexi. "She had been dreaming about machines and crying out, according to that informant. It must have been her. She's been pretending to be defective. Very clever, but after tonight I don't think she'll resist too hard."

"I'll be relieved when we have the map," Vega said.

"Damn Marisa. If it wasn't for her, it wouldn't have taken so long. If only she hadn't hidden it," Alexi said angrily, but Vega laughed.

"Can you really blame her? She guessed what you were up to and she even suspected you of trying to kill her. And it was she who discovered where the Beforetime weapon machines were, not you. She was a brilliant woman. A pity she was content to know where they were and nothing more. It was her sour idea of a joke," she said.

"I only hope she didn't destroy the map," Alexi said.

"She would not have done that," Vega said with certainty.

I could not stop thinking about what I had learned. Alexi was the adopted son of Michael Seraphim, and therefore a legal brother to the present Master of Obernewtyn..How it must gall him to know that by lore, only blood relatives could inherit. Alexi had tried and perhaps succeeded in killing his adoptive grandmother, Marisa Seraphim. I wondered where she had hidden the map showing the location of the Beforetime machines they wanted.

But I still did not understand what Cameo and Selmar had to do with their search. The Zebkrahn must be some sort of machine built or hidden near Obernewtyn, where they were doing something to Selmar and Cameo. And I was sure now that it was what I had grappled with.

The sooner we were away the better.

Selmar had walked away from the others and she began to come toward the alcove where I was concealed. I held my breath.

"I'm so tired I can hardly keep my eyes open," Vega said with a yawn.

"Get her away from the books," snapped Alexi. "She'll ruin them."

Ariel came over and led her away. I was trembling; the perspiration poured down my cheeks. Not from fear, but because at last I knew what they were searching for— Oldtime weapons!

After they left, I waited until nearly morning before daring to return to my chamber. The drugged smoke had dissipated and I needed no help to stay awake. I hid the map and arrowcase under a loose stone near the window in my room and climbed into bed, watching the sky lighten. A whole night had passed but I did not feel tired.

At last, I fell asleep and woke wishing I had not. I felt heavy-eyed and sluggish. I splashed my face with freezing water. Cameo tried to tell me of a dream she had but I forestalled her, saying I had my own nightmares to contend with.

If I had known what was to come, I would have listened.

XXIII

I *ate alone at firstmeal having missed the first sitting, but when* midmeal came on the farms, I hastened to sit with Matthew and Dameon, wanting to tell them what I had discovered. They seemed rather distant. I understood why after Dameon asked whether I had been out the previous night.

"Why?" I demanded, puzzled. A severe look came over Dameon's face and Matthew would not meet my eye.

"You were careless," Dameon said coldly.

"No!" I said indignantly.

I was almost certain I had not given myself away. Surely Alexi would have done something if they knew I was there. Ariel had said he heard something, probably the slamming of the cabinet door, but they had not seemed concerned and had talked quite freely.

"You said nothing about your intentions because you knew I would stop you," Dameon said. Ashamed because that was true, I clasped my hands together. "They have decided to keep the wolves out for longer because of you," he added.

"Outside? But why? I didn't go out," I said in puzzlement. "I went again to the Doctor's chamber. I have a map and an arrowcase hidden in my room."

Startled, Matthew looked at Dameon. "Willie said someone was outside." I quickly told them some of what I had overheard.

"Cameo," Matthew whispered fearfully. He looked around as if to reassure himself of her safety, but she had not come to the farms that day.

"But she knows nowt of any map. She couldn't possibly. Marisa died years before she even came here. And I can't see how Selmar could know anything useful either," Matthew said, after a minute.

Dameon coughed and we both looked at him. "I . . . I think I might be able to guess," he said hesitantly. "I think they are trying to use Cameo's powers to find out what this Marisa did with her map. That's why Cameo keeps having those dreams and acting like she's someone else."

"But she has no power. I don't know how they can have got the idea . . ." I said, then I stopped, aghast.

"It was me! They think she was the one whom the machine caught," I cried in an agonized voice. "That's what she meant! She even said they wanted me."

"I don't know how they intend to use the powers of whomever they find. But obviously, this Zebkrahn machine is part of it," Dameon said.

"We have to get her away," Matthew said.

I told them about meeting Daffyd then and about recognizing his uncle. I said I thought they might be mixed up with the Druid who also appeared to be searching for Oldtime weapons.

"In his case it is more understandable. He would want revenge," Dameon said. But he did not agree that we should try to join the Druid. "He was a Herder and no doubt he still has Herder instincts. If so, we would be no better there than here. I would rather strike out anew, on our own. And besides, this search for Oldtime weap-

ons is wrong. We want no part of such things," he added
firmly.

I felt a sudden shiver down my spine. I had not really
thought about that before now. But what if the Druid or
Alexi or Vega did get hold of some terrible Oldtime
weapon? We talked about our escape some more, but
Dameon stuck fast to his belief that we should wait until
the wintertime was over. It was hard on Cameo, but
hopefully, once they realized she was no use to them,
they would let her alone. "We could not drag her into
the wilds in the condition she is in. She would never
survive." He did agree though that we must have everything prepared so that we could leave if we had to.

That night and the following one, Cameo slept in her
own bed. The cows and other livestock were being sta-
bled for the wintertime and all hands were needed to
transfer the food and some animals to the house environs.
Dameon asked me not to tell Matthew if she was taken
out or if she had another nightmare. He was concerned
that Matthew would do something crazy. I noticed for
the first time that Dameon had grown subtly older, all at
once closer to man than boy. Somehow I felt saddened:
this life had robbed us of some sweetness.

One morning he said, "I am as worried about her as
Matthew, but I know we cannot leave now. Cameo
would die. One blind man, a half-lame boy, and a sick,
defective girl. You are the only one among us who is
completely fit. We must wait," he added with a touch of
desperation. "Matthew expects me to produce some
magic that he thinks comes with being a leader. He thinks
I only have to wave my hands to fix things and save
Cameo. If . . . if anything happens to her, he will blame
me." He hesitated. "Last night I had a true dream. In it,
Cameo died."

I gasped and wished it was not so, but Dameon knew

the difference between a true dream and a nightmare. Even so, I prayed he was wrong.

∽

Two very cold, clear days marked the official start of wintertime and the very next day, the first snow fell. Looking back to the house, from the farms, Obernewtyn was graceful in its mantle of snow. I looked from there to the mountains, my breath making little puffs of mist in the cold air. The mountains were white too and barely visible against the pale sky.

"In case you have any notion of escape," Ariel said, so close that the hair on my neck stood on end, "I should warn you again about the mountains and the wolves. I have seen them tear rabbit and deer apart while literally on the run. No one has ever been mad enough to try to escape in this season."

I looked away from him, and behind us, to where the deep imprints made in the snow by our boots were already filling up with a fresh drift of velvet-white snow. Soon there would be no trace of them. I did not wonder that no one had ever tried it. Perhaps Dameon was right.

But that very afternoon, shouts and the sound of the wolves echoed throughout Obernewtyn, and later we learned someone had tried to escape. We did not have time to wonder who it was, as the afternoon brought a fresh flurry of rain that was not quite rain or snow but something worse—it was as cold as ice but could not be brushed off before it soaked in. I had been sent down to the far field to bring up three goats that had escaped rounding up. They were to be taken up to the main house. I was soaked through and shivering convulsively by the time I got the contrary creatures where they were supposed to be.

Rushton heard my cough, took one look at my fevered

face, and sent me up to the house to see guardian Myrna. By night I was running a high fever and my voice was a painful croak. I felt terribly thirsty and finally fell into a fitful sleep in which red birds swooped at my face and the ground opened up malevolently and tried to swallow me.

The first person I saw when I woke was Rushton. "You are awake at last," he said. "The horses missed you."

I frowned, wondering what he meant. Then I wondered if I could have been asleep longer than I thought.

Before I could ask, Rushton was talking again. "You look a bit better now."

Guardian Myrna came in and Rushton sat up slightly. "I wanted to know exactly what medicines you gave that lame horse. . . ." She went out again and Rushton leaned close. "I told them I wanted to find out what you had fed one of the horses, since you had made it worse, but that isn't true. I came to give you this."

He held forward a small cloth bag. A wonderful summery smell filled the air. I frowned in puzzlement but he pressed it into my hands and urged me to eat it when no one was around. Then he rose. "It will help you regain strength quickly," he said enigmatically before departing.

I drew the strings when he had gone and looked inside—the little bag held a moistened ball of herbs. My mother had made such things. That was herbal lore and now forbidden. In the end I ate the herbs because they smelled delicious and because they reminded me of my mother. I pondered the fact that they had come from Rushton but could come to no conclusion other than that he genuinely wanted to help me.

Soon after I slept again, a deep restful doze that did not end until I was woken for nightmeal. The girl who brought it whispered to me, "Selmar is dead. She tried to run again but Ariel got her. He . . . shot her so she couldn't run, then . . . set his wolves loose." Her face was

ashen as she spoke and I thought mine must look the
same. They had had no more use for Selmar, so Ariel
had decided to use her for sport.

The next day Matthew came and when I asked if it
was true, he bowed his head sadly. "He . . . he keeps
boastin' about it like it was a good joke on her." He
faltered. I thought he did not look in the best of health
himself and said so, but he seemed not to be listening.

"What is the matter?" I asked him.

He looked at me and to my astonishment, his eyes
were full of compassion.

"The Council have found out about ye. They have sent
two Councilmen to bring ye back. They are in Guanette
at a hostel because of th' storm. It seems your friend
Enoch impressed the dangers of the journey on them, an'
they have decided to wait until the weather clears. Enoch
sent his lad with a message to Louis an' Louis told me
to tell ye the Council are after ye. Ye'll have to gan right
away but I dinna know how wi' th' storm. . . ."

"I'll go in the night, but what about the rest of you?
Cameo can't stay here. . . ." I stopped, seeing a thought
dart over his mind before he could hide it.

He saw at once that I had seen it.

"I didn't want you to know," he said despairingly.

"Cameo . . . What has happened?"

"She . . . she's disappeared altogether. You've been
sick for nearly a week and she's been gone almost all that
time. But you must not think of her now. You have to
get away." We heard footsteps and Matthew reached
down and squeezed my hand. "Take care. We love you,"
he said, and was gone.

I lay back with an odd emptiness in my heart. Still I
could feel nothing, not even for poor Cameo who was
surely dead by now. She was very frail and she could not
give them what they wanted—what I was able to. I lay
until it was very late, then rose and dressed. Walking

quietly, I headed for the front entrance hall and the main doors. While no one was yet looking for me, I would go the most direct way. I was standing in a small pool of moonlight, my hands on the door lock when, very quietly, a voice spoke behind me.

"If you make one sound, I will kill you," it said, and to my utter terror, I felt the tip of something sharp press into my neck.

Part III

The Master of Obernewtyn

XXIV

"Nod if you will not cry out," the voice said.

With a queer sense of desolation, I recognized whom that whispered voice belonged to. I moved my mouth to speak but the hand over my mouth tightened. Limply, I nodded.

He unlocked the door in front of us and propelled me into the room. Candles were lit and a fire warmed the air.

I stared with a kind of despair, for this was not the room of any hired servant. Like the rest of Obernewtyn, the room was hewn of gray stone, but unlike the chambers of Misfits, the window in this room was wide and easy to see out, though shutters were pulled across to keep out the night. The floor was covered in a thick, beautiful rug, and the table and chairs and the comfortable couch were enough to make anyone suspicious.

Forgetting my initial fear, I turned angrily to stare at my captor—Rushton.

"I thought you worked for pay," I said accusingly.

He shrugged, seemingly unashamed of himself. "My position here is . . . ambiguous," he said softly. "Keep your voice down," he added.

My confusion increased. If he didn't want us to be

heard, then he must not intend to denounce me. I looked at him warily as he crossed to the front of the fire. He poked at the fire embers with a stick and gradually, I went closer, wondering what he was up to.

He looked up at me, the firelight flickering over his grim face. "You don't seem frightened. Are you?" he asked.

"No," I said simply, because it was true. He gestured for me to sit on the couch. I shook my head coldly and he moved swiftly, so that I was plonked unceremoniously back onto the seat.

"Then you are a fool," he said. I had bitten my tongue and I looked up at him resentfully. "Only a fool would not be afraid in your situation. I could have been one of the guardians. . . ."

My anger melted at his grave tone and he sat down opposite me. "It is time for us to talk. Lud knows, we should have done so before now." He shook his head as if at his own folly.

"Why were you sneaking around in the dark?" he asked with a touch of anger. I bridled at his tone and gave him a secretive look that turned his anger into weary contempt.

Ashamed I looked at the fire. I did not want to tell him, but it was stupid to antagonize him.

"I could march you off to Vega right now," he said, but his tone told me he had no intention of doing that. "You have caused me a great deal of trouble and that might be the best thing. I knew there would be trouble the first time I saw you," Rushton added. "And Louis warned me . . ."

I stared. "What did he tell you?"

He actually smiled at that. "It is rather late in the day to become cautious, Elspeth," he said in an amused voice that made me angry all over again. "Perhaps I should tell you that I know Alexi is searching for a Misfit with particular abilities to help him find something hidden. I believe you have the abilities he seeks."

I gaped, my heart thundering. How could he know so much? If he was to tell Alexi or Vega, I would be lost. "I . . . I don't know what you mean," I faltered.

He ignored me. "I am also aware that the Council has sent some people up here to get you. And I have heard your friends have been unable to help you except to advise you to run, as far and as fast as you can. I also know that the Council is very interested in people like you, and that there are far more of you than anyone knows. The Council interrogates them, then burns them. The same fate awaits you, I am sure, if they get hold of you."

I looked at him dumbly, aware that I was shivering from fear. There was an odd feeling of inevitability about his words. Seeing that I made no effort to deny what he said, he nodded slightly and continued.

"Your only hope of avoiding the Councilmen is to get away tonight, but you must know that if you go out into the wilds now, you will be dead before morning. Maybe you hoped to hide yourself somewhere in the buildings, but put it from you. They will search, and if you are hidden, Ariel will find you. I tell you quite simply that you have no hope unless you will put yourself in my hands and ask no questions."

I looked at him and once more my doubts clamored. "Who are you . . . what are you?" I asked.

He gave me a guarded look. "It is enough for you to know that I am no enemy to you. Or to your suspicious friends, though you have all caused me great difficulty with your endless questions and curiosity. Security around Obernewtyn is worse than ever."

"I just wanted to find out . . . Alexi . . ." I stopped, confused.

"I know all about Alexi," Rushton said rather curtly. "There is little about this place which I do not know. I

care nothing for the ambitions of Vega and Alexi to dig
up the past. It is better dead and buried. Nor do I care
for the fears of the Council over your sort of person. I
have my own plans and before you came along they were
proceeding nicely."

"Plans?" I asked, and unexpectedly he smiled.

"Even now you are curious," he said, his tone half
amused and half exasperated. "I wonder if you really understand how much danger you face. You are a strange
girl. My first impression of you was, I fear, the right one."

"I can't help what life has made of me," I said defensively. Again I wondered how he knew so much about
me.

"Life will not always be like this," he said.

"Sometimes I think life is nothing but fear and strife,"
I said sadly. "I seem to have spent my whole life being
afraid. I was scared of being burned, or denounced, or
of coming here. . . . I don't know if I could even be normal now, even if I could stop being afraid."

"Selmar was like that," Rushton said sadly. "The same
hunger to know everything, whatever the cost—and it
proved dear." He stood abruptly. "Come. There is no
more time for talk."

I stood. "What shall I do then?"

Rushton handed me a cloak from a wall peg and I put
it on. "It is impossible for you to leave the grounds tonight. The weather will get worse, and even an arrowcase
would not help you, for the storms which run from the
Blacklands affect the bearings. You cannot follow the
road because the Councilmen will be coming that way,
and anyway, even if you made it through the mountains
there are badlands which cannot be crossed as slowly as
you would afoot." He spoke calmly and very deliberately,
as if he had all the time in the world. "I cannot let you
stay here because the house will be searched from top to
bottom and I am not exempt," he added.

"Then there is nowhere for me to go," I said despairingly. I had begun to hope he would let me hide in his rooms.

"I will take you down to the farms. They will not be able to search there until the storm ends, and even after for some time, since the maze is snowed in. For that reason they are unlikely even to think of the farms to begin with. As soon as the way is clear, I will return for you, and I will tell you of a place where you will be able to take refuge until the wintertime ends."

"But if the maze is impassable how are *we* going to get to the farms?"

Rushton crossed restlessly to the window and peered through the shutter. "We won't be going *through* the maze. I thought I heard something..." He shook his head and came back to the fire, pulling on his own coat.

"The wolves?" I asked, thinking of poor Selmar.

Rushton only smiled. "They are locked up. I put them in myself, just to make sure." He looked at me searchingly. "You are pale. I hope you are properly recovered. You took the medicine I gave you?"

I nodded. "It was herbal lore, wasn't it?"

"Yes," he said simply. "I know there is no evil in those old ways. The Council are old fools, frightened of everything. Now they have decided you are a danger because they don't understand you."

He shook his head again and glanced out the window. "You must go now."

"Yes, I..." I began, but Rushton waved his hands urgently. We both listened and this time I heard something too—the sound of running footsteps.

"Lud take it! I think they have found you out."

"Maybe they have found my bed empty," I guessed in despair.

Rushton shook his head tersely. "I think it is worse. That must have been the coach I heard some while back.

The Councilmen must have changed their minds about waiting until morning. Perhaps the weather cleared. By now Alexi will know the truth about you. We have to get you out of the house or you will be trapped. They will search the house and in the end they will come here. Vega does not trust me though she will not at once connect me with your escape."

There was a loud knock on the door and we both froze in horror. Rushton tore his coat off and gestured me toward the smaller door in the room.

"All right, all right," he called grumpily. I pulled the little door shut and pressed my ear up against it. "What is it?" he asked, opening the door.

"Still dressed?" Ariel asked him suspiciously.

"I was reading in front of the fire. I fell asleep," Rushton said casually. "What's going on? I heard the wolves."

"One of the Misfits has escaped," Ariel said. "Elspeth Gordie. Skinny girl with dark hair and a proud look. Sly bitch." There was a pause and when Ariel spoke again his voice was full of mistrust. "In fact, you must know her. She has been working on the farms."

My heart thumped wildly.

"I know the girl," Rushton said with a smothered yawn. "Quick with the horses but insolent. But why all the fuss over one Misfit? Lots more where she came from," he said coolly.

"Alexi wants her," Ariel said evasively, his misgivings apparently quelled. "The Council has sent some men here after her. She's wanted for questioning."

"She'll be dead before morning if she's out in it. Storm's nearly on top of us. Anyway, why do the Council want her?" Rushton asked with a natural-seeming curiosity.

"I don't doubt she will die," Ariel said viciously, ignoring his question. "One of the sneaks said she had been planning to escape, but she won't get far. I have let the wolves out."

"A bit drastic don't you think?" Rushton drawled through a yawn. "I suppose you want me to help look for her."

"You are paid to work," Ariel snarled impatiently.

There was a long pause, but Rushton's voice was calm. "I am paid to manage the farms," he said. "But I might as well come. Otherwise I'll be up all night listening to your beasts."

"Good. It's started snowing so you'd better put on boots. I'll come back for you. Don't wander off," he added imperiously. There was the sound of footsteps and the outer door closing, then I heard Rushton's voice.

"It's all right. He's gone."

I came out, staring around fearfully. "He sounded like he thought you might have had something to do with my escape," I said in alarm, but Rushton shook his head.

"He's always like that. I don't think it means anything. Alexi must want you badly to conduct a search while the Councilmen and the soldierguards are here. There is too much here that is forbidden for him to risk having them offer to help. They won't want me to get near the Councilmen either," he added thoughtfully. Howling sounded again in the distance.

"Damn those wolves. How will I ever get you past them? I wanted to take you myself. I might be able to keep them under control, but I can't go now that Ariel wants me. Lud damn it!" Rushton cried with helpless fury.

"I . . . think I might be able to handle the wolves," I offered hesitantly. "You see . . . I can. I mean sometimes I can communicate with animals. Talk to them."

Rushton nodded slowly and there was even a touch of humor in his eyes. "So that is why you were so good with animals. I have not come across that particular ability before. Fascinating. I wish we had more time . . ." He bit his lip impatiently. "But there is no time. You say you can manage the wolves? You know they have been trained to be utterly savage?"

I nodded with more certainty than I felt. I did not know if I could make them listen to me and let me go past unharmed. But I had to try; there was no other choice and the longer I stayed, the more dangerous it was for Rushton.

"Before . . . when you caught me, you said you would kill me," I said in a low voice. "Did you mean it?"

Rushton looked up from lacing his snow boots with the same unreadable expression I had seen on his face that day in the barn.

"It would have been safer for me if I could have," he said at last. "Best for my friends and for yours. If you are caught, you will reveal the way to the farms and my help. No one resists Alexi. And if the Council gets you, the Herders will make you talk. Alive, you are a danger to all I have planned."

"Is your secret so important then?" I asked with a kind of despair.

"More than you could possibly imagine," Rushton answered simply. "I risk many lives beside my own in helping you."

I stared at his troubled face and made myself strong. "Tell me the way through to the farms. I will not betray you. I will manage the wolves." Or die trying, I thought.

"The drains are like a maze themselves, but they were not designed to confuse. Remember to take the right turn always and you will be safe. To get from here to the courtyard, you will have to use the tunnels. I am not so certain about them. My mother told me of them but she had never seen them herself either." He explained about the tunnels then looked up warily as footsteps approached and then passed his door.

"When you get to the farms, keep to the walls. The storm will be much worse by then and if you get lost you will die. Follow the walls to the farthest silo. The door will be open. Hide there until I come."

"But . . . but is that all? For that I am to risk wild beasts and capture?" I asked hysterically.

"You risk no more than I," Rushton said coldly.

"But what if you don't come?" I faltered.

His expression softened. "Understand this. I have already told you too much. If I tell you any more and you are caught, I will endanger others. It is my decision to risk my life for you. I will not decide that for them."

Chastened, I nodded, for what he said was surely the truth. The least I could do was trust him.

"You do not know what an irony it would be if you betrayed me," Rushton added cryptically, pulling on his snow coat.

He stepped up to the door and listened hard. "Down the end of this hall is a tapestry. That covers the first tunnel. The second . . . well, I hope it will be as I recall. If not, use your abilities to find the way, but very carefully." He opened the door.

"Will you be all right?" I asked absurdly.

He did not laugh. "I think so. Ariel may be suspicious but he will not act without some proof. I will try to direct the search away from you." Rushton stepped closer and looked out into the hall before giving me a slight push. "Perhaps someday we will have the chance to talk. There are many things . . ."

He stopped abruptly. We could hear footsteps. "Go quickly," he said urgently, pushing me into the hall.

"Good-bye," I whispered as I slipped away into the darkness.

XXV

I crept silently along the darkened corridor, pulling aside the tapestry and slipping into the dark crevice behind. I felt along the wall for the catch and the wall slid aside with a loud click. Terrified, I froze, but no one cried out or tore aside the curtain. The tunnel behind was festooned with clinging cobwebs and I brushed them aside, trying not to think about their occupants. The tunnel system had not been used in a very long time. Fleetingly, I wondered how Rushton's mother had known of tunnels she had never seen. Again there was the mysterious feeling that Rushton was somehow linked to Obernewtyn.

Dismissing curiosity, I concentrated on walking noiselessly down the passage. The darkness was total and I bumped my nose at the other end. Again I searched for a catch and found it. This time the mechanism that worked the tunnel opening slid aside noiselessly and I found myself behind yet another tapestry. I listened, then crept into the hall praying Rushton's mother had remembered correctly. It was doubly dangerous sneaking along the halls. Anyone might see me.

Almost sobbing with relief, I found the next tapestry and climbed in behind it. I was crouched behind it when I heard a slight sneeze.

Terrified, I waited to be dragged out of my hiding place.

The tapestry trembled.

"Greetings," came a thought.

My body sagged to the floor with relief and astonishment. "Sharna?" I asked incredulously.

"I sensed your need," he told me, squeezing himself into the space beside me. "I dreamed you were in danger, so I came."

"What did you dream?" I asked him fearfully.

"I dreamed your life has a purpose which must be fulfilled, for the sake of all things," he answered.

I frowned into the darkness wondering why the beast-world continually wove me into its mythologies. He told me he could help me through the tunnel system, but when I told him I had to get to the small courtyard, I felt him tremble.

His fear shattered my calmness, but I made myself speak. "I have to pass them. There is no other way. I will die if I don't."

There was a long pause while he ruminated. "I will help," he told me at last. "Innle must be shielded," he added rather dreamily. I frowned, wondering if he was going a bit queer in the head.

We moved like shadows through the darkness, Sharna leading me infallibly from one tunnel to the next, all of which were choked with spiderwebs and thick dust. One tunnel was so low that I had to crawl along it, the cold dusty stone bruising my knees and hands. I bumped into Sharna who had stopped. I thought we were at the end of another section, but he cautioned me to be silent. Someone passed in the hall alongside the tunnel.

"She must be found," said a voice. "It it weren't for the Council . . ." It was Madam Vega.

"The fates are with us," said Alexi. "She is the one I need. It was fortunate that the Council brought her to our attention. We might have let her go and die in the wintertime. She must be found and brought back unharmed. It might be years till another like her is found."

"What of the Council?" Madam Vega asked.

"We will tell them she perished."

Ariel spoke. "She won't get past the wolves."

"I want her found, not torn to pieces. That affair with the other girl was quite unnecessary. You are a barbarian," Alexi added, but as if he found that amusing.

"She will be found alive," Madam Vega promised soothingly.

It terrified me to hear how calm and certain they sounded. It did not enter their heads that I might get away.

"The beasts have been trained to mutilate," said Ariel. "They kill only on command."

"She must not be allowed to die," said Alexi in a flat voice that sent ice into my blood. "A pity we wasted so much time on that defective. I was so certain, but she had only minor abilities after all."

They passed out of my hearing and, despairingly, I knew they meant Cameo. What had they done to her?

"Come," Sharna commanded and we went on.

At last we came to the outer wall. I pressed the latch and slid open the wall. A flurry of snow came in through the opening and I shivered. The chill of wintertime bit into my bare skin. Sharna told me the wolves were at the entrance, having sensed our approach. Their eyes gleamed redly in the dark and I shivered again.

"Greetings, Sudarta," he sent, flattering them with a title that applauded their strength. But it seemed to have no effect on them.

Sharna turned to me, his own eyes gleaming. "These are not ordinary beasts," he told me worriedly. "They were once wild cubs, but were caught by the funaga and made mad. There is a redness and a rage in their heads that stops them from being able to think. Best to come back when they are locked up."

"I can't," I told him despairingly. "The entrance of the drain is just across the small courtyard. Maybe I can think of a way to distract them and then make a run for it."

But Sharna was not listening. He was staring outside, an odd thrumming sound vibrating in his throat. Silently the beasts withdrew.

"Sharna, what . . . ?" I began, but suddenly the old dog launched himself from the tunnel, and with a terrified cry I understood how he meant to distract them.

"Sharna!" I screamed. "Don't!"

"Go!" he commanded. I heard the primitive snarling of the wolves with a primeval shudder. I heard Sharna taunting them, calling them away from my exit.

Trembling so hard I could scarcely walk, I climbed out of the tunnel and stood for a moment, paralyzed with fear as the wolves attacked.

"Go!" shouted Sharna into my thoughts. A madness came over me and I flew across the courtyard and flung myself into the tunnel. It was high off the ground but I did not notice that. And when I was inside, I began to wriggle mindlessly along the round, narrow drain. The noise of battle was muffled as my body filled the tunnel. I fought off the sensation of being buried alive.

"Go!" Sharna cried again, but I felt him weakening and knew he had sacrificed himself to provide the distraction I needed, and I had been too cowardly to stay and help him. Sick with shame and despair, I wanted to die too. Perhaps if I had not been half stuck, I would have thrown myself out of the drain. But I could barely move and a growing panic urged me on to where Rushton had said the tunnel widened slightly.

Tears poured down my face as I crawled and scrabbled, the pain in my knees a distant throb.

After an eternity, the tunnel widened and a blast of snow-laden air told me I had reached the end. I felt no joy. Only the icy cold encouraged me to move. Staggering to my feet, I set off from the wall in the direction of the barns. At least a foot of snow had fallen since I had entered the tunnel, but there was a break in the storm and only a few snowflakes fell. The night was crisp and utterly still, the snow seeming to absorb all sound. The clouds allowed the moon to peep through briefly, lighting a bleak yet strangely beautiful barren scene. The snow had blown in great drifts against the right-angled walls of the old stable and the other two outbuildings that formed three sides of a square. It began to snow again, at first softly, then very thickly. It seemed impossible that this was the farm where I had basked in the sun and smelled the apple blossoms.

The snow obscured my view of the silo and I turned to get my bearings from the wall, only to recall Rushton's strict instructions not to wander in the open. I could see nothing, and in turning, I lost whatever small sense of direction I had. I had once seen a man who had died in the wintertime. They had found him in the thaw, stiff and blue as a statue. Trying to quell the panic I stumbled forward thinking, "I must come to a fence or a wall soon." Trying to forget the endless fields of Obernewtyn.

"Who is there?" called a voice, seeming a long way away. I could see nothing and wondered if I was going mad.

"Is someone there?" the voice called, marginally closer.

"I am here," I called recklessly. Anything was better than being left alone again in the flying white hell. "Here!" I screamed, terrified the person would not hear. I saw a flash of light and broke into a shuffling run. I noticed dimly that I could not feel my feet at all.

"Who is it?" asked the same voice, much closer. Suddenly, a face seemed to appear in front of me out of the swirling whiteness. I knew him. It was an unsmiling youth called Domick whom I had sometimes seen with Rushton.

He seemed to recognize me, and his face grew wary. "Elspeth Gordie?" He held the lantern up to my face. "What are you doing here?"

I stood in the midst of the storm, my mind reeling. What could I say? What possible reason could I have for wandering around on the farms? The silence between us lengthened and I saw doubts fill Domick's face.

At last he said uneasily, "Well, you had better come back with me. We'll talk where it's warmer."

He struck off to the right and I followed him closely, wondering what I could say to him. Very quickly we came to a squat, sturdy building I had not seen before.

"What is this place?" I asked through violently chattering teeth.

Domick bundled me through the door. "This is the watch-hut," he said shortly and hustled me across to the fire. He took a thick blanket and threw it around my shoulders, then piled more wood on the fire and poked at it with a stick.

"Are you numb anywhere?" he asked. Wordlessly, I pointed to my feet. He wrestled off my boots. My feet were white and bloodless. I couldn't feel them at all.

"Frostbite," muttered Domick and began to rub them vigorously. In a short while sensation returned with burning painful clarity. Only when I was writhing with pain did he stop.

"You were lucky. Don't you know anything about frostbite? You could have lost a foot," he scolded.

I shuddered, but what else could I have done?

He poured a mug full of tea and pressed it into my hand, then fixed me with a disconcerting stare.

"Well, what are you doing out here?" he asked.

I sipped at the soup, then looked up at him. "I've run

away," I said, for there was no other answer.

He nodded. "How did you get past the maze?"

I sipped again at the drink, trying to think what to say. If I told the truth, I would be giving away Rushton's part in the matter. On the other hand, perhaps he was one of Rushton's friends, and I could trust him.

"I . . . found a drain," I said at last, lamely.

Suspicion hardened in his face. "I should report you," he said coldly. "But there is the storm. I'll have to lock you in until someone comes from the house," he added.

He promised to bring me something to eat in a while and departed, locking the door carefully behind him.

I decided I would stay here until my feet had recovered, and let Domick feed me until I felt better, then I would get out and hide where Rushton had bid me go. The other room was dark and there was a sacking bed in one corner. Gratefully, I climbed onto it and not even my fear and despair at all that had happened could keep me awake.

I slept.

XXVI

I slept a very long time, but it was a healing sleep. When I awoke, I felt rested and alert. For a while I lay still enjoying a feeling of well-being and warmth. Outside, I could hear the whirling roar of the wind. The storm had worsened, and though it prevented me from leaving, it also meant I was safe for the moment.

I heard a knock and sat up, terrified it was Ariel. Had I slept too long? I wondered if the herbal tea had been laced with sleep potion and felt an aching despair. If it was him, there would be no escape.

"Who is it?" That was Domick. I heard a rumbled answer and for a moment thought it might be Rushton.

"It's me, Roland," said another voice. I did not know the name. I heard Domick unlatch the door.

"Is Louis here?" asked the newcomer. I crawled out of the bed and crossed quietly to the door. I wondered if Roland had been sent to search for me. Yet if so, why did he ask for Louis? I knew the old man stayed down on the farms with his cows throughout wintertime. It was only logical that the two sole wintertime inhabitants of the farms would know each other. But where had Roland come from? Perhaps he was not a Misfit at all. I listened.

"He wasn't where he was supposed to be," the voice

said. "He wasn't there. I waited. Then we heard the wolves. Guess what has happened now?" the newcomer asked.

"Elspeth Gordie has escaped," Domick said. My heart began to thump wildly. There was a surprised silence.

"How could you know that?" he asked.

"She's here," said Domick. "I locked her in there. She says she came through the drains. She says she stumbled on them by accident, but I doubt it."

"I don't know anything about her. Only that she has escaped. But the important thing is that Rushton has gone missing," said Roland.

"Maybe he's with Louis," Domick said.

"He might be. But neither of them turned up to meet the Druid's man. I was the only one there and he was pretty nervous. I think he thought we were up to something," Roland said in a troubled voice.

"What will we do?" Domick asked. He sounded all at once young and uncertain. What had I got myself mixed up in now?

"It might be nothing," said Roland. "Rushton could just be searching for the girl. But he said yesterday that he thought they would not want him around much longer. What bothers me is that he said he would definitely be there tonight."

"I wish Louis was here," Domick said.

"That old nutter," Roland snapped.

"Well, he was the first to help Rushton," Domick said defensively.

There was another silence.

I was trying to decide what to do. It sounded like these two boys and Louis Larkin definitely were allies of Rushton. But where did the Druid fit in? I could only hope Rushton had been delayed in my search. But I remembered uneasily the suspicion in Ariel's voice.

"We'll have to look for him," Roland said.

"Rushton said to do nothing without his word," Domick said. "We should wait for Louis."

"Louis or no Louis, we'll have to act," the other answered. "If Rushton's in trouble, I'm not going to sit back and do nothing."

"We don't even know if he is in trouble," Domick said urgently. "Anyway, what happened to the Druid's man?"

"He went back. What else could we do?" said Roland. "He said the Druid trusted Rushton because he knew him, but he said *he* wasn't so sure. The idiot. Lud knows what he'll tell the Druid. I still can't work out why they want to help us anyway," Roland added thoughtfully. "What's in it for the Druid?"

I wondered too.

"You know, he actually thinks we let Vega find out that last time. A lot of the Druid's people think we set them up, and that's why that man got killed," Roland added.

"Rushton won't like any of this," Domick said.

A log in the fire cracked loudly and I heard the sound of running feet outside. Again I froze, this time hoping it would be Rushton at the door. There was a knock and the other door was flung wide open.

"Louis!" Domick cried in relief.

"Where's Rushton?" Roland asked swiftly.

"They've got him," Louis said in an angry growl.

My heart plummeted. Impulsively I unlocked the door and stepped into the warm main room.

For a moment it was still like a wax display. Louis, warmly clad with snow melting and dripping in a pool at his feet; Domick and the other boy near the fire. We all stared at one another, then Domick made a little warding off movement that unfroze the tableau.

"I locked that," he said faintly.

"You!" Louis said and, to my astonishment, a look of anger filled his face and he stepped threateningly toward me. I had never seen him so animated. "You have some explainin' to do!" he growled. "Why do th' Council seek ye?"

"The Council?" Domick echoed.

Louis flicked him a quick quelling glance. "Aye, th' Council. Two Councilmen arrived tonight. They had a permit to remove Elspeth Gordie. They said th' Herder Faction wanted to question ye' as well."

I felt my face whiten. The Council wanted me, but I dreaded the fanatical Herders more.

But there was Rushton. "I had a brother. He was involved in some Sedition. They want to find out more about him," I said, leaving out a world of detail.

Louis squinted his eyes and looked at me skeptically, but I pretended not to see the look.

"You say they have Rushton? Who?" I asked.

No one answered.

"Look, I tell you I am a friend to him. Rushton helped me get away from the house and through the maze," I said urgently. "When I last saw him, he was waiting for Ariel. They were going to search for me."

"Why would he help you?" Roland asked sharply.

I looked at him helplessly, for I did not know that myself.

"She is not important now," said Domick. "We can deal with her later. I don't know how she undid that lock but I'll tie her up in there and we can talk."

"No!" I shouted. "I might be able to help. He told me to wait for him in the last silo. He helped me and now I want to help him."

"Do you know what Rushton is doing here?" Louis asked very carefully.

I hesitated then shook my head. "He wouldn't tell me. He said it would put other people in danger. His friends—you I suppose," I added soberly. "Before I left I heard Ariel talking to him. He sounded strange—suspicious. He knew I worked in the stables with Rushton. Something must have gone wrong." There was no disguising my distress and Domick regarded me searchingly for a moment.

"Where have they got him?" asked Roland. "I'm not going to stand around here and talk. He needs help. I knew it."

"I dinna know where he is," Louis said in a defeated voice. "But I do know he had some interest in her." He pointed to me. "Maybe she speaks true. How else could she have got through the maze? They don't know about the drain system."

"Somebody must know where he is," Roland said persistently. "Didn't Selmar say once they'd taken her to a place away from Obernewtyn. A cave?"

I gasped, remembering the passage concealed behind the fireplace in the Doctor's chamber. Madam Vega had said it led to the outside. Could that lead out to the cave that Domick meant?

"I think I know where they took him," I said, trying to contain my excitement.

Louis looked at me, his eyes faded with age and watering from the cold but sharp as a knife. "An' where would that be?" he asked noncommittally.

I told him some of what I had heard in the Doctor's chamber, and what I had seen. Only Domick allowed his face to show any expression.

Louis mused. "That might be so. Selmar said something about a track leading from a secret way. If we could find the outward path, we could go straight to this place."

"Rushton said to do nothing," Domick said.

Roland gave him a wilting look, but Louis only shrugged.

"Perhaps you can help us," Louis said, looking at me speculatively.

My heart skipped a beat at the knowledge in his look.

"Stupid idea. One girl against Alexi and Vega, not to mention that rattlesnake Ariel. I say we go there and take him out by force. There are enough of us to do it," Roland said.

But Louis was still staring at me. "You alone can speak to him. Find out what he wants us to do. He will be able to advise us," Louis said.

Domick and Roland looked at him as if he were mad. But I knew what he was getting at. Somehow, he knew the truth about me.

Slowly, I nodded. "What do you want me to do?"

"Go to him. It will take us time to gather some people and bring them through the maze. Speak to Rushton and find out what they are planning to do with him."

Realization dawned on Domick's face. "You . . . you are like Selmar," he said in awe, tapping the center of his forehead.

"I'll help," I said. "But I don't have much courage."

Louis said briskly, "There's strong an' weak in th' world. If yer born without courage, ye mun look in yeself an' find it. There's a hard way ahead of ye. From what Selmar said, this place is some way from here."

"How will I get there?" I asked, trying to be sensible.

"The best I can offer ye is advice," Louis said. "Ye mun get outside the walls an' gan round to where this path starts. But I think I know where th' caves are. If ye'll trust me, ye can go there direct."

He strode to the door without further formality and opened it. Snow whirled into the room. "I fear th' weather will be against us, but there's nowt for it. Come on." He grasped my gloved hand in his so that the wind would not part us. It was terrifically strong. He looked back to where the two boys stood, still open-mouthed.

"You, Roland. Gan back to th' house an' get th' others. It's time to move. Dinna tell them about Rushton for they might not act without him. Just get them back here.

Domick ye best gan an' dig up the weapons. I fear this is it. I'll be back soon." He pulled the door shut behind us and we walked into the night.

It was freezing after the warmth of the cabin and I wriggled my toes to make sure I could feel them. I could see nothing but Louis, who walked as if pulled by a rope, unerring in his sense of direction. We crossed a dark, half-frozen stream.

Eventually we reached the outer wall. We walked a short way along it, then Louis let go of my hand and dropped to the snow. In a moment I saw what he was about and bent to help him pry some foundation stones loose. We crawled through to the other side, and the wall acted as a natural windbreak.

"From what Selmar said and what I know of these mountains, I think this cave place is set in a clump of granite hills some way from here," said Louis. "My father spoke of them. He said they were marvels, filled with tiny creatures that glowed and flew in the night. Selmar said there were such creatures where she was taken. I have never heard of such a thing, save in those two instances. That is where ye will find him, I think. He is not at Obernewtyn, I know that much." He took a small arrowcase from his pocket and pressed it into my hand. "I dinna know how true this is especially with this storm, but when ye can see, head for th' western mountains. They frame th' granite hills. Selmar said th' path was hard to find. If he's there, ye'll know," Louis said certainly.

"How did you know about me?" I asked.

He smiled his old smile. "Watchin' an' listenin'. An' Rushton started to wonder too."

I nodded. "I'll find him if he's there."

"Dinna get caught. Stay outside, some distance away, an' wait for us to get there. Tell him we'll come as fast as we can."

I looked up at the sky. The snow had paused briefly
and now that my eyes were accustomed to the light, I
saw that it was quite light. "It's nearly morning," I
thought, then realized I had spoken out loud.

"Ye mun go," said Louis. "Move swift as ye can an'
remember to watch out. There are dangers other than
from Obernewtyn out there. Tell him we're comin'." He
squeezed my hand then without ceremony, climbed back
through the gap in the fence, and replaced the stones.

I was alone.

All at once, it began to snow again.

XXVII

I *woke to the dense whiteness of a blinding snowstorm. The events* before my fall were tumbled together in a wild kaleidoscopic dream. I had been walking, looking for the granite hills and hoping the arrowcase was accurate. The snow had been falling too thickly to discern more than the occasional black outline of trees or rocks.

Now I was lying in a ditch of some depth, my head aching and a numbness creeping over my limbs. Dizzily I thought there was something dangerous about that, but I couldn't remember what. I coughed and discovered my head hurt. I had walked and walked until I had to rest. I had gone toward a clump of trees seeking shelter.

I sat up abruptly, remembering the low growling that had sent me into a headlong, mindless flight. Wolves, I had been sure. That was when I had fallen.

I peered around, thinking I must have managed to lose the beasts since they had not eaten me. I reached up and felt the huge bump on my forehead. It was a wonder I had not killed myself. It was impossible to know how long I had been unconscious, but I was not really very wet and there was not a great deal of snow on me. I felt numb. Again I shuddered with fear, remembering what Domick had said about frostbite. Brushing the snow off me, I sat under the edge of the ditch overhang, wrestled my shoes off and began to rub my stiff toes vigorously. Before long the feeling returned. I rubbed every part of me that felt even slightly numb then stood up, wincing at the pain in my head. A sense of urgency filled me as I remembered what I had to do. I hoped I was not already too late.

I heard a noise. I looked up and a pair of yellow eyes gleamed at me from the darkness. This time I could not run and a weakness in my legs made me think I was going to pass out. Dimly I remembered the gruesome tales I had heard of the terrible creatures that dwelt in the mountain country.

Then a calm probing question in my thoughts shocked me so much I very nearly did run. To my utter astonishment, I knew the thought pattern.

"Maruman?" I whispered incredulously, then repeated the name in thought.

"It is I," he answered calmly.

I burst out laughing, half in relief and half in hysteria. He blinked at me disapprovingly and that made me laugh all the more. I laughed until I was gulping for air and when the last hiccuping giggle faded into the still night, he moved forward so that I could discern his dark feline shape.

"You fell," he observed, again as if that was impolite.

I felt the laughter rise but fought it down. "How on earth do you come to be here?" I asked.

"You did not come, so I came. It was necessary," Maruman said. The tone of his thought was offended. I had forgotten what a strange, contrary creature he was. If I ignored his mood, I risked him refusing to communicate at all. Again a sense of urgency and impatience came over me.

"I could not come. I was a prisoner at that place. But

now I have escaped and I go to aid a friend who is in trouble," I explained briefly.

He mulled over that for a moment. "This night I came over the black ground in the wheeled creature drawn by the equines. Two rode within the coach. I came because your face was in their thoughts. But as we came near to the place you call Obernewtyn, I could not sense you. So I began to search. I followed your trail but it was not easy."

"You were clever to find me," I said diplomatically. "But there is no time to talk."

"Your friend?" Maruman inquired, with a hint of coldness.

I ignored that. "He helped me, now I must help him," I said.

Maruman's thoughts approved of that, since as a beast he had a very keen sense of loyalty. "Where is Innle friend?" he asked at last.

I explained the directions I had been given but confessed I did not know where exactly I was going.

"There is danger for you in these mountains," Maruman said pensively. "But it is in the mountains that you must fulfill the prophesy. And there is your debt to this friend. I will help," he decided.

I told him cautiously that I thought it would be better if he waited for me, but he refused, telling me a garbled tale about prophesy and his duty. Sighing, I wondered how long it had been since he had faced a bout of madness. Now would be a bad time. I marshaled my arguments, but Maruman fixed me with a penetrating look.

"Innle must seek the darkness and destroy it forever. All else is second. We each do what we must." Sharna had called me "Innle" too. I shivered, though I thought it was all nonsense. All at once the darkness of the night and the mountain fastness seemed steeped in some poisonous force that drew me regardless of my own will.

Once more I had the sensation of being drawn inexorably toward something. Once more I felt that mad urge to forget everything and run as fast as I could from the mountains and all of the dangers and mysteries that lay within them.

But then I thought of Rushton, and his cool green look when he told me he did not mind risking his life for me. There was a debt I must pay.

"Come then," I said. "But we have to move quickly. I have wasted too much time here."

∽

Several hours later I knew that I had sadly underestimated Maruman. I had expected him to slow me, but he was still as fresh as ever, stepping daintily and scarcely leaving a mark in the snow while I floundered along heavily, feeling exhausted and depressed. I had not expected the cave to be so far. There was a tickle in my throat that warned me I had not escaped my sleep in the snow unscathed, but the air had warmed marginally and there was no numbness in my feet or hands.

We reached a wide, flat plain. Now that the snow had stopped I could see, and though there was no moon, the snow itself seemed to give out a ghostly luminous light. The land around us was barren but strangely fascinating, as if it were a dreamscape—alien yet beautiful.

Maruman revealed an unexpected instinct for avoiding trouble and many times prevented me from stumbling into a hole filled with snow. Once he stopped me from walking onto wafer-thin ice covering a frozen pool of water and camouflaged by a deceptive layer of snow. It was a strange, treacherous journey, and I admitted to myself that without Maruman, there was every likelihood I would not have made it.

Another time he stopped just ahead of me, his fur

fluffed in a manner that I now recognized as his uncanny instinct for danger.

"What is it?" I asked of his thoughts.

He told me there was no immediate problem but that we had just entered wolf territory and that we should pass through it as quickly as we could. We went on very quietly and he would not even let me slow down when we reached the border of that area, saying it was unsafe even on the perimeters of such land. Wolves were beasts, not funaga with lines on bits of paper signifying borders, he told me.

I thought how patronizing I must have sounded, trying to talk him into staying behind. Looking up absently, I noticed several big humped shapes along the horizon, and farther back, framing those humps, the faint jagged line of the western mountains. We were almost there.

"That is where we will find my friend," I told Maruman.

His eyes roved warily along the horizon, taking in the dark hillocks. "There is danger here," he observed.

There was no answer to that. I knew trouble lay ahead. We went on, but warily, watching for any movement that might indicate we had been seen.

It took less than an hour to reach the granite outcrops, but though we searched diligently and with increasing frustration, we could find no path or cave opening.

"The snow must have hidden it," I said despairingly.

Maruman gave that low eerie growl that had so terrified me before. I looked down, wondering what had prompted it. His eyes were glowing and his spine twitched convulsively. At first I thought he had heard or seen something, but when I questioned him he did not respond. I knelt and looked into his face with consternation.

"Forever and forever is pain. . . ." Maruman said, his

eyes whirling. Helplessly, I touched his paw. The cat was heading for another period of madness.

"Please, not now," I begged, but hopelessly, knowing the time or length of his fits was impossible to direct. He turned his raggedy head to look at the hills, then back to me.

"Here is danger but it cannot be avoided. It is necessary so that you can come to know your task," he said. "Here is darkness, but it is not the darkness you must destroy."

I stared at him wishing this had not happened now. It was growing colder.

"The flies!" Maruman shrieked suddenly into my mind. I reeled back with intensity. He trembled violently from head to toe, then fell sideways like a stone. Poor, tormented beast. I picked him up. He was surprisingly heavy. I carried him to a very small cave we had passed some minutes before. Taking off my outer coat, I wrapped it around him and lay him inside the hole. At least he would be warm until he woke. I was torn between worry for him, because his fit was so much more devastating than any I had witnessed before, and fear that I would be too late to help Rushton.

I stood irresolutely, knowing I must reach out with my thoughts. Farseeking. But this would open me to another attack from the strange machine I had defeated only with the help of my unknown rescuer. Would it be better to wait simply until the others arrived, and keep looking for the cave entrance, or should I call? I felt the light touch of snowflakes on my face and looked down at Maruman.

He was safe enough for the moment. I would try once more to find the path and the cave opening, then I would farseek Rushton.

I walked away from Maruman quickly, and when I looked back only moments later, the gently falling snow hid the cave from me.

Five minutes later, I found the entrance.

XXVIII

It *lay hidden from sight behind a rockfall.* Now I could see *where* other feet had scaled that height. Or perhaps the fall was deliberate to keep the place from prying eyes. The entrance was wide and artificially smoothed, as if someone had filed the rock down. Some distance in, I saw the faint light of a lantern, suspended from a jagged bit of rock. Farther in I could see that the tunnel leading into the hill was strangely glassy, and perhaps was not even rock.

Carefully, I reached out a seeking probe. Not enough force to make it dangerous, but enough to tell me if someone approached from the other direction. My heart thumped madly as I crept along the wall. Wonderingly I noticed the tiny glowing insects that Louis had mentioned. I passed the lamp and saw another in the tunnel some way ahead, but there was only darkness beyond that. The farther I went into the tunnel, the more musty it smelled. It began to slope down slightly and was very smooth where the wall changed from stone to a dull gray surface.

Near the second lantern the surface was broken and the stone wall of the tunnel protruded. A thick pool of multicolored ooze lay below the gap and slowly, drips of the substance slid from the fissure down the wall. I kept well away from the slimy mess, certain it would be tainted. Quite possibly the caves lay beneath the Blacklands.

Somewhere ahead I heard the sound of running water. The tunnel curved around and opened abruptly to a huge warm cavern of monstrous proportions. The cavern was lit not by lanterns but from a round white sphere on top of a stand. The shining ball hummed faintly and the light it gave out was extremely bright, like summer sunlight, but less cheerful.

There was no one in the cavern, but there were three other entrances besides the one I had left. They might lead out or they might lead to other caves. The cavern was walled in the same gray metallic substance as the tunnel. Each of the tunnels leading in was ragged and broken as if the entrances were late additions to this ancient place. There was no doubt in my mind this was built by the Beforetimers. The light source stood in the center of the room and all around the walls were square silvery boxes of varying sizes, but all higher than my head. Buttons and gleaming jewel-colored lights covered the surfaces of what must surely be machines. There was a faint patina of dust along the surfaces of all but one machine, which had been forced away from the wall and tampered with. It was a very large machine, with a flat extension and lots of thin, colored strands. I guessed this might be the machine with which I had grappled. I could not tell if it was operating or not.

I felt a whisper of movement in the outer edge of my thoughts and reached out, but it eluded me. That brief touch of thought was familiar, though it could not belong to Alexi, Ariel, or Madam Vega. Nor could it belong to Rushton, since I had never touched any of their minds. Praying that I had been mistaken, and that Madam Vega and the others were all back at Obernewtyn searching for me and dealing with the ire of the Councilmen, I went to the nearest tunnel.

If Rushton were here, one of the passages would lead to him. I did not dare farseek him. I would have to find him physically. Once I could see him, I would be able to make mental contact without using enough power to engage this machine, if it was operating. I hoped Rushton would not turn out to be one of those people with a natural mental block that would prevent contact.

There was no source of light in the tunnel I entered, and the wall felt faintly damp to the touch. As I proceeded, it widened, becoming, I assumed, another chamber. The darkness seemed dense and the lantern I held made little impression. Nervously, I stared about, trying to tell if there was anything in the room.

All at once the light reflected back from two small round eyes. Paralyzed with fear, I dropped the light. But when moments passed and nothing happened, I realized there had been something unnatural about the eyes. Still trembling, I retrieved the lantern and held it up. Again the eyes flared unblinkingly. I stepped closer, seeing now that there was no life in them.

To my disgust, the eyes belonged to a stuffed Guanette bird. Revulsion filled me at the sight and I was struck anew by the way the bird continued to crop up in my life. Even in death, the bright, round eyes of the bird seemed penetrating and full of wisdom.

"Who could do this?" I whispered to myself, then froze as I heard a sound a bare distance away.

Trembling, I turned and held the light up, but no one had entered behind me. Puzzled, I looked around. I saw a movement in the farthest corner of the cavern. Someone lay on a bed.

"Rushton?" I whispered.

But it was not Rushton. To my astonishment, I saw that it was Cameo! The light fell on her face as I approached, making her skin look marble white.

Her eyelids flickered. "Elf?" she murmured, but vaguely, as if she were dreaming. Her eyelashes fluttered open like tired butterflies. She was gaunt-faced and painfully thin, great dark bruises under her eyes. Hesitantly I reached out and touched her face. She frowned. "Elf?"

"I'm here," I whispered.

Consternation crossed her features, bringing them to life. "You mustn't be here. He . . . he wants you. I heard him say it. You must go now."

"Don't talk," I begged. Her voice was barely audible and even that much speech had taken its toll. She fell back, exhausted. She closed her eyes, obviously gathering her strength. Then she looked at me again.

"I knew you would come," she whispered. *But too late,* I thought to myself.

"No!" she protested and I gasped. She had read my inner thought. "I don't know why, but somehow whatever they did made me . . . able to do this. It made me . . . smarter. But I couldn't do what they wanted. I'm not strong enough. While they used their machines, I had a true dream, only I did not sleep. I dreamed there is something you have to do. You alone. I dreamed it was more important than anything else in the world. It has something to do with this place and with the map that Alexi seeks. The map . . . shows the way to a terrible evil. . . . It shows the way to the machines that made the Great White."

"No!" I gasped.

"They don't know that. I saw it in the dream and I did not tell. They think only that it is a weapon." Her eyes fluttered and I saw the effort it took for her to go on. "You have to stop them from finding it. You have to destroy it." She faltered, sighing softly. The veins in her neck stood out like cords.

"Stop," I begged, my mind whirling. So Maruman had

been right—men were responsible for the Great White.

"You are the Seeker," she croaked. I could feel her life force flickering. "So long as it exists, fate will draw you to it."

"Please," I cried, not understanding, and discovered that tears were running down my face. She was dying.

"You came," she whispered, as if she understood my horror and despair, and perhaps she did in this brief awakening of her mind. I buried my face in her side and she stroked my hair with hands no heavier than a breath of air. Then her hand was still.

I cried until I could weep no more. Only then did I hear someone. I recognized Ariel's cruel laughter and a rage such as I had never known filled me. I stood then, vowing that he and the others would pay for what they had done to Cameo and to Selmar. I could not bear to think about what Cameo had said. That was too much.

Listening, I became aware they were in the cave next to the one I was in. Blowing out the lantern, I crept along the wall, making sure no one was in the main cavern, and crossed to the other tunnel. Like the one leading to the other cavern, this was rough, but a lantern hung to light the way. I could hear nothing from the main cavern and reasoned that the wall between the two caves was thin.

I went along the tunnel, careful but determined, certain this was where I would find Rushton. In helping him I would find a way to exact revenge.

Vega suddenly spoke, so near that I held my breath. She walked right past the cavern opening. The light was dim, obviously candlelight.

"You are with the Druid, aren't you?" she said. "I suspect you know something about most things here. What the Druid's man told us reveals that much. Did you really imagine we would let you come in and establish yourself? You should have gone straight to the Council and told them your story."

"I didn't know then," said a voice I recognized as Rushton's. "My mother sent me here; she thought Michael Seraphim was alive and would recognize me as his son."

"Too bad." Madam Vega laughed.

I listened with a sense of amazement. That explained so much. All along I had possessed the clues to the truth about Rushton. But there had been no obvious reason to link them. Even the unposted letter Michael Seraphim had written to his lover was a piece of the puzzle. Rushton had even told me he had a half brother.

"I will enjoy killing you," Madam Vega said softly. "As long as you were ignorant of your true status, it suited me to let you live. But first, there are a few questions I want answered."

"Bitch! I will tell you nothing," Rushton grated savagely, and there was the sound of a sharp blow.

"Have some respect," Ariel said silkily.

Creeping forward, I could see what looked to be the tip of Rushton's boot. I reached out my thoughts carefully.

"How obliging of you to come to us," said Alexi, behind me.

Something heavy crashed into my head and a wave of blackness filled my mind.

❦

Alexi and Madam Vega were talking when we woke. Through my eyelids I saw a bright light and knew I was in the main cavern.

"Why did you have to hit her so hard?" she complained. "You could have killed her!"

"She will not die," Alexi said grandly.

"What about him then?" Ariel said. "He fainted and you said he wouldn't. We'll have to wait till he wakes to finish questioning him."

"I'm not interested in him," Alexi said coldly.

"I bet he helped her," Ariel persisted. "Why else would she have come here?"

"Perhaps they are allied," Alexi said, after a thoughtful pause. "She might respond if we threaten him."

"He'll talk if we use her as a lever," Ariel said. "You should have seen his face when we came to that mess the wolves had made in the courtyard. He thought it was her. So did I at first. He seemed to go mad. That's why I had to shoot him."

"I'm not interested in any of that," Alexi snapped. "I want that map."

"We will have it soon," Madam Vega said soothingly. "And what power it will give us over the Council. They will grovel in terror. And if they do not, we will give them a demonstration."

Horrified, I realized she meant to use whatever the map led her to. If Cameo's dream was true, what they sought were the very machines that caused the Great White. Did she and Alexi know that?

I felt a caressing touch on my face and my eyes flew open.

"Awake . . ." purred Alexi, his face close to mine, his dark yellow eyes curiously like Maruman's. I shuddered away from his hands, but he laughed wildly until Madam Vega took his hand.

"Calm yourself. We don't want to make any mistakes this time. We don't want another Selmar."

"She will be able to do it," Alexi said, ignoring her. "If she can unlock doors, she will unlock the thoughts behind Marisa's diaries." His nose wrinkled delicately. "She is sweating. That might affect the machine. Clean her," he ordered imperiously, looking over his shoulder, before he strode away.

"Am I a servant?" Ariel hissed. Obviously Alexi was out of his hearing.

"Be silent," Vega snapped.

Sullenly, Ariel wiped my face with a cool cloth. "Crazy as a loon he is. Lud but he's creepy with those monster eyes," he muttered under his breath.

"You forget yourself, Ariel," Madame Vega said. "You have proved useful since your arrival at Obernewtyn as a Misfit. But do not forget your place and presume you are more than that now, for all my generosity and your privileges. Without him, all of my plans will come to nothing. Only he understands these infernal machines. Now come with me."

They went out and I heard their voices receding in the distance and surmised they had entered one of the tunnels. Bitterly I reproached myself for failing to obey Louis's instructions to remain outside until help arrived. I had practically given myself as a gift to them.

And they meant to use me.

If Marisa had written her notes thinking about where she hid the map, then I would know too, where she concealed it. I only had to think of Selmar and Cameo's fate to know that I could be made to tell where it was, and I would be directly responsible for unleashing the horrors of the Great White on the world again. Bleakly I hoped I would have the courage to hold out until the end, but I had no illusions about myself.

Remembering why I had come, I considered trying to contact Rushton now while we were alone. I was lying flat on a table, and when I turned my head, I found that I was strapped to the extended table on the machine I had seen earlier. Beyond that, I could see from the corner of my eye a hand tied to a chair—Rushton's.

"Rushton?" I whispered.

"Elspeth?" he croaked in disbelief. "I thought you were dead."

"It was Sharna the wolves killed," I said sadly. "You . . . you gave yourself away because of me," I added, not knowing what to make of that.

"I thought you were dead," Rushton said again, as if that explained everything.

I did not pursue it. Instead, I answered the question I knew must be forming. "I got away, then I heard . . . I heard you had been caught." I stopped, thinking it was not safe to say everything. Not when we might be overhead.

Alexi and Vega returned then and we fell silent.

"I have the diaries here," Alexi announced, holding up a small pile of letters and a brown notebook. "In themselves, they are less than useless. I want you to use your . . . ability to see what she was thinking when they were written. I know that is possible because Selmar could do it. But we hadn't the right papers then. This is her scientific diary and certainly she will have thought of the map while writing these notes. If you cooperate, I will not need to use the Zebkrahn. If you tell me where the map is, you will be allowed to go back to Obernewtyn."

"You will kill me whatever happens," I said defiantly.

"You will tell me," he screamed in rage. He turned to the machine and Vega hovered behind him with anxious eyes.

"Be careful, Alexi," she said.

"She will talk. I will not have her defy me," he snarled. He did something to the buttons and several colored lights began to pulsate. The machine hummed very faintly. He took a bowl-shaped helmet and placed it on my head, his strange, black eyes burning down at me.

Looking at the machine crouched over me, I wondered if it were possible for a machine to be evil. What kind of people had the Beforetimers been to invent such machines?

All at once I felt a faint buzzing in my head. It was only slightly distracting. If this was the extent of their torture, the secret of the map would be safe with me. I wondered if Marisa had known the truth of the map she had hidden. I thought of that cold enigmatic face, and I knew she had.

"Even if you find what you want, the Council will not let you rule them," Rushton said, obviously trying to distract them.

"I will be the next Master of Obernewtyn," Alexi said, grandiosely. "It is my destiny."

"Can't you see he's just trying to get you mad?" Ariel sneered.

"I will kill you too if you say anything else that annoys me," Alexi hissed, turning his hot, mad gaze on Ariel, who visibly quailed. But the damage was done.

"She will talk, and so will you," Alexi said, more calmly. He went back to the machine, turned a knob, and the buzzing increased. It was still a long way from being painful, but again I thought uneasily of Cameo and Selmar. Especially Selmar. Could this machine do to me what it had to her? Alexi brought the diary and letters and placed the book under one of my hands and the letters under the other. I sensed Marisa's thoughts but I did not try to understand them. I clamped a block over my perceptions.

Alexi leaned close, his eyes glistening. "I have dreamed of the power that will come to me," he said. "I have dreamed of the great and beautiful darkness that will rise to my bidding."

It was odd that he used the word "darkness" to describe the terrible power of the Great White. Somehow Maruman and Cameo and Sharna had shared something that was beyond a true dream, for they had seen that the weaponmachine that caused the Great White slumbered only, and that I must be the one to find and destroy it. That was almost laughable. There was no help for me now—even if the others arrived in time.

Alexi moved a lever on the machine and the buzzing became more forceful. Still painless, it set my teeth on edge.

"Release your power, tell me where the map is," Alexi said. I might be able to endure a great deal, but I did not think he would stop. He had destroyed Selmar's mind and he would destroy mine if I did not obey.

His madness could not allow me victory. I wondered if I could reach out to Rushton. Again I craned my neck and sought an entrance to his mind. I encountered a block, similar to Jes's, but was undeterred. If I could find a weakness, I would force my way in. It would be painful, but at least he would know there was hope for him. I found a weakness, forced myself against it, and tore my way in. Distantly I heard him moan.

"What is the matter with him?" Vega asked.

"He's fainted again," Ariel said contemptuously.

But he was wrong. Rushton had retreated into his thoughts to deal with my intrusion. Quickly I identified myself.

"You." I heard Rushton's thought, and with astonishment, recognized the mind of my rescuer.

"How?" I demanded, for I could find no farseeking ability in his mind.

"But there are many among my friends here who have mental abilities, though none like you. We worked together," he answered, and I remembered the echoing effect in the mind probe of my rescuer.

Knowing I would have to be quick, I told Rushton his friends were on their way with help.

"Who?" he asked urgently.

I told him everything that had happened since we

parted last. It took but a moment because I used mental pictures rather than words. I also read in his mind that he was unaware of the truth about the map and what it led to. I decided not to enlighten him. Such a secret was safer with one. He asked if I could do what Alexi wanted. Before I could answer, the effect of the Zebkrahn increased dramatically. I tried to withdraw from Rushton's mind but he held me.

"Let me go!" I begged. It would have been easy to tear free, but he would be hurt.

"No. I can help. Draw on me," he insisted. "I can help you endure." I warned him that he would feel whatever I did so long as we were linked but he still insisted. Gratefully, I allowed myself to draw on his strength.

"The weapons shown in the map are terrible ones. They must not have them," I said.

"This is taking too long," I heard Ariel say impatiently. The power of the intruder increased sharply and the vibration was like twenty men with hammers. Even with Rushton's help I would not be able to resist forever. I prayed his friends would hurry. On the other side of my shield I could sense Marisa's thoughts clamoring.

"Don't be afraid," Rushton told me. I heard him moan and realized with horror that he had been keeping the pain from me. He had only a weak ability, and he was suffering far more than I.

"What is wrong with him?" Vega snapped. Alexi sprang forward and looked into my face.

"He's helping her!" he screamed.

"No!" I cried.

His eyes drew together in triumph. "Tell me where the map is or I will kill him," he whispered. I dragged my mind away from Rushton and took the full brunt of the machine. "Vega, get a knife," Alexi instructed. He looked back at me. "Tell me or he will die."

"Elspeth!" Rushton shouted.

In that moment, despair weakened me so badly that the block that separated me from Marisa's thoughts was as thin as a web. I saw right through it and knew where the map was. The doors! It was carved into the pattern on the front doors. And I saw more, a vision of a dark chasm in the ground from which rose a thick brownish smoke. I knew I was seeing the very place indicated on Marisa's map!

Terrified at what else I would see, I found the strength to block the vision and push Marisa from me.

"Very well, kill him," Alexi snarled.

I threw back my head and saw Vega's hand raised with the knife. "No!" I begged.

"Tell me," Alexi whispered.

"We come," said an unknown voice in my mind. Startled, I opened my eyes wide. I recognized the disjointed tone and realized it was Rushton's friends, and they were not far away.

"Tell me!" Alexi snarled. "Tell me or I will kill him."

I hesitated. I could not tell him where the map was. That was too high a price for either my life or Rushton's.

Yet I could not bear the thought of doing nothing while they killed him. I had to delay them long enough for his friends to arrive, but how?

Alexi's eyes narrowed. "All right. Kill him."

Madam Vega lifted her arm slowly.

I heard running footsteps and at the same time the machine seemed to be overheating. Sparks started from it. One of the sparks fell on my boot and began to smolder.

Vega's hand lifted slightly, to give her downward blow strength. Something inside my head crackled violently, a power stirred in me completely unlike any other ability I possessed and all at once I knew that Rosamunde had spoken the truth. Jes had killed that soldierguard, *and I knew how.*

The wild surge of power rose from the deepest void of my mind and I felt a sense of exaltation at the knowledge that I could control it. It was part of me! I directed every bit of that uncanny power into Madam Vega, and I felt my battering mind plow a terrible furrow into her. She screamed horribly just as I felt flames lick at the soles of my feet.

"Rushton . . ." I called him dreamily with my thoughts. I felt the heat of the flames but could feel no pain. I seemed to be floating away from everything. Dimly I saw people running and shouting.

"Is she alive?" asked a voice I knew but could not recognize.

Am I? I wondered and a dark wind swept me away.

XXIX

"*Ye nowt well enough!*" Matthew said stubbornly. The look on his face told me what I already knew. I looked haggard even after all this time.

"It might be better . . ." Dameon said diplomatically, but I would not let him finish.

"Stay herĕ and miss this mysterious meeting, not on your life," I said. I sat back after that outburst, feeling the now familiar weakness roll over me. It was still incredible to think the machine had taken so much from me. That and the strange power I had tapped in myself. I had been unconscious for days after.

"You look different," Matthew said, and for a moment I thought he had read my deepthought. I did feel different, stronger somehow, despite my physical weakness. Even now I could feel the tingle in the depth of my mind that told me the power was there, waiting to do . . . whatever it was to do.

"So would you be different if some machine was inside your head," I snapped.

Matthew grinned.

"Where is Rushton today?" I asked casually.

He looked quickly at Dameon, but the blind boy's face remained as inscrutable as ever. I had not seen Rushton since the cavern. Louis and his friends had freed him. Both Alexi and Vega were dead. Ariel had rushed out into the night and it was believed he had perished in the blizzard.

It was known now by all those who dwelt at Obernewtyn that Rushton was its legal master, and that the mysterious Doctor was his defective half brother. None doubted his claim and he openly spoke of taking it to the Councilcourt, where it would be formally recognized.

I was amazed at how many different varieties of mental prowess lay among Rushton's friends. There were even two with abilities identical to Dameon's. Rushton did not believe that people with new abilities were demon-tainted or deformed. If anything, he was fascinated by the powers, and slightly envious that he had so little above the ordinary.

He planned to have Obernewtyn in order before the thaw, when he would make his legal claim. I did not doubt he would achieve it. This meeting was to explain his plans. From what I understood, only those trusted by him would be present. That meant almost all Misfits. Quite a number of others, such as the cook, Andra, would not attend. I wondered whether Andra would transfer her matchmaking thoughts to Rushton and smiled at the thought.

The meeting was the cause of our dispute. I wanted to go, but Matthew and Dameon felt I was not fit enough. Rushton had apparently left word that I was not to get up until I was completely better. The numbness and pain in my mind had gone, but there was still a crushing weakness in my strength and the burns on my feet were yet to heal fully.

"He's the master here now," Matthew said, as if answering my thought. "He's everywhere. But he'll be back for the meeting. He has plans for Obernewtyn, and for people like us."

I frowned.

"He has been busy making sure things run smoothly. Wintertime is no time to be idle," Dameon said. "He came to see you several times, but you were always asleep and he would not let us waken you."

"No doubt he was busy," I said coldly, wondering why I felt annoyed that he had not spoken to me, given he did not know I had stopped Vega from killing him. In truth, I was not sure I wanted anyone to know that. I admitted to myself that my desire to attend the meeting arose from a wish to see Rushton again. I felt oddly shy at the thought. I had been inside his mind, but I hardly knew him really.

"We're going to stay," Matthew said. "Nearly all the Misfits want to stay. He's going to make Obernewtyn a secret refuge for people like us. He has plans."

"So you said." I smiled. Dameon seemed to be staring at me with an odd expression on his face. I was tempted to read him but the bruises in my mind dissuaded me. Besides, I had decided it was immoral to barge into the minds of people with mental abilities like mine. It occurred to me there would be some adjustment before a community of so many people with unusual powers could harmonize.

"What about the Druid?" I asked suddenly. Rushton had met the Druid several years before, when he had first traveled to Obernewtyn. Then, he had known nothing of his parentage and had made the trip at the request of his dead mother. He had stumbled accidentally on the secret encampment of the rebel Herder, but instead of being killed or made prisoner, the Druid had befriended him and allowed him to go free.

I thought there was bound to be much more to that story than was known.

Rushton had arrived at Obernewtyn and been hired to work. He had stayed because he was curious about why his mother had wanted him to come. She had told him nothing, expecting his father, whom he resembled closely, to recognize his son. She had never considered that Michael Seraphim would die before her. The wonder of it was that recognizing him at the outset, Madam Vega had not killed him.

Reading between the lines, I guessed Louis Larkin had given Rushton the first real hint about his origin. After discovering the truth, Rushton thought to go to the Council with his claim, but friendship and allegiance with the Misfits he had come to know, and his growing knowledge of their special nature, made him think again.

Instead, he had returned to the Druid with the offer of aid from the Master of Obernewtyn in exchange for the Druid's help in establishing himself at Obernewtyn. I knew the old Herder sought the same things as Madam Vega and Alexi. He had accepted, no doubt seeing the joint benefits of help from Obernewtyn, and free run of the mountain country.

Matthew shrugged. "They haven't contacted Rushton since he failed to meet them the night you escaped. He says he'll deal with that when the time comes."

I thought of the front doors and remembered there was something I, too, had to deal with, but not now. Matthew said the Druid would probably send someone after the pass thawed, and by then Rushton's hold would be secure. Secretly I vowed to myself to make sure no one ever knew the truth of Marisa's map or what it led to. There were too many people greedy for power, no matter what the cost.

"What about the Doctor?" I asked, because everyone still called him that.

"I don't think Rushton is quite sure what to do with him," Dameon said in an amused voice. "He really is rather harmless."

Looking at my two friends, I thought this business had

wrought a change in them, too. Dameon was quieter and rather sad, while Matthew bore the scar of Cameo's death. Yet they were more certain of themselves, more purposeful. Perhaps it was because Rushton had offered them a place in his world and his scheme of things.

I found myself yawning and knew I did not really want to go to the meeting. I grinned at their relief when I said so and wondered what I would do once I was recovered. I did not think I would stay at Obernewtyn. I felt restless, partly because of the new power I had discovered, and partly because the mountains held a darkness that called me.

I also felt an urge to look at the sea again, and also to return to Rangorn. That was the effect of freedom. What a sweet taste it had. That made me think of Maruman and I wondered fleetingly if I would ever see him again.

"Will you be staying?" Dameon asked, with again that faint bitter twist at the edge of his mouth.

"I don't think so," I said.

"There would be a place for you. Rushton said you're stronger than all of us. He has the notion of starting his own Council," Matthew said enthusiastically.

I stared and Dameon nodded, sensing my curiosity and incredulity. "He wants to govern Obernewtyn with the help of a Council elected from our ranks. He wants it to be fair. He wants us to work to better our abilities and to train others like us to be better at what we do."

"He wants us to form groups, guilds of special abilities," Matthew added.

"And this Council will be a sort of guildmerge," I quipped.

Dameon's mobile mouth twitched. "A good name. I will suggest it," he said.

I laughed.

Then another question occurred to me.

"What happened to those Councilmen?" I was amazed

that something so intimately important to me was so readily forgotten. To my surprise, Matthew only laughed.

"There's a story," he said with a twinkle in his eyes. "Madam Vega made the mistake of leaving the Councilmen to Alexi's tender mercies. Alexi, lacking any subtlety, fed them drugged wine and threw them in one of the underground storage chambers."

I gaped.

"By the time they were discovered, it was all over. Rushton got them out and told them what had happened—with a few omissions."

"A few omissions!" I gasped. Matthew grinned widely, enjoying his audience.

"He told them Madam Vega had been up to mischief for ages, plotting against the Council, and that she had organized to have the Councilmen knocked out and murdered in case they found out what she was up to. Rushton gave them the impression the whole revolt had been made to free them. His own claim was secondary. They were sick to their stomachs from the stuff Alexi gave them, and only too happy to believe anything they were told. They rushed back to Sutrium and civilization with the promise to present Rushton's claim to the Councilcourt. Rushton said he couldn't leave in wintertime, but that he would come in the spring to make his formal petition."

I laughed aloud at the thought of the self-important Councilmen thrown into a storage cupboard. Then I sobered.

"What about me?"

"What about you?" Matthew inquired pertly. "You're dead. You ran away during the battle and were almost certainly eaten by wolves."

I laughed again at the sheer audacity of the story.

Domick poked his head around the door. "Rushton's coming up." Dameon and Matthew moved to depart.

"Wait. Don't . . ." I stopped. Don't what? Don't leave me alone with the person who risked his life to help me? I shook my head at the absurdity and they went.

Rushton entered. He was familiar to my eyes in a way that surprised me. That was what came of linking minds. He seemed too tall in the turret room where I had been since I woke. There were faint shadows in his green eyes, though he looked remarkably content.

"Hello," I said, helplessly formal. "I don't know what to say," I added, as the silence lengthened—and because it was the truth.

"I heard you want to come to the meeting," he said.

I shrugged. "Not really. It was a whim. I hear you have plans," I said.

He didn't seem to hear me. "I thought you would die or wake up senseless like Selmar."

I shrugged again, embarrassed at his intensity. "Well, I didn't," I said with some asperity. "I never thanked you for helping me with the machine that time."

This time he shrugged. "Will you stay?" he asked, rather as Dameon had done.

"I don't know." I sighed. "I feel restless. I want to get away from the mountains for a while."

"Did they tell you my idea about the guilds? You could stay and help set it up," he offered diffidently.

"What guild would I belong to?" I asked a little mockingly.

He smiled. "Choose whichever pleases you. I think you will be an exception. I expect you will overlap all guilds." He smiled. "We're going to bring others up here too, you know. In secret. And when we're strong enough, the Council will have to accept us.

"Stay," he said again. I looked at him and some of my restlessness faded. After all, it was an adventure and something to live for that he was offering. There was some good in that.

"I'll stay for a while," I said at last and he nodded.

"That will do to start," he said cryptically. "Now the meeting calls."

He looked through the small window at the pale wintertime sky, a faraway look on his face. "It will not be easy, you know, to do what I want. But we have made the first step. Who knows, you might even be able to teach me some tricks. Obernewtyn will be a force in this Land. And I am the Master of Obernewtyn now." He smiled down at me, but there was a fierce pride in his face that made it strangely beautiful.

He went away.

He would be a good leader, I thought. Guildmerge or not, he would remain the Master of Obernewtyn. There was a quality in him that inspired trust and a kind of love. He was born to lead. People like Rushton never thought much about the past. It made them impatient. His mind was full of what was to come. It was left to those like me to remember the past—and doubt.

Deep in my belly, I felt again the tingle of the power I had wakened. Such power must have a purpose. I thought of a dark chasm somewhere in the mountains and again the restlessness filled me.

If Cameo and Maruman and Sharna were right, it was my destiny to stop anyone from ever unearthing that terrible power.

I would not fail them.